DEDICATION

To Winston:
Damn good dog
through thick & thin.

BJH

THE CLEARING
Benson Jacob Hyler

Table of Contents

CHAPTER ONE
The Way In

Shit, I don't wanna be doing this. That's the first thing that goes
through Lawrence's mind when Brett parks his dad's 1950 Chevy
pickup on the gravel and red clay cliff overlooking the gloomy
landscape. A green sheet of Riddle Pines covers the Chattahoochee
National Forest. A warm breeze picks up just enough to remind them
of the daunting fall a mere two feet ahead.

It's early spring. The ground has finally soaked up the heavy rain
that covered the area a week earlier. They planned this outing weeks
ago when Lawrence's rent was only a month past due. Somehow he
has managed to avoid or fend off his landlady up to now. The
opportunity waiting for them in that forest can't wait another second.

The lukewarm air of the spring afternoon has kept their forty ounce
bottles of malt liquor just cool enough to stomach. Brett slams a pair
of binoculars down and jumps on top of the hot, metal hood. The sun
shines brightly in the distance and he furrows his thick, dark brow
before tossing on his shades. Sweat stains have started to show
through his black t-shirt and faded jeans.

"When we get this money I can finally afford not to drink this shit anymore." Brett tries to smile through the distasteful grimace on his face. Ever since they were little kids, it has always been he who discovers the trouble they get into.

Lawrence lowers his cap over his brown eyes. "How do you find out about shit like this?"

"Just one of the perks of coming from the wrong side of the tracks, Larry." Brett likes to point out the subtle differences in their upbringings. Their fathers earned the same amount of money at the same job. But in their little town, an out of commission set of rails that runs in front of a refashioned train depot separates the two castes. Brett and his kin live on the unlawful side.

"Seriously, man. This is some dark shit." Lawrence tires of Brett acting like it's cool that his dad was an alcoholic who beat him.

"You remember my cousin, Joe? The one that got busted fencing stuff for my dad?"

"Vaguely." Lawrence untwists the cap on another warm one.

"I went down to the prison and paid him a visit a few weeks ago. It's like graduate school for hardasses in there. He kept telling me about all the stuff he's learned in prison. Shit he wants to pull when he gets out and what not. Told me this is how he plans on kicking up his bankroll when he's finally paroled."

"And he doesn't mind us showing up here and taking his idea?"

"Not at all. He's still got a couple of months. He said if he ain't getting it, might as well go to family." To the rest of the town they might be low class scum, but the Perry family had their own thing going on that they consider a source of pride.

"How do you know they bring everything with them?"

"Think about it man. You're all depressed… you're crying. Wah, wah, wah. Daddy didn't throw the ball with me and mommy stopped breastfeeding me when I was four. Do you stop and make out a will to leave all your things to people who don't care enough about you to stop you from fucking killing yourself? No, you wrap yourself up in as much as you can carry and take that shit with you."

"It just doesn't feel right. You know?"

"No!" Brett snaps defensively. "I don't know. These lowlifes took life – God's most precious gift – and just threw it away. If they can't respect such a simple thing as the God given ability to walk, talk, breathe, eat, and shit, I got no respect for 'em." Brett stops to gather himself for a moment.

Brett picks up the borrowed binoculars and scans the woods. He starts at the western side of the tree line and scans the front edge of the forest. After spotting nothing of particular interest, he points the lenses at a giant opening and the circle of trees that surrounds it.

An eerie wind picks up from the forest. Brett's eyes dry out and his vision blurs. It's nearly impossible to focus. He yanks the binoculars down and takes a chug. With his eyes and throat remoistened, he scans the clearing for a second time. It's only a matter of moments before he sees them.

Two gangly figures hanging a full fifteen feet from the lowest branches of two towering pines.

"Boom! Found two. Right there in the back." He hands the binoculars to Lawrence and jumps down.

Lawrence focuses on the opening and catches a glimpse of the twin bodies dangling in the wind.

"Alright, we gotta go." Brett sticks his head out the window. "I told Keith we'd meet him before midnight. And I damn sure don't want to be stuck in this forest after dark."

Lawrence takes one last look into the abyss of trees before climbing into the cab. Brett welcomes him with a warm bottle wrapped in a paper bag. "Do you really think the bag's gonna fool anybody?"

"Unless you grabbed a couple of red solo cups, this is all we got." Smoke pours out of the tailpipes when Brett shifts into reverse and slams his foot on the gas. They are bounced out of the bench seat when the tires crash in-and-out of the deep ruts left by the logging trucks that run up-and-down the mountain. Brett points the nose downhill and takes off, his foot heavy with liquid courage.

Lawrence throws his arm out the window and grips onto the rusty roof as tight as possible. Brett fumbles as he lifts the brown bag to his mouth with one hand while steering through the perilous curves with the other.

Lawrence's torso slams against the door when Brett takes a hundred degree turn going thirty miles per hour. The look in his eyes is one of focused intensity Lawrence has never seen before. He opens his mouth to ask him to slow down, but bites his tongue when he realizes the words would only make Brett drive even more maniacally.

After what seemed like days trapped in the world's scariest roller coaster, they turn onto an old two-lane highway at full speed.

"How do you know where we're going?"

"They're in the clearing." Brett puts a dip between his cheek and gums. The engine sputters and roars under the pressure as Brett stands up on the gas pedal. "This reminds me of going on vacation with my family. You remember those cheap old motels with those vibrating beds?" Brett yells over the roar of the engine and vibrating of the hood.

Lawrence's anger boils over. "You didn't tell me we were going to the clearing."

"Who gives a shit?" Brett yells over the sound of the wind ripping through the windows. "We're robbing dead people. Who gives a damn if it's from a supposedly haunted section of the forest or Jesus' kitchen?"

"It's bad voodoo, man. I don't want that onus on me. And you shouldn't either."

"I'm not turning back now." Brett tosses an empty out the window and motions for another. "You can sit out here in the truck while I do all the work. But that means we'll be out here after dark *and* you won't get paid."

"Shit." Lawrence relents and stares out the window at the rolling vista of lumber.

Brett dastardly laughs as he turns off of the main road and onto the poorly-worn dirt tracks leading to the trailhead. He speeds down the patchy lines, barely squeezing the side view mirrors between the trees.

Brett brings them to a stop dangerously close to a dead end formed by two pines standing in the center of the trail. Brett jumps out and grabs the plastic cooler that has been slamming around in the bed.

Lawrence takes a moment to steady himself before joining him. He reaches into the bed and pulls out two coiled lengths of rope, a bow, and a quiver of arrows. Without a word, he takes off into the forest.

They trudge through the thick bed of dirt and foliage that makes up the barely worn path. After a fifteen minute hike, they spot the clearing in the distance. Brett leaves behind a wake of broken twigs and crinkled leaves as he jogs ahead.

Still spooked by the whole idea, Lawrence is driven by fear as he marches along.

After climbing over a series of downed trees that forms a gate at the end of the trail, they walk into the glowing light of the clearing. Brett scans the tree line for their intended victims. Lawrence drops the supplies on the damp ground and plops down. He opens up a fresh forty and drinks half of it before working up the nerve to look up.

"There's one of them." Brett points with an arrow. "Yep. There's the other one. Right next to it. You any good with a bow?" Lawrence shakes his head. "That's what I figured."

Brett readies the bow and takes aim. He adjusts for the wind and the weight of the rope before firing. It falls just short of the branch and plants itself in a rotten log at the edge of the ring.

After taking another pull from the warm bottle, he moves in for a second attempt. He pulls the line back tight. His forearm twitches under the pressure as he aims higher. Several deep breaths help him gather his composure before he releases the line. The rope loops around the branch and the arrow falls to the ground.

Before Lawrence has time to tether his line, Brett has secured his to the branch and is on his way up. After several embarrassingly fail attempts at archery, Lawrence finally secures his to the branch. Meanwhile, Brett has sidled up next to his responsibility and is hacking at the rope with a serrated army knife. "Heads up!!"

Lawrence looks up to see the spread eagle body of a dead man falling to the ground. He dives out of the way just before the bloated corpse explodes. Blood and chunks of human body parts splatter all over the place.

"Holy shit man! How about a little more warning next time?" Lawrence yells with pieces of dead man dripping from his clothes.

Brett laughs like he's on vacation. "How about you get your ass up here and do your job so we can get out of here?"

Lawrence is halfway up when Brett's feet hit the ground. He looks up and watches Lawrence climb against the backdrop of the setting sun. "Just an FYI, the sun's setting pretty fast!"

Unfortunately for Lawrence, he is situated eerily close to the decayed corpse. He sidles by her as quickly as possible and starts hacking away at the rope. Her body shakes and shimmers as the rope lurches back-and-forth. Wondering what his thirteen year old self would think of what he's doing right now, Lawrence lets out an audible groan of frustration and disappointment. He pulls the knife back and takes a break. His arms feel like jelly.

A vulture takes off from above. The shaking of the branch causes Lawrence to lose his grip and slide down a few feet. Despite the burning in his hands, he is able to stop and finds himself eye-to-eye with the wife. The vibrations rolling through the branch jostle her. The noose tightens around her neck and her dehydrated eyes pop out of her gaunt face. Lawrence's scream echoes through the forest.

The woman's head falls sharply to the left and the rotting flesh around her neck starts to rip. After dangling in the wind for a few seconds, her neck rips free from her head and sends the body crashing to the ground. The thick stew of blood and guts that had once been her internal organs blend in with those of her husband's.

"Holy shit!" Brett runs over to get a closer look at the Pollock-esque scene. Above him, the woman's spine has hooked itself on the noose and is maintaining a tenuous hold on her head. The friction between her spinal cord and the noose weakens as the rope swings in the air.

Lawrence watches with a look of odd wonderment as the head continues wobbling in front of him. "Heads up!"

The head - complete with its de-socketed eyes and spinal tail - drops toward the forest floor. Brett looks up to find that it has only fallen a foot or two before being stopped by a clump of hair stuck in the noose.

"Jesus, man! Get down from there before you get me killed!"

A rotten-flesh flavored wind whips circuitously through the clearing. The ropes dangling from the trees whip around like lassos. A small patch of decaying skin that attaches the hair to her scalp gives way and sends her head to the ground. It lands squarely on her own back with her empty eye sockets staring back up judgingly at her abuser.

"Come on down before you shit yourself." Brett looks around the ever darkening forest. "I don't wanna be in this creepy place any more than you do." He pulls an arrow from the quiver and marches over to the lady's corpse. After taking the last pull from his malt liquor, he tosses the bottle into the forest and takes a golf stance. Legs spread evenly, shoulders level, eyes focused squarely on her head. "Fore!"

Due to Brett's poor judgment, the blade of the arrow scrapes the top of her head and leaves a wretched knot of decaying skin and blood-stained hair on the tip of the arrow. The head slowly leans forward and teeters over the edge of her back. It lists back-and-forth for a moment before rolling onto the ground.

Halfway down the rope, Lawrence is too afraid to look down. "You still there?"

"Yeah." Brett burps into a fresh forty. "Barely. You'll probably have to drive back to town."

"You know I hate driving stick." Lawrence touches down and takes a second to examine the gruesome scene.

"Yeah. And I hate having a little bitch for a best friend." Brett wraps Lawrence's head in his arms and gives him a one knuckle noogie. "But we do the best we can with what God gave us."

"Let's just do this and go home." Lawrence bends over and gathers up the blood covered necklaces gathered at the top of her shoulders.

The drying blood and rotten veins stuck to the jewelry crust over on his hands as he stuffs the valuables in an old gym bag. Why neither of them thought to bring gloves is beyond him as he peels an assortment of bracelets and watches from her disgusting wrists and forearms.

He considers yanking her ears off and throwing them straight into the bag, but thinks better of it before painstakingly removing the earrings one at a time. Thanks to the mummification of her hands, removing the rings from her fingers is a surprisingly not unpleasant experience. Not that it was pleasant. Just not as unpleasant as one would expect.

Brett laughs when he finally gets a good look at Lawrence. "Holy-shit you look like hell."

"Dammit!" Lawrence stands up and looks at the dried blood and guts covering his clothing. "This is gonna look great when we get pulled over."

"*If* we get pulled over." Brett says cheerfully before picking up his bag of loot and leading them through the darkened path back to his dad's pickup.

· · · · · · · ·

Before they even get to the interstate, Brett has passed out in the passenger seat. Lawrence spends most of the drive fighting to keep himself awake. A job made that much harder by the fact that the radio hasn't worked since Brett's dad's gun went off and shot out the dash.

Three hours and two cups of gas station coffee later, Lawrence pulls the truck into an empty parking lot just outside of Atlanta. He wakes Brett up and they gather around the tailgate and empty their goodies into one big pile of gold and silver. They divvy up the loot into three piles. One for each of them, plus another for Brett's friend Keith.

"Hot damn, boy! We done good!" Brett motions to the bounty of precious metals in front of them. "This'll get that landlady off your ass."

Visions of the woman's head dangling from that rope has Lawrence all out of sorts. He shakes the cobwebs of guilt out of his head and quietly allows himself to revel in the glory of blood-stained victory. "I can't wait to shove some cold, hard cash in that bitches face and get her off my back. I might go ahead and pay next month's too."

"That's the spirit." Brett continues splitting up the treasure. "We'll take this over to Keith's. This should be enough for a ki."

"How much do you think you'll make off of your half?"

"The cocaine? I'll probably get about ten grand. Give-or-take. Depending on factors such as personal consumption and quality. How much I decide to cut it."

Lawrence is embarrassed that he needs to ask the next question. "How do you cut it?"

"Let me have first pick from these three piles and I'll walk you through it."

"Deal."

Brett grabs the pile with the most watches and loads it into his bag. Lawrence takes the one closest to him. Together they load Keith's stash into a paper sack and hop back in the cab of the pickup. This time with Brett behind the steering wheel.

"Diffcrent people do it different ways. But you asked me, so I'm gonna tell you how I do it." Brett swerves in-and-out of traffic. "First you need to get some glucose powder."

"Glucose powder?"

"Yeah, you can get it at the mall. Don't be too obvious about it. Pay with cash…Big Brother looms large. If you haven't got any scales, you're gonna need to get some. You can probably find those at the mall. Don't be a dumbass and buy both things at the same store.

"When you get home, set up a clean table. You want it so clean you would literally be willing to eat off of it. This stuff's going up people's noses, show it some respect. At most you want to cut it twenty percent. That's what your *Dirty Thirty, suburbanite, married, just trying to have a good time while we got a sitter* set is going to expect."

"So you just go to the bars and sell it to people?"

"Sometimes. If I know the bartender or bouncer somewhere they'll point me to the partiers. Other than that, it's not worth the trouble." Brett makes a wide right on red without slowing down. "Now, if you wanna squeeze a few extra nickels out of this – I'm not recommending it, but I've seen people make a lot of money this way – you can go as high as forty percent and sell that shit to the college kids."

"If you can make more that way, why not do it?"

"Eventually one of them'll notice the difference. After that, they all want to kick your ass on principle."

"How much goes in each little baggie?"

"They're called 8-balls. That's three and a half grams of cut powder."

"Might as well get a real job."

"Real jobs don't attract loose women like cocaine."

"Ahhhh." The mere suggestion gets Lawrence excited. His sister pointed out just last week that he needs to get laid.

"That's about it unless you got any questions." Brett stares at the empty setting of an engagement ring he's wearing on his pinkie. "You notice none of this shit has any of the jewels in the settings… no diamonds or rubies or whatever?"

"I didn't want to rain on your parade. I wonder what they did with everything?"

"Probably buried it in the forest somewhere. I checked my guy's pockets and didn't find anything."

"How much do I charge?" The sudden change of subject confuses Brett. "For an 8-ball, how much does one cost?"

"I'm gonna tell you to charge a buck twenty. You can probably go as low as a hundred if you get desperate to get rid of it. Or as high as a hundred and fifty if you find a sucker." Brett runs over a bump in the road and the radio crackles to static-filled life just long enough to get their hopes up.

"Thanks, man. I appreciate the help."

"No problem, bud." Brett pats his old friend on the shoulder and waits for the light to turn green. Five blocks and two red lights later, he pulls into the parking lot of Keith's four story apartment building on the edge of downtown.

"It's probably best if you wait here."

Lawrence lays his head against the window and waves for his friend to go on without him. Once Brett is out of sight, he locks the door and closes his eyes to catch a few winks. The images of those bodies falling to the ground haunts the back of his eyelids.

• • • • • • • •

Brett knocks on the door to Keith's apartment and doesn't get an answer. He raises his fist to knock again when a petite girl in a tank top and barely-there underwear opens the door and exhales a plume of marijuana smoke in his face.

Keith's girlfriend Stephanie greets him with the excitement of a spectator at a snail race. "Hey, Brett. What's up?"

"Keith here?" He can't help but feel awkward around her. She knows how much it burns Brett that his coke connection started hooking up with his ex-girlfriend.

She annoyingly smacks the bubble gum in her mouth. "Yeah, he's upstairs. He might be asleep though. Said he got tired of waiting."

"Well, you know Lawrence. Things always take a little bit longer."

"Where is he? I haven't seen him in a while."

Brett has already started thinking about the old times. What she now considers pleasant memories only fill him with pain and regret. "Is it cool if I go up?"

"Just knock first, he tried coming on to me earlier and, well... he may be in a compromising position in front of his computer."

Brett runs up the stairs and is disappointed to find Keith playing video games in his boxer shorts. "Dammit."

"What are you upset about?" Keith pauses his game leaving an animated dog on the screen laughing at his lack of skill.

"Steph thought you might be up here playing with your joystick instead of your control pad."

"Finished five minutes ago, Why do you think the door's unlocked?"

"Smart man. We just got back from that job I told you about. Can you still hook it up?"

"Yeah." Keith peels his sweaty skin from the duct tape covered bean bag chair. One of the many signs of a drug dealer that dips too far into his own supply. "I'm glad you showed. This guy called an hour ago that wanted this pretty bad. I told him I'd already promised it to somebody."

"Appreciate the faith." Brett empties the mostly clean gold and silver onto the desk next to Keith's laptop.

"What the fuck is that?"

"It's what we talked about. You were saying how you needed to start investing in more precious metals. Because of the declining dollar or some shit. Then I told you I was about to do this job and I was gonna have a lot of jewelry to get rid of." Brett watches as Keith tries to decipher what he's spelling out. "This is my half of the deal."

"Are you fucking kidding me?"

"No. We went through a fair bit of trouble to get this." Brett hints at something more risky than what they had actually done.

"Alright. A deal's a deal." Keith shakes his head. "Man, I should have let that other guy take it."

"But you didn't because you're a good guy. And so am I. I'm gonna throw in my own watch to make up for the misunderstanding." Brett unwraps a stolen watch from his wrist.

"You don't have to do that. I need to learn not to mix liquor and pills. Maybe now I'll learn my lesson." He tosses a brown package across the room.

"Well, I'm going to leave this watch here with the rest of it. There's some good stuff in there, you might even come out ahead."

"If there were any chance of me coming out ahead, you would have sold this shit and paid me in cash."

"How about I come back later and give you some money?"

"No, you bested me and I need to learn my lesson. From here on out though, no matter what I say when I'm messed up, all deals are cash." When Keith plops back down in his chair, the pressure sends a flurry of foam beans streaming into the air.

"No problem. Good luck with those ducks." Brett lets himself out and locks the door.

"Thanks dick, now she's gonna think I'm still jerking it!"

•   •   •   •   •   •   •   •

Back in the pickup, Lawrence has been having a rough time holding onto his sanity. The nightmarish visions keep vanishing just long enough to let him nod out before reincarnating in his dreams.

Each time it's the same thing. He finds himself climbing out from behind the wheel of a strange vehicle at the forest entrance. Completely alone, he makes his way across the rugged path. He doesn't want to go, but his feet keep driving him forward. It's as if his legs have stolen the keys and are driving the car.

Despite the darkness and fear enveloping him, he remains calm. The realization hits that there is nothing to fear. Everything he seeks is in the clearing.

Now that he has synced his brain back up with his legs, Lawrence marches along at a much faster clip. The silence of the woods is broken only by the occasional sound of a twig snapping underneath his heavy footsteps.

A pain suddenly rises from his left foot. He looks down to find that both feet are bare and bloodied. He doesn't remember taking off his shoes and regrets having done so. Then he notices that he is wearing a dark cloak. Up ahead is a torch burning in the middle of the clearing.

Lawrence hasn't the slightest idea what to expect when he enters. He climbs over the gate made up of fallen trees and stops at the top to survey his surroundings. His heart races.

After climbing down, he walks to the center and looks up for a sign or a warning. When nothing happens, he meanders to the opposite edge and walks the circumference. A quarter of the way around, Lawrence turns to inspect the sound of a small bird taking flight and finds himself face-to-face with a rope that has a noose tied at the end. Frightened by what he might find, he courageously looks up.

His body tenses up as he feels a presence closing in around him. The branches overhead grow closer together as the trees move in. Lawrence looks down to find that the trunks are leading the charge as the ground continues swallowing itself up. Before he can react, the trees have imprisoned him. Climbing up the rope appears to be the only way out.

By using the trees for leverage, he is able to climb up to the lowest branch. His arms and legs have grown weak. His whole body is weak, but his soul is still driven. He climbs higher and higher before realizing that the climb is taking much longer than it should. Lawrence looks up to find that he is no closer to the top than when he started. The ground below has disappeared completely.

Without any conscious effort of his own, Lawrence suddenly finds himself standing on a skinny branch near the top. "Now what!?"

The answer comes from below when he notices a thick rope tied to the branch. It is made up entirely of braided hair. Complcte with intermittent pieces of dead flesh thrown in for good measure.

When he finally pulls the rope up, he finds a perfectly constructed noose. Lawrence shows no fear while something deep inside of him wraps it around his neck. More like a disinterested third party than someone about to commit suicide, he watches as his hands tighten the hair around his neck. In the darkness below, he catches the reflection of the moonlight on a silver necklace in the center of the clearing.

The faint reflection blinds him. At the same time it beckons him to lean foward. He shuffles closer to the edge, pushing himself closer to the tipping point. Finally, his mangled, bloodied feet lose all traction and he falls.

For a brief moment, he forgets that he is soaring to his doom and feels free. The faint pressure of the braid around his neck is the only reminder of his impending demise. A smile crosses his face as he slips deeper into the darkness with his eyes steady fixed on the necklace. He feels like a child diving into a swimming pool on the hottest day of the summer.

Sweat beads from his brow. He covers his eyes with his forearm to shield them from the increasing glare of the jewelry. Flames erupt out of the necklace and his smile fades into an anxious frown. He lets out a nightmarish scream as the braid tightens and snaps his neck. His legs flip over his body and leave his bloody feet searing over the ring of flaming metal. Steam hisses out of the fire as his blood drips on the silver.

His head droops to the right and the flames disappear. Leaving only a circle of ashes in their place. The hair braid snaps and releases his limp body. Lawrence lays motionless on the ground.

All thinking has ceased. Blood no longer pumps through his veins. Death is nothingness.

Through sheer determination, he wills himself back into existence. His heart pounds to life as he heaves labored breathes in-and-out in a desperate fight for survival. He becomes self-aware.

Brett tosses a brown package through the window before jumping into the pickup. "What'd you do, rub one out while I was gone or something?"

Lawrence fakes a smile and assumes he is referencing the sweat gleaming from his brow and his hurried breathing. "Let's get out of here... I need some sleep."

• • • • • • • •

Lawrence rubs his sore throat with his left hand as he unlocks the street level door to his apartment building. It has been a long day. All he wants to do is walk up the daunting flight of stairs to his apartment and go to bed. The visions have stopped, but they left behind one bear of a headache.

All along the baby blue walls lining the white stairwell are an assortment of pictures, mirrors, and square-framed knick knacks the land lady purchased from a variety of flea markets and yard sales. Lawrence once viewed them as a misguided attempt at artistic expression. Under threat of eviction, it seems more like a failed attempt at trailer park pretention.

He passes a mirror on his left with an animated picture of a deer in a snowy field running along the top. Lawrence keeps his eyes fixed on the hundred watt bulb lighting the hallway from the top of the stairs. He doesn't notice the ghastly figure of the wife's gaunt, decaying face floating down from the painted white frosting. Just before she disappears behind the bottom border of the frame, she lets out an agonizing scream.

Ignoring what he assumes to be the wind howling outside, Lawrence finishes the long haul up the stairs and busts into his apartment. He flippantly tosses his gym bag of treasure on the couch. In what could have been a foolish decision, Lawrence agreed to let Brett split their cocaine back at his place.

Pete, his goldfish, hasn't been fed all day so he stops by and pours in a couple of flakes. Lawrence opens the window and is welcomed by the flashing lights and sounds of a nearby police cruiser. He glances outside and sees an officer tackle a bumbling suspect directly below his apartment.

From the right pocket of his jeans, he feels a sudden flash of fiery pain. He reaches in and pulls out a forgotten ring.

He is surprised to find that it is cool to the touch. Further examination reveals an empty line of settings that appear to have been holding a row of small diamonds. He wonders how much the ring would be worth if those diamonds were still there. How much would all of the missing jewels be worth?

The grotesque look on the woman's face regains a foothold in his consciousness. The next image that flashes before him is her head falling to the ground. After shaking the cobwebs out his mind, he bolts to the kitchen and grabs a beer.

The relaxation brought on by the suds is short lived. The muscles in his neck twinge and his headache worsens. He pulls a rocks glass out of the cabinet, drops his last cube of ice in, and fills it to the brim with whiskey. Underneath a stack of frozen dinners he uncovers a bag of peas. Between the plumpness of the couch cushion and the coolness of the plastic bag on his forehead, Lawrence is as comfortable as he has been all day.

His cell phone starts vibrating from the desk all the way on the other side of his apartment. Instinctually, he moves to get up before his body starts aching. Whoever it is will have to wait until morning. His body and spirit are hurting from the long day and he's holding a glass full of cure in his right hand.

The glass is emptied while the bag of peas thaws out on his forehead. The clock on the wall ticks away the seconds. Before the lone cube has melted away, he has polished off the whiskey.

After bouncing around for a little while, his mind wanders back to the time he and his ex Linda went window shopping for engagement rings. Excited about a new life with the woman he loved, Lawrence started saving up money the very next day.

The time to actually make the purchase never arrived. Money had always been a contentious issue between the two of them and it didn't help when he started pinching pennies to buy her a ring. One afternoon, push came to shove and he moved out. The two of them haven't spoken to each other since.

He shifts his hand away from his thigh to the gym bag filled with jewelry. For a fleeting moment, he can feel all of his problems fade away. Before long he will be able to pay his back rent and hopefully even buy a used car. His life will still be far from perfect, but this could be his ticket to something better.

Who knows? More money and a car could lead to a new girl – possibly even another shot with the old one – and then he could get his life back together. Without a doubt he'll be able to find something better than a crap job mowing yards for rich people and local businesses.

Maybe something with a salary, health insurance, and a couple of paid weeks off a year. Eventually at this new job he'd get a promotion and move into a nice house somewhere. He and his beautiful wife.

Sooner or later there would be kids. Two. Maybe three. He'd be a role model to his son and a hero to his daughter. Other fathers would wonder how he manages to spend so much time with his kids and maintain such a demanding career.

The string of events leading to a better life for him and his grandchildren has been laid out before him. It all starts with that bag of silver and gold he's gripping tightly in his right hand.

Fear flows through his body. Fear of the dark night. Fear that his headache could be a brain tumor. Fear that he would never find love. Fear that he'll be poor his whole existence. Finally fear that something bad would happen to his bag of goodies before he has the chance to cash in.

How could he possibly leave his future wrapped up in some old gym bag on the couch? A criminal could come running through that door any second and steal his dream away. After locking the door, he looks out the window to see if that shady police officer is still lurking around before lowering the blinds.

He charges into his bedroom and shuffles through his drawers and closet in search of a place to hide his treasure. Every little nook and cranny he can find is either too small or too obvious. Following a great deal of debate and hesitation, he settles on simply shoving it under his mattress.

Once the loot is hidden, Lawrence notices that he has broken out in a feverish sweat. Between that and the dried blood still covering his body, a shower is way past due.

As the warm water rushes over him, his body shivers from head to toe with relief. His muscles relax and the anxiety filling his heart is replaced with calm. Lawrence rinses the sweat, grime, and guts from the forest off of his body. The water washes down the drain in a pink swirl of shame and regret.

The water goes from warm to cool to cold in a matter of seconds before Lawrence puts together that he has spent too much time daydreaming. He hurriedly begins washing himself. While scrubbing his hair with his right hand, he blindly reaches for the metal neck of the shower head and grabs the soap on a rope.

Through the blur of the suds in his eyes, all Lawrence sees is a prunish body in his left hand.

He loosens the rope from his wrist and throws it out onto the increasingly wet tile floor. Lawrence hastily rinses the shampoo out of his hair and looks down.

The soap looks like every other bar he has ever seen. He cuts off the water and grabs a towel. After throwing on a t-shirt and a pair of basketball shorts, he decides it's best if he goes to bed instead of staying up and having a few more cocktails.

Minutes later he climbs into bed and contemplates his new life and how much better things will soon be. Now that he's got his life planned out, all he needs to do is pawn that jewelry and sell some powder. Following that, everything else will be gravy.

Suddenly he finds himself riddled with worry over the treasure
buried underneath his bed. He hops up and flips over the mattress
before roughly grabbing the bag and hiding it in the bottom drawer
of his dresser underneath a collection of worn-out socks and
underwear. Realizing this is much worse than under the mattress, he
yanks the bag out and looks nervously around the room.

Foregoing all thought processes, Lawrence jams the blade of his
pocket knife into the side of the bed. The blade wrestles with the
cheap metal springs of his mattress as he crudely carves out a chunk
of padding. Once he has pulled out a sizable amount of foam, he
shoves the bag into the crevice and fills in the rest of the hole with
loose material.

He's gonna feel a lot safer once he's traded in all of those valuables
for some good old American cash. But if anyone wanted to get at it
tonight, they would have to go through him.

Without that bag, his life is back in the same worthless place that it
was when he woke up. A life without hope and devoid of any chance
at better things. A life he is not willing to accept. Not anymore.

CHAPTER TWO
Gold4Cash

The next morning Lawrence wakes up with a stiffness in his neck. Despite the pulsing pain, the first thing he does is dig out the bag of gold and silver to check its contents.

Feeling reassured, he carries the sack of bloody jewelry into the kitchen and dumps everything in the sink. The hot water dissolves most of the crusted redness. The rest is removed with a dry rag before he tosses it into a leather satchel.

Following another long, hot, shower, Lawrence walks the fifteen blocks or so to Brett's apartment. When his friend opens the door, he is taken aback by his disheveled appearance. "You alright? You kinda look like shit."

"Did you sleep last night?" Brett hurries Lawrence inside and closes the door.

"I did alright." Lawrence tries not to look confused. "I took a shower right before bed that was rather refreshing. Washed off all of the nastiness from yesterday. Sobered me up a bit in the process. I didn't realize how much of that shit got on me."

"That's good. That's real good." Brett noticeably stares at the floor as they pass by a mirror on the wall. "I tried to take a bath, but every time I looked into the tub," he bites his lip, "I just couldn't do it."

"Why not? Afraid you'd wash off that stank of your's that the women find so appealing?"

"Yeah, that's it." Brett plainly answers Lawrence's ill-timed joke. "So you slept alright?"

"I suppose. I had a couple of nightmares. Nothing too crazy."

"Couple of nightmares?" Brett sounds envious. "I didn't get one wink."

"Did you get into any of that stuff?"

"No. Not that I didn't think about it. I wanted to wait until you got here."

Lawrence motions around the studio apartment at the empty forties and beer bottles. "Did you drink all of this last night?"

"Haven't stopped. I keep hoping one of 'em will put me out. So... everything's been alright with you?"

"Except for those nightmares. And that's probably just nerves because I've never seen a dead body. Not like that anyway. One time I touched my uncle's face at his funeral."

"Nerves? Maybe you're right. Nothing but some dreams?" Brett scans his apartment for a bottle without any cigarettes in it. When he finally finds a half full one, he doesn't think twice before drinking it down.

"There might have been something else, but I'm pretty sure I was just imagining things."

Brett takes a seat in front of the brown package and his scales. "What did you see?"

"I had a hard time getting that lady's face out of my head. Her open mouth… that rotting skin… her eyes dangling from their sockets." Lawrence shakes his head to clear the cobwebs. "I couldn't close my eyes without seeing that. Then I took a shower and went right to bed."

"Maybe I just need a shower. That'll wash off all the bad mojo." Brett dumps a pile of coke onto the scales.

"Do it. I guarantee you'll feel a lot better. That and some rest."

"No doubt, man. No doubt." Brett dumps five hundred grams into a large plastic bag and hands it over. "I hate to be a dick, but I really need some shuteye. Remember the instructions I gave you yesterday?"

"Yep. I'm going to buy the supplies this afternoon after I get rid of some jewelry." Lawrence places the package in a brown paper bag before shoving it into the leather satchel on top of his gold and silver.

Brett is already removing his clothes and making his way to a tiny bathroom in the corner. "Sounds great, man. Lock the door on your way out."

•　•　•　•　•　•　•　•

After dropping the cocaine off at his apartment and a quick ride on the subway, Lawrence arrives downtown. He has absolutely no idea where to start fencing a load of stolen jewelry as he aimlessly wanders the streets.

Several blocks into his journey, he notices two acrobatic young men juggling Cash4Gold signs. Lawrence peers down the street where the sidewalks are lined with metal hoarders and junk resellers.

Standing in front of a satellite police station, Lawrence waits for the glowing man to give him permission to cross the street. Once on the other side, he passes by a short, narrow alley (little more than a deep indention in the wall) where a man in an unseasonably long, leather duster steps out from the shadows.

"Heyman." He knows Lawrence can hear him despite his attempts to ignore him. "Heyman! Where you going?"

"Just trying to run some errands, dude. I ain't got no money."

The guy grabs Lawrence by the shoulder. "You got me wrong."

"Then explain it to me." Lawrence is grateful that he can still see the police station behind the stranger.

"You look like a guy that might be trying to free himself of some valuables."

"Possibly."

"I can help you with that." The stranger turns to watch two cops lock up their patrol bikes.

"How can you do that?"

"Are you trying to tell me you weren't about to head over to that pawn shop and sell your grandma's old jewelry or whatever you got in that bag?" Alarmed by the stranger's assertiveness, Lawrence tightens his grip on the satchel and takes a step back. He watches the two cops head indoors. Nervous as all get out, he licks his suddenly chapped lips. "Alright then. What I'm trying to tell you is, you don't got to do that. I do the same thing they do. Buy up stuff on the cheap and resell it. All they gonna do is rip you off."

The fast-talking nature of the stranger makes Lawrence feel ill at ease. "How do I know you're not trying to rip me off?"

"Cause man, this is what I do. I sit out here all day every day and run my game. I'll pay you more than they do then I'll sell it for less than they charge." The hustler's face beams with pride.

"How do you do that?"

"No overhead. They've got to pay rent, employees, the city, the state, the county, and the federal government. Me? I got to pay me."

"What are you looking for?"

"Whatever you got."

Lawrence fights the urge to go back home and have a beer. "How do we do this?"

"I'm gonna take a walk around the block and meet you in the back booth of that burger joint over there."

"How do I know you're not just gonna show up with a gun?"

"If I was gonna rob you, I'd tell you to follow me down a dark-ass alley instead of a fast food restaurant.

Unable to argue with his logic, Lawrence agrees to the meeting.

•   •   •   •   •   •   •   •

Lawrence nervously walks up to the counter and orders a sweet tea before taking his seat at the corner table. His leg shakes vigorously while his mind plays the entire interaction over in his head. On two separate occasions he stands to leave before convincing himself to stay.

Finally the man walks through the double doors and makes a beeline to the corner booth. The stranger clasps his hands together in excitement. "Alright, let me see what you got."

Lawrence looks around nervously. "You mean… right here?"

"Let's do this. Unless you got Fort Knox in that bag."

Lawrence leans forward and whispers across the table. "I got a lot."

"I knew there was something about you. We both about to make some money."

Lawrence tilts the bag open before the man grabs his hand and lowers it to the table. The stranger looks around to make sure nobody is watching and slowly opens it back up. Sweat beads on Lawrence's forehead as he keeps a watchful eye for some sort of slight-of-hand while the man digs around.

"Hooooly shit," the hustler says under his breath. "Your grandmother a Rockefeller or something?" He pulls out a couple of pieces. "What happened to all the jewels?"

"I have no idea. My grandma was eccentric."

Lawrence's lack of street smarts amuses the merchant. "I bet she was."

By this time, Lawrence is ready to pounce on whatever the man offers just to get the whole thing over with. "What do you think?"

"Oooh boy! I didn't bring enough money for all this. You see, I generally don't like to keep this much inventory." The stranger continues picking through the collection of gold and silver in search of the best pieces.

"How much cash do you have?"

"Not near enough. I can't believe you're walking around here with all this." He wraps a watch around each wrist, fills a hand up with rings, wraps a couple of bracelets around his wrist, and then a couple of Jesus pieces around his neck.

Lawrence licks his lips. "How much is that worth?"

"I put an envelope with some cash in that bag if you care to take a look." The proposition comes across as a challenge more than a genuine offer.

Not wanting to offend, Lawrence closes the satchel without looking and takes a gulp from his tea. Not until the man is completely out of sight does he relax and breathe a sigh of relief. After scanning the room for peeping Toms, he opens the envelope and fans through a thousand dollars in twenties.

By Lawrence's conservative estimate, the man in the duster had walked off with about a fifth of his take. If he could get anywhere near that for the rest, he'd be looking at close to five grand.

He closes the satchel, tucks the envelope in his back pocket, and ducks out the side door into a filthy alley. He walks to the end of the street into the bright sun of the early afternoon. *Dale's Discount Pawn Shop* looks to be just as good as any other place to sell a few things.

Never has so much merchandise been squeezed into such a small space anywhere else in the world. The ten foot high walls are stacked to the ceiling with a cornucopia of treasures. Nearly all of which once belonged to some deceased or downtrodden individual.

A young man stands between Lawrence and an opening in the bulletproof glass. He is trying to talk the old man behind the counter out of a few more bucks for his dad's CD collection. To the kid's right, a portly, middle-aged couple who appear to be in town on vacation are arguing over the rings locked under the glass case.

"Excuse me, sir." The husband demands. "Excuse me. Is this jewelry legit?"

"My name is Dale. I don't know how you possibly could have missed that, it's written on every freaking thing in this store. Secondly, it says 14K gold. If you can't trust the sticker, why would you ever trust the man that put it on there?"

"I'd rather take my chances with that fella in the long coat than this mean old son of a *you-know-what*. Let's go." The man grabs his wife's pudgy hand and storms down the second row. "Excuse me." He huffs politely as he scrapes by Lawrence.

Lawrence sees an opportunity and chases the couple out the door. "Excuse me, sir."

"I'm sorry about that son. I've got a short temper. Add that to my claustrophobia and we were about to have a situation."

"It's not that. You were completely right. That's why I wanted to talk to you."

The man sizes up Lawrence. "I reckon since I was a little rude to you back there, I owe you one."

"It's like this. My grandma died a couple of months ago and, since my folks have already passed, she left me everything she owned."

The wife gasps. "Oh my goodness. We are so sorry for your loss."

"Thank you. But I didn't stop you good folks looking for pity. I was thinking we can help each other out. My grandmother wasn't a wealthy woman and a big part of the reason for that is her appreciation for the finer things in life. Like jewelry. She always liked to look her best and figured jewelry was a safe investment."

"Sorry to be rude son, but we've got a train to catch."

"I've got all this jewelry that she'd been hoarding and I saw ya'll looking at the rings so I thought... well, I'd rather some nice folks like ya'll walk away with it for cheap than to let an asshole like that rip me off and profit from my grandmother's death."

The husband looks down at his wife and realizes the young man has already made the sale. "What do you have? Something nice. In the hundred dollar range."

"I've got just the thing." Lawrence shoves his hand in the bag and pretends he's looking for a specific item before pulling out the first ring he finds that isn't missing a setting.

"She was particularly proud of this one. Grandpa gave it to her on the day my mother was born." The woman is in awe of the ring more for its romantic history than its aesthetics. "Beautiful, right?"

"Absolutely." She squeezes the ring onto her oversized finger. "Like a glove."

The husband pulls his wallet out and counts out five twenties. "So we can have it for a hundred bucks and this is all on the level?"

"Yes, sir. If this wasn't on the up-and-up, I wouldn't be doing it this close to that police station."

The husband hands over the cash. "You have a good afternoon now."

"Thank you, sir." Lawrence thrusts the money into his back pocket. "Ya'll be safe on that subway. Lot of shady characters running around here."

The wife holds her hand out and stares at her new prize as they walk away. As soon as they are out of sight, Lawrence ducks back into the pawn shop.

"Weren't you just in here?" Dale asks from behind the safety of the bulletproof glass.

"Yes, sir."

"You casing the joint?" His right hand disappears under the counter. "What's in that bag?"

Scared shitless, Lawrence drops the satchel on the ground and throws his hands up. "No… it's nothing like that. I just went outside to…"

"Ohhh," Dale moves his hand back where Lawrence can see it. "You went and sold some jewelry to that hefty lady?"

"Yeah."

Dale laughs. "At least somebody got some money out of that tight ass husband of her's? What can I do you for?"

"My grandmother passed away and left me some of her jewelry."

"Never heard that one."

"Excuse me?"

"Nevermind. Show me what you got." Dale slides out a security drawer. Lawrence reaches into the satchel and drops in two small handfuls of treasure.

"That all?" Though he doesn't say it, Dale assumes the young man before him has stolen everything.

"That's it."

Dale examines the collection and walks behind a black plastic sheet for further evaluation. Several minutes later he comes back with the items in a plastic tray. "I can give you five hundred for everything you got here."

Sounds like ole Dale is trying to rip him off. "That all?"

"Yep. Take it or leave it."

"I'm gonna have to leave it, Dale." Lawrence motions for him to put the precious metals back in the security drawer.

"How do I know it's not stolen?" Dale's attempt to rattle him fails. "What do you think it's worth?"

"I'm pretty confident I can get at least eight somewhere else."

"Deal." Dale hides the stash under the counter and counts out the cash before Lawrence can think twice.

Lawrence gleams with excitement as he walks outside. Even though he got ripped off, the thrill of haggling the guy out of an additional three hundred dollars really has him going. Ready to collect more fruit from his labor, Lawrence heads into a random Cash4Gold business across the street.

At the end of the unusually long, narrow, and overlit room. he is welcomed by a lonely woman sitting behind a bulletproof counter "Hi. Let me guess. You're here to sell some gold?" Her joke falls flatter than her hair. Or her chest. Both are applicable.

"Yes ma'am." He answers halfway down the long room. "Don't go for any frills around here do you?"

"No, sir," she answers proudly. "We pride ourselves on efficiency. The money we save on decorations we pass on to you in the form of higher payments."

"That's what I like to hear." Lawrence smiles and deposits a handful of valuables into her security box.

Unlike Dale, she tests the quality and weight right in front of him. She crunches the numbers and offers him six hundred and sixty three dollars. He counters with a thousand. Thanks to his burgeoning haggling skills, they eventually settle on eight hundred and fifty.

After walking in-and-out of two more Cash4Gold establishments, Lawrence comes back with another $1750. All told, after three hours of work, he is walking away with a total of $4500. Suddenly too bourgeoisie for public transportation, he hails a cab to take him to the nearest mall.

●　●　●　●　●　●　●　●

After procuring a supply of glucose powder from a health store and a set of scales from a tobacco shop, Lawrence has the cab drop him off in front of his apartment. He whistles a happy tune as he walks up the stairs. If he continues on with all of this hard work, he'll be able to move into a bigger place by the end of the month.

Having already made enough cash to catch up on his rent and buy a cheap used car, the money he is set to make from the cocaine will go to building himself a better life. Even though he has no idea what to do with expendable income lying around, he is more than ready to figure something out.

Off to his right is a painting by a little known artist from Texas that depicts a family celebrating their daughter's quinceañera. The parents and other children have gathered around a tree and are watching the little girl take her swing at the piñata.

The sky darkens and the children snarl at him like dogs. The angry birthday girl uses a sling blade to slash away at the decapitated female hanging from the branch.

Blissfully unaware of the kids playing Murder on the wall, Lawrence rushes through the door and rips open the scales. He tosses the instruction booklet aside and plugs them into the power strip. Rather than clean off the kitchen table to make room for his new office, he sets the scales up on his polyboard desk and drops the bag of coke in an empty candy dish.

After a half hour spent calibrating the machine and setting the defaults, Lawrence weighs out a hundred grams of the cutting agent. According to his calculations, he should get at least a hundred and fifty 8-balls out of his stash. Times that by $120 and Lawrence is looking at around twenty thousand dollars off of this deal.

As gentle as an old woman preparing a cake for her fiftieth wedding anniversary, he carefully blends the glucose powder and cocaine in a plastic bowl. Once this process is complete, he grabs a plastic spoon from his dishwasher and starts measuring out 3.5 mg bags of cut powder.

The boredom kicks in after about ten bags. This process is going to take a while. He decides to have a few beers to help speed things along. He turns on some music and falls into the rhythmic groove of the work. Before long he has made his way through another ten bags and is getting closer to the one-dip-weigh that has become his life goal.

As the monotony kicks in, Lawrence starts imagining a better life. This time things are different. More exciting than his last vision. He's laying out poolside at a villa on the beach. Girls strut by wearing only the skimpiest of the skimpy bikinis.

Body guards loom around every corner and in front of every entrance. While he can't personally see their weapons, he knows they are armed and ready to fire the instant his perimeter is penetrated. There is no wife and there are no kids. There is only the next shipment of cocaine and the next suitcase of cash.

The horde of beautiful women surrounding him are willing to do whatever he wants whenever he wants. Lawrence snaps his fingers and the cocaine groupies respond by removing their tops and jumping into the pool for a rousing game of Mr. Lawrence's favorite pastime. Topless volleyball. He watches intently as the collection of wanna-be-models and don't-wanna-be-strippers bounce, wriggle, and splash around for the most attention.

Back in the real world his head slips off of his balled up fist and sends him crashing face first onto the scale. A sharp pain fills his mouth and he pulls a handheld mirror from underneath an assortment of power cords stowed in the bottom drawer of his desk. "Holy shit!" His fingers feel around the inside of his bloody mouth. There are nothing but two bloody gaps where his top incisors used to be.

Lawrence looks down and finds his teeth resting on the edge of the scales. He picks them up and tries to cram them back into place. The mirror in his hand is too small. He crosses the room to one on the back of the front door. Holding the teeth in his left hand, he leans in for a closer look.

Everything is fine. Aside from the cocaine residue lining his upper lip, his mouth looks the same. When he sits back down at his desk, Lawrence realizes he must have been dreaming when he started shoving cocaine into his mouth thinking they were his teeth.

Regardless of how it happened, his incidental cocaine ingestion has resulted in a state of arousal. Luckily there is a special place where young men with a pocketful of cash, a buttload of cocaine, and some pent-up sexual tension can go to relieve themselves.

•   •   •   •   •   •   •   •

After a quick shower and a change of clothes, Lawrence pours a whiskey on ice into a used fast food cup and runs downstairs to catch a taxi to *The ATLounge* (unofficially, *Ass & Tits Lounge*). Not once in his life has he ever felt like this much of a player.

He feels like a guy with two thousand dollars cash and a couple of 8-balls on his way to a strip club. There really is no better way to describe it than to tell it like it is.

After a couple of overpriced, watered down, top shelf drinks with corresponding lap dances, he tires of the no-touching policy and insists on a private room.

The darkness of the room and the warm, moist stank in the air fills him with excitement. Lawrence takes his seat in front of a small stage centered around a brass pole. After listening around for anyone coming from either the stage or the little entryway, he pulls out a sack and takes a quick bump with his pinkie nail. His eyes dart around to the left and the right before he takes another sample and shoves the bag back in his pocket.

There is a quick rapping at the door followed by a waitress with his cocktails. Two double neat whiskeys with a beer back and a fancy cigar. "Yolanda will be with you in about five minutes." She reaches over and sets out a couple of cocktail napkins on the table next to him.

"Will you bring back another order exactly like this one before she comes in? Then don't come back for another fifteen minutes." Lawrence doesn't recognize the person who is running his mouth at the moment, but he likes him and is pretty sure the waitress is feeling it.

"Yes, sir." As she sets the last drink on the table, she takes care to place her bosom as close to his face as possible.

He pulls out a fifty and sticks it in her garter. "Thanks, baby."

Smoke fills the room. The taste of the whiskey paired with the flavor of a fine cigar overwhelms his pallet. Just as he finishes the second cocktail, the waitress walks back through the door.

As her breasts near his face again, he can tell she had put on more perfume since the last time. Lawrence picks up the fresh cigar and runs it down the bottom of her lip to the top of her knee. Her body wiggles and squirms before the black lights fade to darkness and music starts blasting through the speakers.

"Sorry baby, gotta go. This is a no poaching zone." She pokes out her plump bottom on her way out the door.

Lawrence can't tell if she's working him or if she is genuinely interested.

All worries fade away when a leggy, faux blonde struts out from behind the curtain. She wraps her right leg around the pole and tosses her hair all over the room. A seductive finger beckons him to come forward. He looks at her through the bottom of an empty glass and twirls his finger in the air for her to keep dancing. Engrossed in his confidence, she skips ahead in her routine.

Lawrence leans back and exhales a deep puff of smoke. She wriggles down the steps and firmly plants herself on his enthusiastic lap. For a second he fears she may have broken it.

She confuses his moan of discomfort with a groan of ultra-comfort and moans back at him. "I know baby, there's just something about you in this room right now. Do you feel it?"

"Yes." He whispers back. She leans forward and pops her ass up in his face before dropping back down hard on his lap. She continues grinding her routine away on him while Lawrence takes a sip from his whiskey and smiles a covetous grin.

The dancer turns to face him with her breasts thrown in his face. Lawrence can't fight the feeling anymore. He pulls her close and dives in tongue first for a kiss.

"Touching costs extra." With their eyes locked, she falls back and swings in motion with the music.

"How much extra?"

She pulls up and tugs on his ear with her teeth. "How much touching?"

In Lawrence's haste to grab his wallet, he almost knocks her to the ground. Before he can budget out a small stack, she takes it from him and fans through it.

"This will get you an hour of whatever you want."

He dangles an empty bottle in her face. "I'm gonna need another round."

"Of course you are." She gathers the empty glasses and heads out the door. "This round's on me."

. . . .

After returning with Lawrence's next round - without even so much as a hello – the stripper gets down on her knees and unzips his pants. Wanting to squeeze every dollar out of his show, Lawrence grabs her hand and guides her back up to the stage. She resentfully hops back on and gets to work.

After demonstrating a few things his mother warned him about, she climbs back on the pole and introduces him to a few that she intentionally left out. The acrobatics aren't nearly as impressive as the fact that she does it all with two DDs worth of silicone jammed into her chest. Her hips sway in tune with the beat. She flicks her index finger with her tongue and wraps her legs around the pole.

The room starts heating up. Lawrence adjusts in his seat as he watches the sweat run down her neck and surf the curves of her ample bosom. She climbs to the top of the pole, lets go with her hands, and falls toward the black marble floor.

Yolanda's head slams hard against the pole and crushes in the back of her skull. Dead on impact, her legs stay wrapped around the pole while she slides down. Her head hits the ground and her body bows out. The grip her lifeless legs have on each other and the pole slowly gives away. She slams hard onto the marble floor, losing several teeth and shattering an ankle in the process.

In a matter of seconds her blonde hair has faded to a grotesque black color. The above average face - previously covered with a healthy dosage of makeup - has decayed into a gaunt, blue-black contorted mess.

Unsure whether what is happening is real or not, Lawrence decides it doesn't matter and darts out into the main floor of the club. Blinded by the flashing strobe lights, he trips over nothing in particular and busts it right next to the stage. When he regains his composure, he realizes everybody is staring at him.

The nearly naked women and excited men are coming-and-going with piles of cash strapped loosely in their garters or clinched tightly in their fists. With his eyes fixed squarely on the exit, Lawrence stumbles through a maze of tables and chairs to the glowing sign.

The waitress spots him from the server's station at the end of the bar and gives chase. "Hey, honey. You okay?" She caringly places her hand on his shoulder.

Lawrence straightens up and tries to recover as much of his mojo from earlier as possible. "I'm alright. It's been a while since I've had a nice cigar. I think it got to my head."

"It's alright. It happens to the best of us." Lawrence turns to walk away without thanking her. "You sure you're okay?"

"I'll be alright. I just need to get some rest." He turns before she stops him yet again.

"If you decide you aren't feeling well and need some TLC. Or just want some company." She slides a kiss-sealed napkin in his front pocket with her name and number written on it in lipstick.

Still too freaked out to give a damn, Lawrence stumbles away.

CHAPTER THREE
A Sinner Walks Into A Church

LAWRENCE WILL HANG
FROM A NOOSE
FOR HIS SINS

Lawrence shakes his head in disbelief. There's no way that church sign said that.

Fighting through a hangover, he makes his way up the brick stairs to the front doors of the sanctuary. From this new vantage point he can tell that the sign says something about Jesus paying for their sins as opposed to what he thought he saw.

A group of elderly women is unavoidably huddled near the entrance to the worship hall. In the center of their gathering is a beautiful bouquet of fresh flowers placed in loving memory of one of their husbands.

A line of faded red carpet runs between the two rows of pews that are waiting to be filled by the parishioners shuffling through the door. Lawrence squeezes past a boy and his sister playing cards on the carpet and slides down the back row past a group of teenagers. He scoots to the end and takes a seat in the back corner.

Lawrence leans back and crosses his left leg over his right knee and waits for the preacher to deliver the good news. Off to his right, a couple of the teenagers are flirting more than should be allowed inside of a church. Meanwhile, the unpaired boy and girl with them are passing a church bulletin and golf pencil back-and-forth in a game of tic-tac-toe.

While flipping through the announcements, Lawrence finds the usual list of credits and thank-yous that tend to fill these things. The flowers have been placed out front by Ruth Buckhalter in honor of her husband Mack. Alexa Anderson will be performing a special rendition of *Amazing Grace*. The subject for today's *Children's Church* will be Jonah and the whale. Finally he finds what he's been looking for.

Communion will be given after the sermon for those who feel compelled. Considering all that he's been through the past two days, the one thing he needs right now is to feel closer to God. If drinking his blood and eating his flesh is what it takes, then so be it.

The choir director steps up to the white with gold trim podium to welcome the congregation and make the morning announcements. If young Lawrence had paid this much attention in church, old Lawrence wouldn't be in this situation right now.

Once the announcements have been made, Alexa Anderson meekly steps behind the podium for her solo. She is a thirteen year old who has been a member of the church her whole life. She also happens to do an extraordinary rendition of the gospel classic.

Try as he might to stay cool in front of the disinterested teens, Lawrence starts to cry. First one little tear slides down his right cheek. By the end of the performance, he has given up all pretense.

The tears roll down his face and a small snot bubble forms at the end of his nose. The bubble pops and lands on the sheer shoulder of the middle aged woman seated in front of him.

The song ends and Lawrence feels like a brand new man. The goodness of the Lord flowed out of that little girl's mouth and straight into his soul. Lawrence is reinvigorated and filled with hope. He has a new future now. This one is more clean and more pure than ever before.

In his new reality, Lawrence is a well-respected pillar of the community. He has found himself a beautiful wife and they have two children. They decided early on that a good, Christian upbringing will keep them from making the same mistakes he made when he was growing up. Every Sunday they sit together on the second pew in this church and are a shining example for the rest of the congregation.

Eventually he'll volunteer to be an usher and maybe one day even become a deacon. His wife has a beautiful voice and one day she'll decide to use it to lift up the Lord in praise by signing up for the choir. After a while, he might even create a Sunday school class for youths who need a little extra guidance or are having a tough time growing up in today's increasingly anti-theist society.

He doesn't snap out of it until the sermon is over and the pastor finally calls for all sinners to kneel around the altar of the Lord for communion. Normally he would be too embarrassed from all the crying to walk down the aisle, but that little girl's voice has him unusually motivated.

A statue of Jesus on the cross hanging over the baptismal pool stares at him. He gently kneels down at the altar where he is surrounded by a stern man on one side and a frail woman on the other.

Everybody lowers their head and retrieves a dry cracker from the basket being passed around by the preacher. "Take and eat; this is my body." He passively orders each of them as they reach into the basket.

Lawrence's heart fills with hope when the preacher stops before him. "Take and eat; this is my body." With his eyes closed in solemn prayer, Lawrence stuffs the small cracker into his mouth and bites down.

His pearly whites fail to make a dent in the slimy, rubbery substance now tumbling around in his mouth. Still riding high from the glorious warmth of God's love, he shifts the cracker to the back of his mouth and lets his molars have a go at it.

Even though it takes more work than usual, they finally rip through the purple and black flesh of the woman's cheek. The disgusting flavor of blood and puss fills his mouth. Somehow able to ignore the horrible taste and rubbery texture, he continues tearing and grinding in an erstwhile attempt to rip her cheek to shreds.

Then he feels a rising up from his stomach and realizes he is seconds away from vomiting all over the altar. He spits the piece of chewed cheek into his hand and closes his mouth just in time to prevent himself from throwing up everywhere. His cheeks are left swollen with a mixture of last night's dinner and alcohol.

A bead of sweat rolls down his nose and drips on the hardwood floor. With no other option, Lawrence tilts his head back and swallows it down.

He unclenches his fist to examine the piece of decaying cheek that he had been chewing on. The sight of the shredded flesh in his hand elicits another rising in his stomach. Just as he starts to relax, the preacher circles back around with a chalice of red wine.

"This is my blood of the covenant, which is poured out for many for the forgiveness of sins." Lawrence plunges his cracker into the front pocket of his khakis to receive the cup. His hands shake as the golden goblet nears his mouth. He can feel the cross glaring down on him.

The crown of thorns crammed onto Jesus' head unravels. It slowly starts sliding down Christ's face and curling around his neck. Soon it has formed a noose. The vine tightens and his body starts sliding down the vertical bar.

The savior is dropped sharply to the ground and his neck snaps instantly.

The length of the noose leaves his feet hanging just inches above the water in the baptismal pool. Dark red blood flows from the nail holes in his feet and darkens the water below.

In hopes of recovering his earlier mindset, Lawrence envisions the young girl singing and hums along in his head. *Through many dangers, toils and snares we have already come. T'was Grace that brought us safe thus far and Grace will lead us home.* Lawrence has never wanted anything in his life more than he wants the hallucinations to disappear. He can feel everyone around him giving him the stink eye as he bogarts the chalice. The preacher looming overhead lets out a polite cough.

With the pressure now coming from all angles, Lawrence puts the cup to his lips and takes a sip. When the saliva in his mouth makes contact with the wine, it congeals into a thick, puss infected fluid. He wants to spit it out, but that's not an option. He tries to pretend it's nothing more than an oyster shooter and tosses his head back.

On behalf of his stomach, his throat muscles don't allow that to happen.

He pops up and runs out the side door into the courtyard. Once outside, he leans up against a faded brick façade where he finally releases the contents of his stomach into a cluster of wild flowers.

Try as he might, Lawrence is unable to convince himself that didn't just happen. He shakes the cobwebs out of his head and weakly stumbles back in the direction of his apartment. He keeps his head pointed straight at the ground while he tries to figure out the next step.

As he walks along, the distance between himself and his apartment seems to grow larger. The mere thought of weighing out more product bores him to tears. But a man's got to do what a man's got to do.

Then again he could always buy a used car. The good Lord would want him to buy a car so he can go to church (some other church) more often. He could even give rides to the old and infirm and what not. The little girl with the beautiful voice would want him to have a new car so he can take his wife and kids to all of her area performances. Not to mention, with a new car he can make it to work on time more often. Maybe next time he'll get the promotion and the fifty cent raise.

Weigh out a bunch of cocaine or buy a new car? What kind of coke dealer takes public transportation? But what if he doesn't want to be a drug dealer?

What if he just wants to use drug dealing to get ahead and then clean up his life? Joseph Kennedy got on that hustle to build up his stature. Look how that worked out.

. . . .

Lawrence struts through the door and pulls a quarter out of his change jar. Heads equals tediously measuring out small amounts of cocaine. Tails equals shopping for and purchasing a new car.

"Alright! New car!" The outcome is further evidence that God wants him not only to be a good citizen, but also a happy one. The Lord wants him going to church every Sunday. The Shepherd wants his lost sheep coming home once a week where he can be brought to tears by a child's solo.

Lawrence was never meant to live a life of loose women, piles of dirty money, and sleepless nights worrying about the government and their DEA henchmen. With a new car, it's only a matter of time before the universe rolls out the red carpet.

Still tired from partying last night, he puts on a pot of coffee and readies for an afternoon of surfing the web for a used car. If the caffeine doesn't keep him awake, the copious amounts of cream and sugar he dumps into it will do the trick.

Thanks to the bargaining skills he gained from selling the jewelry, within an hour he has agreed to purchase a red SUV with a blue book value of just under $1800 for only $1200. Somehow Lawrence even negotiated a side deal that got him a full tank of gas in exchange for an 8-ball. He doesn't even remember how cocaine entered their e-mail exchange, but he's confident that's what tipped the scales.

He counts out the twelve hundred bucks and throws on his shoes. With only a half hour to walk twenty blocks, he hurriedly tosses everything in his leather satchel and darts out the door.

•   •   •   •   •   •   •   •

Lawrence scans the fast food parking lot for what will soon be his red SUV. Out of the four he sees, none of them fit the description. He strolls up to the counter and orders a large slushy, a small order of fries, and an empty cup. He then grabs the most secluded table in a quiet part of the restaurant and takes his seat right next to the window.

Lawrence keeps a steady eye outside while his stoned mind wanders to days gone by. All the times he and his father would stop by this same restaurant on their way to a ballgame. Or when he and his ex-girlfriend Linda would stop by here late night for something greasy to soak up the booze.

He lowers the spare cup to his side and deposits the 8-ball before nonchalantly setting it back on the table. He puts his old boots up on the opposing bench and takes a drink from his straw. It's been almost an hour since he left his apartment when he sees the guy pull into a parking spot directly in front of the window.

To his surprise, it's in even better shape than the fella had described. Lawrence pounds his fist against the glass and motions for him to come inside.

"How's it going? I'm Sheldon." He is short with little to no muscle definition. Lawrence could definitely take him.

"Lawrence, nice to meet you."

"Did you want to go outside and check her out?"

"You look like an honest guy. She looks like she's in good shape. Is there anything you think I need to know?"

"Title's in the front seat. Probably gonna need a little brake work in the next month or so. That's about it."

"And the gas?"

"That's why I'm late."

Lawrence reaches into his back pocket and pulls out the presorted cash. He counts it out into Sheldon's hand one twenty at a time. As soon as he's paid in full, Sheldon slides the keys across the table. "How about for the gasoline?"

Lawrence passes him the cup and Sheldon peeks inside. "Unless there's something else, I've got a friend outside waiting to go to a party."

"That's it."

"Have a good one." Sheldon rattles the 8-ball against the sides of the cup. "Got any more?"

"I've got plenty. But not on me. You've got my e-mail, if you wanna party some more, hit me up. I'm sure we can work something out."

Sheldon leans forward. "What's the damage?"

"That goes for one-fifty."

"Must be good shit."

"Best I've ever had." Technically it's the truth. "If you try it and you find the price is agreeable, give me a call. If not, thanks for the gas." He sits down and kicks his feet up on the other bench.

. . . .

On his way out of town, Lawrence stops at a gas station to grab a lighter for the roach he found in the ashtray. While he's at it, he grabs a cheap sixer to take on an afternoon cruise.

Not sure where or why he's going, he pulls onto the interstate and kicks it up to eighty. His new car is nothing but a red blur as it zooms in-and-out of traffic. Once well outside of society's reach, he pulls off onto an exit and turns north.

It's another twenty miles or so before he finally clears the residual traffic and tacky billboards of city life. Rows of trees and the occasional farm are the only things surrounding the highway now. After checking for Johnny Law, he sparks the joint and lets the smell of marijuana fill the car.

Lawrence rolls down the window. Fresh, country air flushes out the stank. He kicks back and takes a pull from his first beer. The heat of the sun pouring through the windows has already warmed them a few degrees.

Now that the reefer has taken full effect, his eyes are squinty and the sun is a thousand times brighter than it was seconds ago. On the left, he passes by an old country gas station with a newly graveled parking lot. The brakes Sheldon warned him about squeal something awful when he slams on them. He backs up and yanks it into the lot where he parks right in front of the entry to the cinder block building.

Once inside he grabs the cheapest pair of sunglasses he can find from the counter display and asks the woman for a pack of smokes. Two minutes later he's back outside and on the road. He adjusts the side view mirror and checks out his new shades.

The sly smile he detected across the face of the cashier suddenly makes sense. Turns out he had just spent three dollars on a pair of women's sunglasses. The pink daisy etched into the corner of both lenses is a dead giveaway. Too relaxed to care, he laughs at his reflection and packs the cigarettes against his wrist.

He turns the volume up when the DJ announces a *Hellish twofer of AC/DC* coming at him. In spite of everything that has been going on, he fails to see the irony of speeding down a backwoods highway rocking out to *Hells Bells*. His head bobs back-and-forth and his left leg taps rhythmically on the floorboard. Angus' guitar kicks in and joins the tolling of the bell. Lawrence turns the volume up.

The sweet smell of honeysuckle overpowers the smoke billowing out of the cigarette in his left hand. Deciding he needs the fresh air more than he needs the nicotine, Lawrence flicks it out the window. He hooks an empty bottle over the roof and narrowly misses a deer crossing sign.

Three beers later, he sees a big, green & brown sign alerting him that he has just entered the confines of Chattahoochee National Forest. Frightened by the mere prospect of going further, he pulls onto the grass shoulder and cuts the wheel hard left for a quick U-turn. He takes another pull from his beer and taps the gas pedal.

HOOOOOONK! A semi driver pulls on the brake wire. Coming so close that it left a rubber track on Lawrence's bumper and knocked him backwards into the drainage ditch.

Scared even more shitless than before, Lawrence drops it into four wheel drive and pulls back onto the shoulder. Now that his nerves have been properly wrecked, he chugs the last of his beer, lights a cigarette, and pops the top on another one.

He stares at the sign up ahead and reconsiders his game plan. Maybe the reason the quarter landed on tails was to get him here and force him to face his fears.

After carefully checking both directions, he speeds back onto the highway and climbs up to the clay and gravel cliff overlooking the clearing. He considers actually heading down to the interior for about two seconds before deciding there's no way in hell he's going back down there.

His heart races. Whatever it is that has been following him around or attached itself to him, he and it are about to have a little chat. He turns onto the overlook and drops an empty out the window. After opening his last beer, he turns the volume all the way down and lights a fresh cigarette.

Not until this very moment does he stop to wonder if maybe he should have thought this through some more. How does one perform a séance in the middle of a national forest without any knowledge of the supernatural? Does he need to look around for the eye of a newt and a lock of hair from a virgin?

So far this adventure has turned out just like that time in high school when he asked Dorothy to the prom. Since then, that whole debacle has been a reference point for all the other bad decisions he's made.

Lawrence had a crush on her for at least four years prior. One morning, out of the blue, he woke up and decided to ask her to prom. The whole bus ride to school he imagined himself walking up to her in the hallway and receiving an immediate yes. Possibly even a hug.

Exactly how he would go about asking her never crossed his mind until he had already interrupted a conversation she was having with a few friends. After several long seconds of him stuttering, she touched his arm and asked if he was okay. A familiar tingle rose to life in his pants.

How embarrassing that he had gotten full on erect from one touch of her hand. He knew, but he didn't think anybody else would notice. "Wanna go to prom?"

Dorothy was so focused on the puppy dog look in his eyes that she didn't notice what was going on down south. "I'm sorry. I'm actually going to my boyfriend's fraternity function that weekend." When she leaned in to give him a hug, things got worse.

While hugging his neck, her hip bumped his erection and caused an explosion in his underwear. He instinctually pulled her closer as his body cringed in orgasmic bliss. Oblivious to what had just happened, she flirtatiously slapped him on the shoulder and laughed at his general awkwardness before turning back to join her friends.

He removed his backpack to cover the stain on his pants and ran straight to the bathroom. She walked away with a small, yet noticeable amount of residue on her white skirt. Over lunch, Dorothy's friends got the rest of the story from a couple of basketball players who saw Lawrence cleaning himself off in the bathroom.

That last year of high school was *absolute hell*.

For the last few weeks of his junior year and the entirety of his senior year, Brett was the only person he really hung out with. Whenever the rest of the class was out in the middle of a field drinking beers, he and Brett were in the barn smoking pot and listening to old country records. When everybody else was at their senior prom dancing at arm's length under the strict supervision of their parents and school administrators, Brett scored a couple of fake IDs and they went out to a local strip club. They spent the whole night making lowball offers to strippers they were hoping would take their virginities.

Brett had been there for him during some of the toughest times in his life. Even the ones he didn't cause. Now is Lawrence's chance to repay his friend.

Emboldened by a newly discovered sense of duty, he jumps out of the car and looks over the ledge. Still not sure what to say or how to say it, he chugs the last of his beer and tosses it into the forest.

A vision of himself soaring to the ground flashes in his mind. "Fuck you!" He yells to the forest and the two formerly desperate souls rotting in the clearing.

"I'm sorry. I don't know what you want from me." Lawrence pleads as much as informs. "I'm just trying to get a new life for myself. Those people out there didn't appreciate theirs. They didn't appreciate all that they were given. They flaunted their disrespect by coming out here and hanging themselves with thousands of dollars' worth of gold. You can't just tempt people with free gold and punish them for taking it. It's bullshit!"

Lawrence turns to walk away. A strong gust of wind rushes down the cliff wall behind him and knocks him off balance. He digs in and fights his way back to the vehicle. A pine tree clinging to the side of the ledge starts wobbling. The swaying of the branches dislodges a root that trips him.

From his position on the ground, he watches as more roots break free from the soil and the tree tips over further. Huge chunks of clay and shrubbery slide over the cliff.

He stands up and steadies himself as the ground underneath rumbles. He darts toward the car. The tree jerks farther to the right before being slowed by its roots. A fault line forms that stretches from the trunk to the other side of the cliff. More soil gives way and slides down the mountain.

Lawrence climbs in the front seat and cranks it up. The engine revs under the pressure of his right foot before he can even put it in reverse. Without looking, he yanks onto the main structure of the mountain just before the entire cliff collapses.

After taking a second to catch his breath, he lights a cigarette and stares into the forest. "Just tell me what you want."

The clouds overhead shift and open up a gaping hole in the sky. The last gleams of the afternoon sun are blinding. A fresh headache pounds to life in his skull. He closes his eyes and stares down at the floorboard.

He opens them onto a shiny, red carpet underneath his feet. The people around him are all dressed in their Sunday best, yet here he is in his sweaty work outfit. The nicely dressed strangers have lined up between the two rows of pews and are waiting in line to visit an altar covered with flowers and a closed casket.

In his hand he holds a church bulletin. His sister walks in with her daughter whose ear is covered in bandages. Lawrence waves to them but they don't see him. He tries to open the pamphlet but the paper won't separate. He holds it up to the light and can tell there is something printed in the middle.

Lawrence shuffles two steps forward with the rest of the line as he studies the chilling scenes depicted in the stain glass windows of the sanctuary.

Eve is cowering underneath the tree of knowledge. The snake is hanging from a branch and has wrapped itself around her neck. The forbidden fruit is in his mouth and he is trying to shove it down her throat.

Judas is in a fiery room collecting the thirty pieces of silver he was promised from Satan. A horde of demons watch the exchange from above.

A shadowy devil looms over Cain as he sneaks up behind his brother with a knife in his hand. The demonic look in Cain's eye contrasts mercilessly against the angelic look on Abel's face.

In this ghastly interpretation of the parable, Abraham relishes in the murder of his son. The Angel of the Lord is not there to prevent it from happening. From the murderous look in Father Abraham's eyes, it wouldn't matter who tried to stop him now.

The line around him dissipates and Lawrence finds himself staring blankly at the casket. The flowers and the pews have disappeared along with the mourners. All of the doors have been bricked over. The colorful stained glass windows are now spraying a fury of blood red light over the sanctuary.

Upon further examination of the casket lid, he can't help but wonder who's inside. *It can't be me... I'm right here.* He gives it everything he's got, but the lid won't budge.

Lawrence refuses to give up. He climbs on top and claws at the seam that attaches the lid to the main structure. In a last ditch effort to find out who died, he pounds furiously on the stained wood.

And he keeps pounding until his fists are bruised and his knuckles are swollen. Fatigue sets in and he gives up. After catching his breath, he lifts his head up and scans the room.

He is surrounded by several angry and confused family members. Security is racing through the crowd at him. Next to the front pew, two guys are holding back an older man who is frantically scratching and clawing to kick Lawrence's ass.

Lawrence looks down at the casket to find the ghastly face of the woman from the clearing. The darkened, disgusting mass is now nothing more than a darkened, disgusting blob. The well-suited security guards make their way through the crowd and harshly yank him down.

Upon hitting the ground, he snaps back to the real world and finds himself kneeling on all fours on the side of the road. He vomits and watches it flow over the ledge before falling over backwards. His feet are left dangling over the edge with his bootstrings blowing in the wind.

The clearing had made it pretty obvious that it wants him to report the bodies to the police before he will be allowed to get his life on track. Grateful for an answer, he climbs back into the car and heads downhill.

Unbeknownst to Lawrence, a black vulture has just taken flight out of the forest and is soaring straight toward him. It's heart stops beating. It's now dead body spirals toward the ground. Lawrence doesn't see the damn thing until a split-second before it crashes through his windshield.

"What the hell!?" He slams on the brakes and puts it in park before the dead bird in his lap twitches out its last bit of life. He gently pokes at it before poking it harder a second time. Lawrence opens the door and slides out from underneath the sheet of shattered glass.

He checks the sky for one of those end-of-days situations where dead birds start falling out of the sky en masse. No such luck. There's not one other dead/dying bird. Or any other signs of an oncoming apocalypse.

•   •   •   •   •   •   •   •

The only pay phone Lawrence can think of is tucked in the back of a bodega where it is dutifully surrounded by on-call drug dealers.

One time the store owner had it removed to make room for a video rental machine. Soon after, his store was ransacked and/or shot up every night until it was put back in place. After all was said and done, the owner was out thousands for the cost of the destroyed machine, stolen videos, stolen/compromised inventory, and several broken windows.

Lawrence pulls his windshieldless car into a parking spot out front. His posture stiffens and his chest puffs out as he readies himself to enter the dimly lit store. The old man behind the counter breaks a dollar and points him to the back corner without being asked.

He strolls past the variety of chocolate bars and microwaveable noodles lining the third aisle. In the back corner - next to the heating pads and two on-duty street pharmacists - is the pay phone.

"Excuse me." He nervously slides his left arm between the two men and grabs the phone.

The guy on the right doesn't take kindly to the intrusion. "We're expecting a call."

"I'll just be a second." As scared as he is right now, the thought of more nightmares is worse. The dealers look to each other and decide to let this one go.

Lawrence picks up the receiver, dials 4-1-1, and whispers nervously into the speaker. "Police Department." The two men on either side of him move in closer. He can feel them breathing down his neck.

"Uhhhh... second precinct?" His hand is shaking so hard the phone bangs against his head.

Lawrence splurges for direct dial and slides all four quarters into the slot. The voice of a female comes through the other end of the line. The men guarding him still can't believe he's going through with this call.

His voice drops about eight octaves as he does his best George Takei impression. "There are two dead bodies out in a clearing in the Chattahoochee National Forest."

"Did you say there are two bodies in the national forest? Sir?" He harshly slams the phone into the cradle and turns to leave.

With that completed, it won't be long before this whole thing is over. Now it's time to go home and get his life back on track. Tomorrow he'll get caught up on his rent, then he'll sell off that coke and be in the black for the first time in his adult life.

• • • • • • • •

Due to the busted out windshield, Lawrence parks his car in a covered garage for the night and hopes wandering eyes don't notice. With an unusually spry spring in his step, he walks the three blocks to his apartment and jogs up the steep stairwell.

He hurries past a landscape painting set in a Midwestern wheat field that is hanging just above the wooden rail. The sun is setting in the background. A bird resting on the left shoulder of a scarecrow in the center of the field holds a bloated head in its talons and takes off away from the setting sun. As the bird soars closer to Lawrence's dimension, the head in its claws opens its mouth and lets out a thundering squawk.

Out of nowhere, Lawrence hears the loud crash of broken glass. It doesn't take long to figure out the noise originated from his apartment. He races up the stairs and busts open the door where he finds the window that he had left open has fallen to an abrupt and destructive close.

Earlier today this would have freaked him out, but having resolved his beef with the clearing, Lawrence writes it off to bad luck. After sweeping up the broken glass and duct taping a piece of cardboard over the empty pane, he sits down at his desk to do some work.

It only takes two bags before he is once again bored to death by the whole process. Lawrence grabs two beers from the fridge and turns on his Waylon Jennings playlist. He licks the tip of his finger and dips it in the large bag of powder and rubs it against his gums.

Mission accomplished. The boredom has faded and he is divvying up the powder at twice the rate he was earlier. Halfway through *Ain't Living Long Like This*, Lawrence gets caught-up in an outlaw state of mind and trims off a small rail.

The music sounds better. The beer tastes more refreshing. And weighing out little bags of cocaine has morphed into an art form as fine as painting in its precision and creativity. The drug fueled nerves in his legs have his feet tapping in time with the music.

The little baggies start to pile up in an empty shoe box. With each little bag he finishes, Lawrence laughs a little and makes an internal *ka-ching* sound. He imagines himself living the life of a lesser Pablo Escobar.

In this other world, he has underpaid underlings doing all of this busy work while he wheels and deals with the famous and the elite. They all want what he's got. All the pop musicians and Hollywood stars come straight to him when they're looking for weight.

With several of the right cops and two judges on the payroll, he is all but immune from prosecution as long as he doesn't leave the state.

When you're destined to be so great, why not take another little line right now and enjoy the ride to the top? Just one. That's all he can allow himself tonight.

After he's sold more and made more cash, then he can reward himself. Eventually he'll double down and buy his own kilo. Then he'll flip that. And so on and so forth until he's lying poolside at his fancy new beach house.

"Whooo boy!" He yells before the chorus of *Are You Sure Hank Done It This Way* rises from the speakers. Suddenly he yearns for prescription medication. Valium, vicodine, Xanax, oxy. Almost anything'll do.

An image of the woman's body crumpled-up in the back seat of a baby blue Cadillac flashes in his mind. He slaps himself across the face. "Keep your eyes on the prize." He drops the volume twenty decibels in hopes it will allow him to concentrate. The song ends and the change in mood created by a duet between Waylon and his wife Jessi gives Lawrence a chance to relax.

He reminisces back to his childhood and the first time he saw Jessi Colter's picture on an album cover squirreled away underneath his grandpa's old record player. She was among the many country music queens he used to rehearse his love making to during those awkward teen years.

Between the cocaine winding through his system and the image of Mrs. Colter's bosom heaving out of a tight, black shirt, his engines have fired up and are running at full speed. Lawrence fumbles through the miscellaneous pile of garbage strewn across his desk and finds the *ATLounge* waitress's phone number.

After realizing who is on the other end of the line, she agrees to come over and hang out. She'll be there in fifteen minutes with some wine.

Lawrence wisely uses that time to clean up his apartment. Holding an empty garbage bag in his left hand, he runs around filling it with empty beer bottles, cigarette butts, and plastic frozen dinner containers. It's embarrassing enough that he eats that crap, and it would be only that much worse if she realizes he doesn't eat the vegetables that come with it.

The shoebox of cocaine goes under the television next to his stereo while the unsorted powder gets covered with plastic wrap and thrown underneath the bathroom sink.

Unsure if she smokes, he leaves the pack of cigarettes next to the ashtray on his desk. If she takes one, that opens the door for him to smoke as well. If not, then he'll tell her that he keeps a pack around for company.

The real question is whether or not he should ask her if she parties. Some girls don't like the harder drugs. Decent girls don't want to be around guys that do them. Then again, cocaine is the ultimate party lubricant. And if she's a stripper, odds are she isn't a very good girl.

Finally he decides to hide his personal 8-ball behind the pack of cigarettes. If she wants a cigarette, he'll excuse himself and tell her to help herself. This way, she'll find out about his new habit on her own and it's up to her if she wants to bring it up or not. "Foolproof."

The alarm on his cell lets him know that she should be arriving any minute. He runs to the bathroom for a quick splash of cologne. After doing an underarm check, he wets a rag and rinses down his pits. In an attempt to show that he's not totally poor, he puts the ring he kept on his left index finger.

Considering he may have a chance to score tonight, Lawrence drops trow and washes off his manhood. While he's down there, he freshens things up a bit by giving it a little spray of cologne. He puts on a fresh shirt from the closet, picks up his copy of *Catcher in the Rye*, grabs a cold beer, and sits down on the couch.

Not that he has any actual plans on reading right now, but he wants her to know that he does own a book. If she assumes he has read it, so be it. Nobody wants anybody thinking they just sit around all day smoking cigarettes and snorting cocaine. People will think more of you if they think you at least read from time to time.

He sees a loose copy of *Rolling Stone* - featuring Sir Elton John on the cover - sticking out from underneath the coffee table and decides to switch it out for the book. It seems more plausible for the nicotine addicted cokehead persona he will be presenting to her. He kicks his feet up on the table right before he hears a gentle knock on the door.

She tosses her purse and two bottles of wine on the couch before lovingly wrapping her arms around his neck. "I'm Lydia by the way. I'm glad you called."

A huge smile crosses his face and he pulls her in closer. "I'm Lawrence. It's a pleasure to meet you, Lydia." His erection rubs up against her waist.

She doesn't love it. But she isn't repulsed by it either. After an unusually long and strangely seductive hug, Lydia pulls away and asks for a beer.

Lawrence grabs two cold ones and motions around his apartment. "May I offer you the tour?"

"Good girls don't go to a boy's bedroom so early. Especially since I just learned your name."

"Good girl, huh? Been a while since I've met one of those."

"You might not think so after I ask this. Do you mind if I bum a cigarette?"

"I thought you'd never ask. Help yourself." Lawrence walks into the kitchen to look for nothing in particular.

"Thanks." Lydia pulls one out of the pack. It isn't until she puts it back down that she notices the familiar looking bag of white powder. The smile on her face fades away. She has been through this before and there is no way she is about to start a relationship with another cokehead.

Not that there aren't any benefits to dating a coke addict. The sex is mind-blowing. The two of you can go out on the town, booze it up til all hours of the night, then come home, do a little blow, and make love til the sun comes up.

Lawrence sheepishly makes his way back to the living room with a corkscrew in his hand. "For when we pop the wine."

"What about glasses?" Her question sends him back into the kitchen. Lydia sits down on the sofa and cuts out two lines on Sir Elton's face.

Lawrence strolls back through the walkway holding two *Flinstones* glasses he purchased at a recent yard sale. "These, embarrassingly enough, are the only glass um… glasses that I have."

His strange and plebeian actions continue to weaken his attractiveness as a long-term mate. "That's fine."

"Ohh, you found that?" Lawrence feigns embarrassment. "Sooo… you get down?"

"I'm not like an addict or anything. But from time to time… *if* there's a party or special occasion." She rolls up a twenty. "You?"

"To be honest," he can't decide whether to downplay his cocaine habit or go all Keith Richards on her. "I've only dabbled a bit. This actually kinda fell in my lap."

"That's one lucky lap. You mind?" She takes a thick one down before getting his approval.

"Sure." He envisions her naked body crawling into his bed. "Help yourself." She leans in with the other nostril and takes down the second line. The waitress has just done about as much coke in those two lines as he's done in his entire coke sniffing career.

Her cocaine proficiency turns Lawrence off a little bit. Between that and her working at a strip club…

He plops down next to her and pours out a smaller line for himself. Lawrence wipes off the business end of the twenty with his shirt and tightens it back up. After he's done, he hocks up a loogie and reaches for an empty bottle to spit in.

"You've got to swallow it." She grabs him by the shoulders and tosses him back on the sofa before he has the chance to spit it out. "All the good stuff's in there." His naiveté proves he was telling the truth. With this peace of mind, she comfortably folds herself up in his arms.

"Good." He wraps his arms around her and soaks in her warmth. "The only reason I was gonna spit it out is because you're here."

Lydia laughs and pokes his knee with her index finger. "So you really don't do coke, do you?" She is dying for him to say no, whether or not it's the truth.

"Not as much as you."

"Oh my God." How the tides have turned. "I come over here talking about being a good girl and in the first ten minutes I'm smoking your cigarettes and have done half of your cocaine."

"I did think we were going to *share* those two lines. But, mi casa es su casa." He reassuringly runs his fingers through her hair.

She places her open palm squarely on the top of his thigh and massages the muscle. "What are we listening to?"

"Sorry." He moves her head aside and grabs the remote from the coffee table. "I don't really listen to much new music. What do you like?"

"I have a real appreciation for the classics. You know, *Cherry Pie, Hot For Teacher, Walk This Way, Pour Some Sugar On Me, Girls, Girls, Girls.*"

"That's a pretty specific list."

"They're all songs girls at the club dance to. It was a joke." Lydia pokes out her bottom lip and looks up to him. "Apparently not a very good one."

"Do you ever get on stage?" Lawrence has set aside his preconceived notions and asks with genuine curiosity.

"I've thought about it. I just can't stop thinking about what my dad would think. The money would be beyond great, but as long as I can keep my head above water and save up some money to pay for college, I'm fine."

"You could do it a lot quicker if you started dancing." Not only does he have a crush on a strip club waitress, but he's giving her honest career advice.

"Right now I'm on pace to have enough money to start in two years with my dignity still intact. I'll have to work while I'm in school to pay my bills, but by then I'll have enough saved for four years of tuition and books."

"That's great." It turns out the strip club waitress might be too good for him. "What do you want to be when you grow up?"

"Right now just a college student. I hope to figure that out before I start. But if not I can at least get my pre-reqs out of the way."

Lawrence finds himself genuinely impressed with her and wishes he had met her sooner. Much sooner. High school or even junior high. They could have met, fallen in love, and stayed together. Every Sunday night could have been like this. Life would be different. Better by miles.

If they would have met in high school, he would be a senior in college now and he would be the one saving money. But his would go toward buying an engagement ring. A nice one. And she'd say yes. She'd have to; they're meant for each other.

He leans in and gives her a passionate kiss. The one he imagines himself giving her in front of God and their families on their wedding day. She shouldn't be wearing the white dress he pictures her in, but that'll be their little secret.

She leans in and pulls him closer. It may or may not be the cocaine, but he has never been kissed so passionately in his life. Hands from both parties start wandering south as her body shivers in his lap.

He twists her hair up in his fist and gives a slight tug. This is new to her, but she likes it. The simple pull reminds her of the strong and confident man from the private room at the strip club. The man kissing her is the take no prisoners type that knows where the line is and when to cross it.

He twists her hair tighter around his fist and pulls her in closer. She likes it more this time. In the throes of passion, he yanks his hand down to caress her body.

She screams and grabs her head. "SHIT! What the hell?"

Lawrence looks down to find a handful of hair still wrapped around his fist. Attached to the end is a small flap of bloody scalp. His heart sinks.

"Holy shit. I'm so sorry." Lawrence runs to the kitchen, wets a handful of paper towels, and runs back to tend to her wound. "I don't know what happened. It must have gotten caught in this ring." He stuffs the bloodied clump of hair between the cushions.

"How bad is it?" If she had seen the size of the swatch of skin he stuffed into the couch, she would be much more distraught.

"It's not good. But it's not horrible." Lawrence mixes his lies with the truth.

"Do you have any bandages or anything?"

"Not that would work on this. But we'll figure something out."

Lydia leans back and stares at her bloody thumb. Out of the corner of her eye she sees the tips of several blonde hairs poking out of the couch. She pulls the clump out and laughs when she sees the piece of skin dangling from the end.

Lawrence runs back in with a bottle of alcohol, two bath cloths, and an elastic strap. "This won't be the most comfortable thing in the world, but it'll have to do until the the store opens in the morning."

"Do you think I should go see a doctor?"

"This is probably gonna sting." Lawrence pours some alcohol on a cloth and dabs it on her head. "Do you feel like you need to go to the doctor?" *Please say no.*

"Not really."

"Then you don't." There is no way he is taking her to the doctor in their condition. The nurses would throw a bandage on her head and seconds later the police would take them both to jail.

Lawrence presses a dry bath cloth against her bloody scalp and ties the elastic band around her head. Comforted more by his attempt at care than the actual results, Lydia lays down in his lap.

CHAPTER FOUR
A Case of The Mondays

Lawrence's eyes flutter open and he wakes up alone on the couch. On his chest is an unopened piece of junk mail with big red lip prints planted on the back. Invigorated by the reminder of his newfound love, his face lights up like the morning sun peeking through his window.

He notices what appears to be a flattened piece of grape chewing gum resting on the floor. It feels weird between his fingers. Wetter, yet less sticky than he would have imagined. For the life of him he can't figure out how so much hair had gotten stuck to it.

The memory of yanking a fistful of hair out of Lydia's head rushes over him. His world crashes down and he drops the flap of dead skin and jumbled hair on the floor before scrambling into the kitchen to wash his hands.

Hadn't he done everything the clearing wanted him to do? Surely the authorities have shown up by now to discover the gruesome scene. In the next couple of days the couple will receive proper funerals. What more could anybody expect?

He closes his eyes to picture a throng of local law enforcement filing into the forest. They wind their way through the rugged path and into the clearing. The detectives and medical examiners spend hours piecing together what happened. Eventually they'll put together that somebody let them down from their nooses.

Lawrence snaps back to reality. His hands had been soaking in the warm water the whole time and now he has to piss. The digital watch strapped to his wrist says its five after seven. This leaves him almost two hours to get ready for work, find a shop to repair his windshield, and catch the bus to work.

Feeling a little hungover and freaked out by the fact that he had almost scalped Lydia, he jumps in the shower to wash off the willies.

Ever cautious of another flashback, he does his best to shower with his eyes wide open. This is no small task considering the shampoo may as well have been labeled *MORE Tears Shampoo*. The instant those first bubbles rinse down his forehead, his eyes start to burn. He looks up to wash away the suds.

One-by-one, the tiny streams darken to a deep red color. After the water has darkened to near black, it starts to thicken. It slaps him in the face like blood gravy and drips down the length of his body.

His mind tells him to run, but his body insists on staying. The water thickens into a tactile solid and the separate streams flow together to form a dark red rope that wraps itself around his neck. Once it has tightened, he regains control over his body and tries to loosen the noose.

Lawrence struggles with the ever tightening rope while the showerhead stretches out-and-up, lifting him in the air. He stands on his tiptoes, but eventually finds himself floating. The ceramic tub below him has transformed into a patchy section of grass and dirt.

The rope fibers tear into his flesh as the noose tightens. Realizing his life will soon be over, Lawrence reaches for a towel to cover his privates. His main concern now being found with a shred of dignity. His sister will freak bad enough when she reads about the felony's worth of cocaine under the sink. Being found naked will only make things worse.

He shoves his feet up against the walls and pushes out far enough to reach a towel hanging from the plastic rack. The rope tightens around his neck and pulls him back into the shower.

After struggling to wrap the towel around his waist, his mind clears and the shower is no longer a torture chamber in the forest. Just an old white tub.

Still standing on his tip toes, Lawrence loses his balance, and crashes over the edge of the tub landing hard on his tailbone. He wraps his hands around the welts on his neck as the cooling water pounds on his legs.

A nearby pile of dirty laundry serves for a pillow as he lays on the tile floor for a five minute breather. The only thing he can figure is that the authorities haven't found the bodies yet. "Things will get better when they do."

It's almost a quarter to eight. He still has fifteen minutes to wait before any of the mechanic shops open. He cuts on the television and catches up on the news for the first time since he left his ex. With any luck, he'll find a local morning show reporting twin suicides in the Chattahoochee National Forest.

Weather… traffic… sports… commercials… weather… traffic… Princess Kate got a puppy… ALARM.

He starts dialing a list of mechanics in order of proximity. Three calls away (roughly twelve blocks) he finds a mechanic willing to take cash and leave the keys under the bumper after they close. Lawrence gathers his things and scurries down the stairwell.

Much to his disappointment, the landlady is not in her office so he doesn't get to see her face when he pays all of the back rent. Lawrence grudgingly slides the envelope through the night deposit slot and jogs out the front door. He hits the sidewalk in full stride.

He sprints up to the dark corner where he parked and is relieved to find no thieves had discovered his vulnerable vehicle. Much less to his liking is the discovery that a group of pigeons had made their roost inside. That's alright; he'll just offer the mechanic a few extra bucks to have it detailed while he's at it.

· · · · · · · ·

"Excuse me." Lawrence interrupts the woman behind the counter who is playing computer solitaire. "I spoke to Jim earlier and he said you guys could help me out."

She fights a yawn before answering as politely as she can fake this early in the morning. "Jim had his morning coffee about fifteen minutes ago." She motions to the bathroom door.

"How long does that usually take?"

"He likes to take it slow." She lowers her voice. "That's his thinking time. I do not get paid enough to interrupt him during it."

"He said he could fix my front windshield for two hundred dollars. I'm kind of in a hurry to catch the bus."

"Two hundred dollars? That doesn't sound like Jim."

"He said he liked the cut of my jib."

"That sounds like Jim." The receptionist pulls out a receipt and jots down a few notes. "Anything else we can do for you today?"

"Yeah, I parked in a garage last night and some pigeons decided to crash inside of my car."

"No problem." She scribbles another note on the receipt. "Fifty dollars."

Lawrence lays the money along with a ten dollar tip on the table. "Thank you for being so helpful."

"That's unnecessary."

He's already halfway out the door. "Yes it is." The receptionist looks around to make sure Jim hasn't come out of the bathroom before stuffing the tip in her shirt pocket.

Once outside he can see that the bus is one stop over. This gives him a little breathing room to slow down and walk the rest of the way. A cool breeze drifts through the overpass and dries the sweat coating his body. He smiles and spreads his arms out as the swirling air envelopes him.

The wind catches a mixture of sulfur and human waste coming from a sewage drain and bathes him in it. "What the fuck?"

The other people standing at the bus stop share a good laugh when he rips off his work cap to cover his face. From their laughter, he can tell this isn't the first time that smell has blown by.

It's 8:30. Plenty of time for the bus ride and a brisk two block walk to the adjacent storage units his boss considers their offices. One of them is just a plain old storage unit holding two trailers full of landscaping equipment. The other one is a storage unit with astro turf for carpet, an old brown desk with faux wood paneling, and a card table with four chairs that serves as their break room.

When it's raining out, the boss will often pull out a pack of cards or a set of dice and they'll gamble the time away. If the sun hasn't come up by lunch, sometimes they'll call it a day and head to the nearest bar where the boss buys the drinks. Those are the best days.

The bus lets him off ten minutes before nine. This could be the first time he has ever been the first one to show up. He quickens his pace as he turns a corner off of the main road onto a side street. Behind him, he hears the familiar noise of Rodrigo's muffler roaring.

"Son-of-a-bitch!" Lawrence takes off down the sidewalk.

Risking life and limb, he cuts to the center of the road and blocks Rodrigo's path. He darts back-and-forth across two lanes of traffic. Rodrigo grows desperate and jumps onto the sidewalk between a fire hydrant and a tree. Lawrence raises his middle finger as he speeds to an open spot on the street parallel to the storage units. He has a tough time squeezing in which leaves a window for Lawrence to take the lead.

Sean hears the noise coming from outside of his window and checks to see what's going on. When he sees them racing across the lot, he locks the door. Lawrence runs up at full speed and yanks on the knob.

He looks up to see his boss's horse teeth shining through a shit eating grin over a cup of black coffee. After having a good laugh, Sean opens the door and welcomes him in by pointing to the time clock.

Lawrence makes moose ears as he walks by. "Nanny nanny boo boo. Stick your head in doo doo."

"Congratulations. You get to unlock the doors and hitch up the trailers while Rodrigo and Handy do what you usually do in the mornings."

"I usually hang out and watch them do everything." Lawrence gets it as soon as the words come out of his mouth. Sean sits down at the desk and snickers over his morning candy bar. "That'll teach me to never show up first again."

"So that's why you've been showing up late every day for the last two seasons?" The truth is, Sean doesn't actually care when he shows up as long as it's before they head out for the day. Lawrence's bad attitude and general lack of interest in being a good employee saves him four dollars a day in unearned wage increases. That's a case of beer every week.

Lawrence slams the door that divides the office from the storage unit and raises the garage door to reveal his two coworkers. "What are you assholes doing?"

Rodrigo and Handy have learned to take his moods in stride. "Just wanted to be here to watch you do all the work." Rodrigo grins and jabs Handy to let him know it's his turn.

"Yeah, Larry. How does it feel to actually do work in the morning?"

"It sucks. It's not fair. I've got to do the same job alone the two of you do together."

"There's nothing stopping you from helping us on all those other days." Rodrigo can be such a dick.

"Whatever." Lawrence drags the first trailer out the door. "Why don't one of you at least pull the trucks around here for me? I know I've done that before."

Rodrigo pats him on the shoulder and repeats an oft spoken saying of Lawrence's. "Not til I've clocked in and had my coffee. I'm just not myself til I've had that first cup."

"Hey, Rod," Handy yells on his way to gather the first of the two trucks, "clock me in too." Handy's a little slow, but he's a great guy The fact that he is a little slow isn't why they call him Handy. He earned that nickname because Sean walked in on him pleasuring himself on the toilet one rainy morning. Within seconds, Andrew changed to Handrew. Eventually everybody settled on Handy.

Lawrence drops the neck of the trailer on the hitch. "Thanks, Handy. You want me to go get this one and you can pull out the other trailer."

Handy laughs and runs to grab the other truck. "Nope."

"Dammit." Lawrence sighs and walks back to the storage unit.

He pictures the hot girl he spent last night with and that cheers him up. This trailer seems lighter than the last one. The air smells sweeter and the sun is shining a little brighter.

The other truck speeds around the corner in reverse and squeals to a stop inches shy of the equipment trailer. "What the hell, Handy?"

"Quit being such a vag!" Rodrigo yells out the window as he lines up the hitch with the trailer. "Hook us up and hop in." Lawrence slams the hitch down on the trailer ball and climbs in the passenger side. Before he can even buckle his seatbelt, Rodrigo has taken off across the parking lot and out the gate.

· · · · · · · ·

"Sean wants me and you to go do a job on the other side of town. Some neighborhood group wants us to do their little park. He thinks if he sends his best beefcake over, maybe the housewives will want us to *mow all of their yards*." Rodrigo adds his own inappropriate sub-context.

"That's gross." Lawrence can't imagine why anyone would want a dried-up, old raisin when he's just plucked one of the sweetest grapes from the vine.

"If I can hook it up with one of these women, I'm done. No more mowing grass for me. I'll be a kept man. Shit I'll be her sex slave if that's what it takes." Rodrigo licks his index finger and runs it down the front of his shirt.

"Do we get to stay on the clock while we're fooling around with these women?"

Rodrigo pulls the truck onto the main stretch of road leading to the interstate. "What Sean don't know won't hurt him. What'd you do this weekend?"

"Nothing worth mentioning." Lawrence lies before copping to the one thing he did that wasn't embarrassing. "I hung out with this chick last night."

"Where did you meet? Did you score? Was she hot?" Rodrigo stops Lawrence before he can answer. "Wait, wait, wait. Was she hot? Did you score? Then where did you meet?"

Normally he would lie to avoid the onslaught of bad jokes, but he actually cares for Lydia and doesn't want anyone thinking he's ashamed of her. "Yes. No. And at the *ATLounge*."

"You met her at Ass & Tits?" Rodrigo is both impressed and a little surprised. "She a stripper?"

"No." Lawrence knows how ridiculous his answer is about to sound. "She's a waitress. She's saving up to go to college."

"Sure she is." Rodrigo laughs at Lawrence's simplicity. "You mean she's waiting tables til she gets promoted to the pole?"

It's not what Rodrigo said but how he said it. "Come on, man. Mess with me about it all you want, but take it easy on her." Rodrigo nods his head to accept the truce. "She came over last night and we hung out. It was a nice time."

"Define *nice time*."

"You know. Listened to music. Had a few drinks." Lawrence taps his nose. "Hit the slopes."

"When did you start getting down?" Rodrigo finds himself learning a lot about the guy he has been landscaping with for the past two seasons.

"Just this weekend. Last night was the first time I've done a whole line." Except for that time when he thought his teeth were cocaine.

"Is it good?"

"It worked for me."

"The both of you were drunk and high and you didn't spend the night naked in bed together?" In Rodrigo's mind there's only one way a good date ends. Especially if you wasted good money on cocaine.

"We just hung out and made out a little bit. When that was done, she fell asleep in my lap. Like I said, it was a nice time." Except for when he sorta scalped her a little bit.

"Alright. Seems like a waste of some perfectly good cocaine to me. But alright."

Lawrence turns and looks out the window. "There's plenty more where that came from."

"What's that?"

"What would you say if I told you I found a half a kilo of cocaine?"

"I'd say you were a fucking liar. Then I'd ask you if I could have some."

"Do you got any friends that like to get down?"

"Yeah, I could introduce you around to some people. For a fee."

"It's real good. I've been getting one twenty an 8-ball."

"I can help you get rid of a few if you'll hook me up with my own."

"I can do it for forty."

"What if I tell my friends it's some really good shit and it costs one fifty? Would that be worth a free bag."

"You can get five of your friends to pay one fifty?"

"They like to party and they make more money than we do. When do you want to do it?" Rodrigo holds his non-driving hand out to finalize the deal.

"Wednesday night?"

"Deal." Rodrigo pulls the truck onto the interstate and swiftly maneuvers to the carpool lane.

• • • • • • • •

After a long day spent mowing grass and trimming bushes, Lawrence is relieved when the bus drops him off near the repair shop. True to his word, Jim had left the key hidden underneath the back bumper. To make things even better, he gets home and finds an open parking spot directly in front of his building.

He unlocks the door, grabs a cold bottle of water, and lays down on the couch. Checking his phone for probably the hundredth time this afternoon, he still doesn't have any missed calls or texts.

The desire to call Lydia grows as he flips through the crisp pages of a men's entertainment magazine. It hasn't even been a full twenty-four hours, there's no way he can call her tonight. Probably best to spend the rest of the evening weighing out some more product.

Lawrence fights the urge to cut on some tunes and grab a cold beer. It is imperative that he behave like an adult until he has started making some money off of this venture. Instead, he turns the TV onto CSPAN2 where a woman is holding a question-and-answer session about her book on the post-slavery south. The monotony of his work sets in and he finds himself actually paying attention.

Up until now he knew very little about the civil rights struggle or the history that occurred in-and-around the city. Several of the events she is describing happened within a few blocks of his apartment.

The tedium of measuring the cocaine pairs like a fine wine with the educational experience of the presentation. The white bags start piling up faster and faster. Before long the shoe box is overflowing and the larger mound of white powder is shrinking.

He starts thinking about where he should take Lydia to dinner on their first date. It would have to be some place nice, but not too nice. She needs to think he's cool. Cool people know about nice, little, out-of-the-way restaurants. Definitely not a chain.

Lynching was by far the most atrocious form of mob justice that occurred during that era. Once again his mind wanders off from his current place in space and time.

Suddenly Lawrence is standing in the middle of the clearing surrounded by a headless lynch mob in white robes. None of them are moving, yet they are closing in around him. He starts sweating and breathing heavily. Just when it appears as though their plan might be to suffocate him to death, the figure behind him wraps its arms around him.

The other decapitated bodies part and clear a path to the gold noose dangling from a tree. The noose magnetically stretches out and wraps itself around his neck. The gold melts into his neck as the hot metal tightens around the welts from the shower incident. The familiarity of the pain reminds him this is just another daydream, but that does little to help him snap out of it.

He closes his eyes and counts to ten. When he opens them again he is weightless. The rope is lifting him up as he fights suffocation by standing on the shoulders and necks of his attackers.

If only the rope had broken his neck, he wouldn't have to wait while the life is slowly suffocated out of him. The ride stops when his head bangs against a branch. He looks down at the colony of headless white ants covering the clearing floor. A warm stream travels down his pants as he continues struggling with the non-malleable rope. All the while yelling at God to save his ass.

The thunderous noise of the headless crowd stomping in rhythm with a distant drumbeat is the only sound he can hear. A vulture stares down at its next meal and the drumbeat grows louder. The rhythm of the forest crescendos.

It stops.

The rope drops, sending Lawrence hopelessly to the ground. The golden noose tightens around his neck as he nears the sea of headless white bodies below. His tormentors spread out in preparation of him crashing to the ground.

Having exhausted his shot at redemption, Lawrence again resigns to death moments before the rope snaps taut around his neck. His tongue lifelessly rolls out of his mouth as he struggles for air.

A weak strand of gold snaps at the base. Followed by another. Then another.

Below him, the anthropomorphized sheets are getting antsy for his arrival. The remaining strands are no longer strong enough to support his weight and he falls to the ground.

"Holy shit!" Lawrence yells out to his empty apartment when he falls backward in his desk chair. The sharp corner of the entertainment center takes a big chunk out of his head in the same spot where he scalped Lydia.

The blood flows and starts to form a puddle on the floor. Lawrence gets up and sticks a dirty fast food napkin in his hair.

A rolled up dollar bill is poking out of the cellophane covering his cigarettes. It beckons for him to take a load off. Without hesitating, he jams the dollar bill into the pile of powder and inhales as much as he can stand.

The throbbing and the pain in his head subside. The blood running down his shoulders starts to feel like July rain. The bumps in the popcorn ceiling drift down on him like snowflakes. The roof opens up and gives way to a clear blue sky accentuated by a blinding yellow sun.

His interest in the post-slavery south wanes and gives way to thoughts of Lydia and her sweet smile. He wonders if she's at work. If so, how many guys have hit on her tonight? The mere thought of her flirting with some other guy makes him want to be a better man. The best way to become a better man is to start acting like a decent man. Decent men clean up their apartments.

He puts a load of laundry in the washing machine and loads the dishwasher. Next he sweeps and mops the floors before scrubbing down the entire bathroom. By the time the clock strikes ten, his entire apartment is spotless and he is still wide awake.

Even after all of the cleaning, there's no way he is going to get a good night's sleep at his place. His sister Elizabeth lives in the suburbs and often tells him that he has an open invitation to visit anytime. Lawrence picks up the phone.

"Hey, Lar." Elizabeth opens with his least favorite childhood nickname. "What's up?"

"This is gonna sound strange, but can I come stay at your place?"

"Is this a bootie call or did you and Linda have another fight?"

"We broke up three months ago. Why would we be fighting?"

"I don't know. People fight. I divorced Carol's father three years ago and I'd kill to go a week without having a shouting match with him."

"It's nothing like that. I've been having some pretty bad nightmares lately. I think if I could just get out of this crappy apartment for a little while I'll be alright."

"Sure. I'll leave the door unlocked."

"Thanks, sis. I'll see you in a bit."

· · · · · · · ·

"Sis?" Lawrence yells in a raised whisper as he crosses Elizabeth's living room. She can usually be found sitting at a little table in the kitchen working on whatever new hobby/get-rich-scheme a friend has introduced her to.

"I'm in here." She answers rather loud for the mother of a sleeping seven year old.

He crosses the other side of the dividing wall to find her fiddling with an mp3 player. "You okay?"

"Yeah. I couldn't find my Walkman so I borrowed Carol's music player."

"Why were you looking for your Walkman?"

"You remember how I used to take you to school? On Friday's I'd always put in that mix tape to get us pumped up for the weekend?" Her voice fills with joy just thinking about the good ole days.

"That's what that was?"

"Yeah. Anyway, I borrowed this gadget and downloaded a greatest hits collection from the late nineties and the early aughts."

"Is that what they're calling it, the *aughts*?"

"I don't know, I heard Mr. Burns use it on a rerun the other day." She sticks one earbud back in her ear. "It's a great little mix. Remember Hoobastank?"

"Yeah, they were *The Reason* I didn't like Friday's. You had them on your weekend party mix? What did you do on Friday nights? Snort meth and cut yourself?"

Elizabeth thinks back to the time she tried meth at a post-prom party. "No, I've had that song on repeat for the last half hour. It's the first time I've listened to it since the whole Dion/Carol thing. I get it now."

"I hope I never get that song."

She looks up at him with sincerity. "I hope you don't either, little bro. What brings you here sober on a weeknight? You got a monster in your closet?"

Her joke was exaggerated, but not wholly unfair. "Since you asked…" He pauses to decide how much truth she can handle. "Mind if I grab a beer?"

"As long as you grab two. You know… you can talk and grab beer at the same time?"

"I've been having these dreams." He plunders through a drawer and pulls out a bottle opener. "Nightmares to be honest."

"And they've got you freaked out enough that you have to run to your big sister for protection?"

"Well…" Lawrence flips the chair and sits Slater style across from her. "You're gonna make fun of me."

"No, I won't." She rubs his forearm.

"Not right now because I'm freaking out. But later on when it turns out I'm crazy, you're definitely gonna make fun of me."

"You're probably right. But we're gonna have to cross that bridge when we get there. What's up?"

"These nightmares have been keeping me up all night. The little bit of sleep I do get isn't worth the trouble." The bottle tremors in his hand as he takes another drink.

"What happens in these nightmares?"

"It's not just nightmares. It's daymares. Visions. Hallucinations. Whatever you want to call them. I see these things in broad daylight and it's like I'm living them. They just come and go as they please."

The hopelessness in his voice breaks her heart. "Anything strange or unusual going on when you see these things? Time of day? Noise? Something you saw? A scent?"

"Nothing." Lawrence leaves out all of the sinning he has done lately. "It seems to happen when I least expect it. It's like it knows the instant I forget and finally relax." He polishes off the suds and walks back to the refrigerator.

"Maybe that's it. What if you are so used to feeling tense and unhappy because of the breakup that your mind and body refuse to let you relax?"

"You think so?"

"I'd bet that's it. When's the last time you really took some time to relax?"

"It has to have been before I found out she was cheating."

She knew the whole time they were dating that Linda was too good for him and that it was only a matter of time before she'd realize it too. "So she was cheating on you?"

Lawrence shakes his head. "Before you ask, I don't know how long, how often, who it was, or where they did it. After she told me, I couldn't bear to look at her. Rodrigo helped me move all of my stuff out the next day."

"I'm sorry."

"It's not your fault. What makes you think that's what's causing my hallucinations?"

Since he had actually bought into her dime store psychiatry, Elizabeth hesitates telling him the truth. "I've been watching a lot of Dr. Phil."

"I guess it makes as much sense as anything else."

"So you really don't know why she was cheating on you?"

"I guess she didn't love me anymore."

Seeing the heartache in her brother's face, Elizabeth decides to shift subjects. "What are these visions? What do you see?"

"Weird stuff. Gross things. Decaying heads. Dead bodies hanging from trees. All sorts of other morbid shit." Lawrence offers her a cigarette, opens the window next to the table, and cuts on a nearby fan.

"Describe this morbid shit?"

"The other night, this girl came over…"

"A girl?" Elizabeth literally cannot help herself.

"Big picture, sis."

"Sorry."

"Things were going good. We were having a nice time over a few cocktails. Her name's Lydia. It's a coincidence; please don't go reading anything into it. We're making out on the couch and I'm kinda, you know?" Lawrence grabs a handful of his own hair and starts pulling on it.

"You pulled her hair?" Elizabeth is shocked to find that her brother has a kinky side. "You like that?"

"I'm fine either way. I tried it and she seemed to like it so I kept at it. This goes on for a little while. Each time I keep pulling a little harder. She keeps liking it. Then all of a sudden I just yank really hard." Lawrence pauses and takes a long drag off of his cigarette before taking an even longer pull from his beer. "Then I looked down at my hand and saw a clump of hair attached to a section of skin about this big." His thumb and index finger form a small circle.

"Wow. What happened when you woke up?"

"This was real... At first I thought it was a dream. I hoped it was a dream. I got so caught up in the moment. I told her the hair got caught in my ring. But I honestly think I just yanked the shit out of her hair. Something inside of me did that. Something inside of me yanked so hard on a girl's head that I pulled out a patch of skin."

"But the other stuff you've been talking about have all been dreams?" Lawrence shakes his head and shrugs his shoulders in a combined *yes/I don't know* motion. "What have you seen that you know was a dream? Give me an example."

Lawrence thinks back to everything that's been happening to him. "I went to church the other day. At first it was great. It was a genuine religious experience. I could actually feel the forgiving touch of God."

"What changed?"

"At the end of the sermon I walked up and took communion. I ate the cracker and drank the wine. But it wasn't a cracker and it wasn't wine." He blows a puff of smoke into the fan. "It felt and tasted like rotten flesh and congealed blood in my mouth. I tried to swallow it, but I freaked out and ran out the side door."

"Catholics believe the cracker and the wine turn to Jesus' flesh and blood in their mouths. Maybe that actually happened to you. If you read *The Bible*, all sorts of strange things have happened."

Lawrence grabs two more beers. "Where in *The Bible* does it say anything about Jesus sliding off of a crucifix and being hung by the crown of thorns?"

"Like?" Elizabeth pulls on an imaginary rope around her neck. "Wow. I know you didn't want me reading anything into this, but I mean Lydia and Linda?" The look on Lawrence's face grants her permission to continue. "Does Lydia have blonde hair too?" Lawrence answers with an eyebrow movement. "Maybe somewhere in your subconscious, you confused the two of them in your head and, thinking it was another hallucination or whatever, you took it out on Lydia."

"You're probably right." He hands her a beer and sits back down. "Thanks, sis."

"Yep." She pops open her beer and they toast. "How'd you get here anyway?"

A cocky smile crosses his face. "I drove my new car. New to me anyway."

She runs to the window and looks outside. "Where did all this money come from?"

Lawrence follows her into the living room. "Sean promoted me to team leader. It pretty much means when he's not around, I'm in charge. But I'm making a dollar more an hour now." Lawrence attributes Rodrigo's recent promotion to himself… and adds an extra fifty cents. "I went by this car dealership the other day and they approved me for a small loan. Bing, bang, boom, here I am."

"Wow." Elizabeth beams with pride. "Look at you go. Linda cheating on you might turn out to be the best thing that's ever happened." Expecting an outright rejection of this statement, she is surprised to see a smile cross his face. "What's that mean?" Lawrence blushes. "She's hotter than Linda?"

"She's close to a ten." The only flaw that he can think of is the bald patch on the back of her head. "She's a waitress at a strip club." Usually Lawrence doesn't like to feed his sister's gossip machine, but he is so excited by this new relationship that he can't not tell her.

"Waitress at a strip club?"

"I know. But I promise it's the truth. It pays better than most waitressing jobs and she gets to keep most of her clothes on. She's saving up to go to college." Lawrence recites the same line that every man caught dating a stripper has spoken at one time or another in their relationship.

"I can't wait to meet her." What Elizabeth really means is that she can't wait to compare her to Linda.

"I'm sure you can't." Lawrence stands and pats her on the shoulder. "I'm gonna make up the couch and catch some sleep."

"You don't want to talk to your sister anymore?"

"Does Carol still wake up with her motor on full blast?"

"Yep." Elizabeth smiles at the thought of the three of them having breakfast in the morning. It's nice to have a man in the house. Even if it is her brother.

"Then I'm gonna need all of the sleep I can get." A few feet down the hallway he stops and sticks his head back into the living room. "Thanks, sis… for everything. You know I love you?"

"I love you, too." Elizabeth puts her headphones back in and starts fiddling with Carol's mp3 player.

CHAPTER FIVE
Cougar Bait

"Uncle Lawrence!" Seven year old Carol jumps into his lap with her knee dangerously close to his crotch.

He gasps under the weight of the ever growing little girl. "Elizabeth! Help! The monster that ate Carol is attacking me."

Elizabeth walks around the corner with a hot cup of coffee in her hand. "You're lucky I let you sleep as long as I did."

"What's for breakfast?" Lawrence lifts Carol and sets her on the floor.

"Mommy's tired. She said you kept her up late last night so we're having frozen waffles."

Lawrence tickles her ribs. "What happened to the homemade pancakes and omelet your mom promised *you* were gonna make us this morning?"

Carol looks up to her mother. "Don't worry baby, I told him no such thing. Must have been another one of your uncle's crazy dreams." She pulls the store brand waffles out of the freezer. "Speaking of which?"

"Slept like a baby."

"That's good." Elizabeth looks down to her daughter. "While these are cooking, why don't you run and get ready for school?"

"But I wanna play with Uncle Lawrence."

"We all do honey. It'll just take a minute and then the two of you can play until I take you to school." Elizabeth pats Carol's backside and sends her off to her room before turning to Lawrence, "First off, you're welcome here any time, I hope you know that." Lawrence nods. "Second, you just need to relax. Break ups can be hard. I know. Don't spend so much time chasing girls at the strip club. Call up some buddies and go out. Grab Rodrigo and grill some steaks. Don't keep jumping into bed with every girl you meet."

"She's not just some girl."

"Sorry." She pauses for a moment. "I completely forgot to tell you I've been blowing this DJ at a male strip club. I think he's gonna make a fabulous stepfather for your niece."

"Point taken."

"I know that when you've been in a relationship for a long time, your friends can fall by the wayside. Then you find yourself all alone after it's over." Elizabeth pours him a cup of coffee. "I know you have to work on Mondays, but if you can get off, me and a group of friends are going out to the rope swing. We're gonna hangout there most of the afternoon. Should be a good time."

"Thanks sis. I just got that promotion and I don't want to mess things up. I'm trying to turn my life around."

"I know. I just don't want you to get all stressed out. Drastic changes like this can take some getting used to."

Carol runs back into the room with her backpack. As if the toaster senses her presence, it shoots out two waffles.

"These are a little overcooked. Do you want them or should I give them to your uncle?"

"He can have them."

"That's cool. I'll just put some extra syrup on there to cover it up."

"Mama, can I have extra syrup on mine?"

"No."

Lawrence looks down at his watch and scarfs down his breakfast. "Sorry guys. I've got to go." He kisses Carol on the back of the head and waves goodbye to Elizabeth.

●　　●　　●　　●　　●　　●　　●　　●

The guys are dragging the trailers out of storage when they see Lawrence pull up in his new car. Rodrigo starts in on him first. "I don't know where to begin. I mean, should I gloat over the fact that he's here last despite apparently owning his own set of wheels or should I ask where he stole it from?"

"Lawrence got a new car?" Handy looks up from the weedeater he is restringing.

"Who'd you steal that piece of shit from?"

Lawrence throws back the first insult that comes to mind. "Your mom."

"How'd you get it?" Rodrigo loads a gas can onto the trailer.

"Paid for it. Where'd you get that shirt?"

"Where'd you get the money?" Rodrigo refuses to let it go.

"I got a loan." If the lie Lawrence told earlier was good enough for his sister, then it's definitely good enough for these two.

"What bank gave you a loan?"

"The place I bought it from. It's over near my sister's house. They killed me on the interest, but I've got a feeling I'll be coming into some money soon."

Rodrigo picks up what Lawrence is putting down. "I'm sure something will work out for you."

"Me too." Lawrence is again filled with a sense of clarity. He can see every twist and turn in the road before him.

Rodrigo tosses Lawrence the keys. "Just me and you again today. Sean's plan worked."

Lawrence jumps behind the wheel. "No shit."

"Apparently the reason we got the gig in the first place is that *The Green Gobblers* went bankrupt. Well, the owner went bankrupt and sold everything. A gambling problem or a coke problem or some shit. After he sold everything, their offices mysteriously burnt down. They gave us a test run yesterday and apparently were impressed."

"Is Sean a better businessman than we gave him credit for?" Lawrence has always underestimated his boss's business acumen. Sean started the business when he was twenty. Year-by-year he has built it up a little bigger. The best part is that it allows Sean to spend his winters touring ski villages in his camper truck.

"He's a better businessman than *you* give him credit for. I've been learning all I can from him since he called me to help him pick up these two trucks. Rodrigo lights a cigarette and rolls down the window. "Thanks for driving by the way. I've got one hell of a hangover."

"You went out last night?"

"Yeah buddy. Me and my friends went to the bar and got wasted watching the baseball game. I don't remember shit after the first inning. You still want me to show you around tomorrow?"

"Unless you've had a change of heart."

"Yes, sir. I told a couple of them about it last night. We're all taking the next morning off so we can party all night."

"And they're fine with the price?"

"It didn't come up. They're not gonna fret over a little money if they've already taken off."

Knowing this allows Lawrence to relax a little as he speeds down the interstate. A few minutes later he pulls up to the gated community and waits for the attendant. "How do we get there?"

"I'm not sure. Sean said this guy should either give us a map or directions. People like us probably have to go through a background check and spread our cheeks before they let us near their houses."

The security guard walks up to the window. He's got the little badge and everything. "Hey guys. Where you working today?"

"Ummm, I think the boss said their names are Faircloth and Strait. Pretty sure he said they live on Maplewood."

"Maplewood?" The security guard stops to think. "Hold on a second." He comes back with two maps and a highlighter. "I'm gonna walk you through it and you highlight the map as we go along."

"First you're gonna go down about half a mile and take a right onto Cedar. That's just past the ninth hole. Cedar's gonna fork about two hundred yards uphill. Stay to the right. That's Willow. You're gonna wind and weave around Willow for about five minutes. There's gonna be a sharp right after the overlook. That's Maplewood. They live right across the cul-de-sac from one another."

Rodrigo points to the trailer. "Are these roads safe with this load?"

The guard pokes his head out. "I've seen worse do it. You boys'll be fine." The gate lifts and Lawrence drives forward without having heard a single instruction. After what could politely be called a hairy driving experience, he parks the truck.

•   •   •   •   •   •   •   •

The rest of the morning is spent mowing, weed eating, trimming bushes, and spreading fertilizer. Neither of them sees hide nor hair of the homeowners until after they are done and two women stumble out the front door of the mansion on the left. The formerly frozen margaritas swishing in their hands splash down on the stoop.

"Oh my Goodness!" The fake blonde exclaims. "It looks great guys!" She passes by on the way to her house. "I'll be back with my checkbook."

Lawrence and Rodrigo laugh before the fake brunette standing in the front door waves her checkbook at them. Since he's closest, Lawrence jogs over. "Good morning, ma'am."

"And good morning to you." She takes a seductive sip from her margarita. "Look at my manners. Would you like one?"

Lawrence can't help but be flattered. "No, thanks. Rodrigo's really hungover today so I have to drive. I don't think I could steer that trailer out of here after one of those."

Her hips twitch. "Rodrigo? Sounds exotic. Where's he from?"

Lawrence can tell she's disappointed that she wound up getting him instead of his more *exotic* friend. "Good ole US of A." Lawrence catches a glimpse of her ornately decorated living room. How nice would it be if he and Lydia lived together in a place like this? "Can we do anything else for you today?"

She lifts the glass to her pursed lips and takes another sip. The strip of gold holding a massive diamond to her finger blasts sunlight into his eyes. His head starts to throb and he shields his eyes with the back of his hand. "Not unless your friend wants a margarita?"

"He's more of a beer guy." Lawrence turns to see Rodrigo being drug into the blonde's house.

"It looks like he's going to be busy for a while. You may as well come inside and take a break."

The headache gains momentum as her ring continues blinding him. He imagines how magnificent that ring would look wrapped around Lydia's finger. Lawrence ignores his better judgment and accepts her offer.

She sets to work making margaritas while shaking and twisting her body even when no movements are required. His eyes narrow and grow hungry as he pictures himself proposing to Lydia. With a rock like that, there's no way a strip club waitress can say no.

His hostess pours an icy green concoction into two martini glasses. She catches him looking and assumes he's staring at her chest. Flattered, yet not interested, she lowers her head into his line of vision. "I'm right here, sweetie."

She passes him the drink and seductively licks a drop from her finger. He walks around the counter and stops in front of her. She is frozen in erotic fear. For all the time she has spent teasing him, this is the first time she has felt truly turned on. "Do you see anything else you like?" The tip of her finger dangles from her lip.

Lawrence pulls the finger from her mouth. Misconstruing his intentions, she leans in and shoves her tongue down his throat. The flavor of alcohol and saliva touching his tongue activates his gag reflex. Once again he feels a familiar tingle in his throat.

Assuming their impending tryst had been stopped dead in its tracks, the housewife is surprised when Lawrence pulls her hand to his mouth. Before long he is flicking his tongue at the base of the ring. Figuring he's just awkward like that, she moans and lifts herself onto the counter.

She maneuvers her hand so Lawrence is working the thumb for a second. He promptly moves back to her ring finger. In an attempt to move things along, she leans in and starts kissing him on the neck. The ring finally loosens and he tugs on it with his teeth.

"What are you doing?" The housewife tries to shove away but is pinned between his body and the counter. She yanks her hand back and slaps him before he can completely remove the ring. Lawrence retreats while she wipes her hand on a rag and straightens her hair. "I think it's best if you leave now." She lifts up her hand and examines the bruise darkening her wrist.

The ring on her finger still draws him in. Emboldened by greed, he reaches for it. She squirms backwards over the counter before falling over the edge and slamming her head against the lacquered brick floor.

Too far gone, Lawrence pulls a knife from the cutlery set and walks over to her. The look in his eyes warns her of what's to come. She jumps to her feet before being tackled from behind. "Stop fucking moving." Lawrence finally tires her out and drops his right knee on her left arm and loosens the ring.

"Don't rape me." As if she hadn't been begging for it moments earlier.

"I just want the ring."

She sees him reach for the knife and fights with all of her might. "Susan!" She screams. "SUSAN!"

The knife plunges into her hand and pops the finger off at the first knuckle. Lawrence holds his prize out and stares in amazement. The ring is now his and soon he will give it to Lydia. Then Lydia will belong to him.

The doorbell rings and Lawrence covers her mouth before dangling the finger in her face. "You better shut the hell up or I'll choke you to death with your own finger."

The bell rings again, Lawrence freaks out and jams the bloody knife into her heart. The woman's frozen stare goes blank and her mouth droops open. Blood flows from her chest and soaks into her blouse.

While still kneeling over her corpse, he straightens himself and checks for any blood stains on his clothes. Without thinking, he shoves her finger into his pocket.

Before leaving, he tears out the signed check and stuffs it in his back pocket. The bright sunlight splatters across his face. Whoever was ringing the doorbell has disappeared. His head starts pounding. Her finger starts wriggling in his pants.

"Here you go." The housewife stuffs the check in his hand. His blank stare confuses her, but she assumes he must be on the pot. "Excuse me," she twirls her margarita with a glass rod. "It looks like your friend is waiting for you."

Lawrence looks at the check and then at the giant diamond strapped to her ring finger. He is filled with a combination of relief and disappointment. "Thank you."

Rodrigo can tell his nerves are shaken. "You alright, man?"

"No." Lawrence answers bluntly as he climbs behind the steering wheel. "Are we done here?"

"Yeah. After lunch we're supposed to go meet Sean and Handy at fast food row. You good to go?"

"I don't think so." Lawrence massages the sides of his temples. "Pretty sure I've got a migraine."

"Need me to drive?" Without answering, Lawrence opens the door and walks to the other side where he takes a nap while Rodrigo drives.

• • • • • • • •

Lawrence stops at the foot of the stairs to his apartment and ponders taking a nap on the floor. He throws his right leg on the first step and painfully follows with his left. The vibrating pain runs up the length of his body before releasing its angst on his brain.

A dozen painful steps later, he passes by a landscape portrait of an old, multi-generational farmhouse. A grandmother is sitting in a rocking chair on the front porch watching her grandchildren swing from an old tire hanging in a mossy oak.

When she sees Lawrence pass by, the old woman throws down her knitting needles and runs straight at her grandchildren. She shoves them out of the way as she races toward him. Stopped by the limitations of the painting, she grabs the inside of the picture frame and thrusts her decaying face into the forefront of the shot and yells. A golden tongue rattles inside of her mouth.

Lawrence hears a rumbling noise coming from upstairs. He stops briefly to listen before another crash comes from his apartment. With the luck he's been having, he never even considers it might have come from anywhere else.

Gritting through the pain, he runs up the stairs and busts through his door. Sure enough, the bookshelf over his desk had fallen on top of an old desktop monitor. Pete's fishbowl is resting upside down next to the screen that is now covered with dirty fish water and red gravel. He flounders around before coming to a stop over a puddle of water near Lawrence's feet. His gills pulse in-and-out over the minute amount of water.

Lawrence scoops Pete up and tosses him into the kitchen sink. The water flows from the tap to envelope Pete and lets him take some much needed breaths. Just as quickly as the water saves his life, it sends him straight down the drain. Lawrence reaches out to save his roommate, but it's too late.

Poor Pete is at the bottom of the sink in the center of the disposal blades. Lawrence looks sadly at him for a brief moment. "Sorry, Pete. You've been a good friend." He flips the switch, cuts the water back on, and watches mournfully as Pete's body blends in with a mixture of rice and crumbs.

With his brain pounding angrily, Lawrence stumbles to the couch. The image of the lifeless housewife comes to mind. His brain has been so inundated with headaches, sleepless nights, and the building up and subsequent crashing of dreams that he can't remember which was reality. The murder or her handing him the check.

Resigned to the fact he may very well be going to prison, Lawrence throws himself on the sofa. The pillow underneath his head provides support but almost no comfort. He may as well be laying on a cinderblock. Across the room, smoke starts wisping through the vents of the computer monitor.

He smells something but writes it off as dirty goldfish water. The monitor continues smoldering as the smoke fills the room. Lawrence finds a dirty t-shirt on the back of the couch and covers his face with it. The coolness of the cloth and the smell of his sweat fills him with a sense of calm. The headache begins to fade.

BEEP! BEEP! BEEP! The fire alarm brings him back to his new normal. Paranoid with a headache.

"What now!?" The tension of these hard days is starting to take its toll on him. He looks over and sees smoke pouring out of the screen. "Fuck me."

He picks up his work boot and slings it at the alarm. It slams against the wall just hard enough to loosen the cheap piece of plastic from its mount and sends it crashing to the ground.

The cessation of the noise slows his headache, but the smell pouring out of the monitor has started to bother him. He grudgingly stands up and lifts open the window to let in some fresh air when he notices that there aren't any pedestrians outside.

"Screw it." He yanks the monitor from the wall and tosses it out the window.

As the screen rotates in-and-out of view, Lawrence sees the face of the woman from the forest pressed against the glass begging for help.

· · · · · · · ·

After three uncomfortable hours of daydreams, nightmares, and a significant amount of time staring at the ceiling, Lawrence gives up on his afternoon nap and decides to clean up the mess from the shelf collapse. His head throbs mercilessly the whole time, but he keeps at it. With the mess cleaned up and his desk cleaner than it has been since he first bought it, he pulls out the rest of his stash and sets to work.

"First things first." He dips his finger in the large bag and rubs his gums for a little pick-me-up. This gets his motor running and clears up his headache. After patiently weighing out two bags, he gives in and trims off a rail.

CHAPTER SIX
Necrophilia

Lawrence offers Rodrigo a cigarette. "Your friends still excited about tonight?" They've been waiting on the tailgate for Sean to give them their marching orders.

"Yeah." Rodrigo answers quietly so Handy can't hear. Not that Handy can't keep a secret, you just have to explain to him that it's a secret and he shouldn't tell anybody. "We can talk about that in the truck. Sean's in there talking to somebody from that neighborhood. I think we may have gotten a couple of referrals."

"Alright fellas, same as yesterday." Sean struts through the garage doors. "You two get to go to the fancy neighborhood again while me and this one go hit the furniture district."

The boss leans into the truck and jots down the morning mileage. "Good to see you today Lawrence," he says semi-sarcastically. "Until you can prove to me you can accept payment from a customer without freaking her out, Rodrigo will do all the bill collecting from now on."

"Sorry, boss." Lawrence flicks his cigarette onto the dew covered grass. "I just kinda spaced out I reckon."

"She thought you were having a stroke or something." Sean walks around to check the mileage on the other truck. "Said your lips kept moving and your body was twitching. She said you looked like a dog having a dream."

"Which is it? A stroke or a dog dream?" Lawrence adds sarcastically when he should have just shut up.

Sean snaps. "Listen here you little shit. I know you don't give a shit about me or my company. I put up with it because, despite the fact that you never show up on time, you're a good worker and smart kid. You keep fucking around like this and one day you're gonna cost me business." Lawrence has always heard about his boss's temper, but this is the first time it has been used against him.

"Maybe one day when you're working for Rodrigo he'll put up with your shit. But as far as you and this job goes, you got one more." Sean takes a deep breath and tries to calm down. "That's one more freaking out of a client, coming in late one more time, one more smartass comment, one more… one more thing that Rodrigo wouldn't do and you're gone. And I wouldn't plan on using me as a reference for your next job as fry bitch."

The boss bumps his shoulder as he walks past to the other side of the truck and hands Rodrigo the day's itinerary. He leers back at Lawrence. "We clear?"

"Yes, sir." Lawrence has been shamed. He looks to Rodrigo who has already jumped behind the wheel.

Rodrigo laughs as they head down the street. "Holy shit, man. There's been times I thought he was gonna come hard at you like that, but I never saw this one coming." He holds his hand out for a cigarette.

Lawrence lights him up. "No shit. It wasn't the nicest thing I've ever said to him, but it damn sure wasn't the worst."

"I'd put your nose to the grindstone and behave for the next month or so. Either that or find another job. Maybe after tonight you can start slinging blow full time."

Lawrence's cigarette dangles between his lips as he stares hopelessly out the window. The idea of going to the bar tonight annoys him.

"We're probably going to be there around nine."

The only thing Lawrence wants to do right now is climb into bed with Lydia and let her hold him while he sleeps away the anguish from the last several days. "Sounds good."

Rodrigo can tell he's still worried about getting his ass chewed out. "Don't let that get to you. He was laughing about it when he told me. That's why I was so shocked to see it happen." Rodrigo laughs. "Meanwhile, poor Handy over there had to be shitting himself. He didn't even get the pleasure of pissing him off and now he's got to ride around with him all day. Your life could be worse. You could be Handy."

Lawrence would kill to be Handy. Go to work. Go home. Watch TV. Go to bed. Wake up. Repeat. That's Handy's life. Along with his general slowness, he has no sexual proclivities of which to speak holding him back. All he expects out of life is work, food, and sleep. Nothing more. Nothing less. It's admirable.

Lawrence's headache makes it harder for him to forget his problems. Not the least of which being that later on he will be walking around in public with a pocketful of a Schedule II narcotic.

The worrying makes the time go by. Before he knows it, the day has passed and Rodrigo is dropping him off at his car. "Don't worry. I'll drop the trailer off and clock you out. It's probably best to keep you away from Sean. Give him a little more time to cool down."

"Thanks, Rod. I'll see you around nine."

· · · · · · · ·

Immediately after walking through the door, Lawrence takes down a line and grabs a beer from the fridge. *Sweet Home Alabama* blasts through the speakers while he opens the window to let in some fresh air.

Since his only knowledge of drug dealing comes from movies and television, he searches his closet for something flashy and tight. *What's the first thing a baseball player does before knocking it out of the park? He puts on the uniform.* Lawrence pulls out a low-cut, shiny red shirt to go along with his cleanest pair of black britches.

After getting dressed, he slicks his hair back with gel and checks himself out in the mirror. He opens the top of his shirt to show a teasing of chest hair then fumbles under the sink for a bottle of cologne that Linda gave him two Christmases ago.

Now that he's ready to go, Lawrence cranks out another line before running downstairs and spending his last ten bucks on a cab. The brown leather satchel strewn across his shoulders is packed with 8-balls. If everything works out perfectly, he should be coming home with at least a thousand dollars at the end of the night. Minus entertainment expenses.

·   ·   ·   ·   ·   ·   ·   ·

The cab drops him off at the sports bar a few minutes after nine. One glance at the exterior and Lawrence knows he made the wrong fashion choice. From the glowing neon signs and sports pennants hanging in the window, this is not the type of place where smooth, sophisticated coke dealers come to do business. This place looks more like somewhere that functioning meth addicts come after work.

"Shit." He slips the driver his last ten dollars without apologizing for the eighty cent tip. The short walk to the front door provides him an opportunity to untuck his shiny shirt, button up the top two buttons, and muss up his hair. One quick look down at his feet and he bemoans that it is too late to change out of the black penny loafers.

The crowd of beer swilling nine-to-fivers inside is pretty much what he expected. Most of the revelers had obviously come here straight from work without bothering to shower, change, or even put mousse in their hair. The clean mouth vs. meth mouth ratio is a paltry two to one.

Finally he notices Rodrigo poke his head up and flag him down. "Really?"

"I didn't know you were coming here straight from work." Lawrence points to the variety of work uniforms around them. The most attractive of which belongs to a young woman in a brown delivery outfit.

"I didn't know you were gonna dress up like a broke ass Scarface. And what's this shit?" Rodrigo ruffs up his hair and points to an open seat next to the hot chick. "Everybody, this is Lawrence. He's the one I was telling you about. Lawrence, these are the people who will be late for work tomorrow. So I guess in a way, we're all Lawrence."

The gang laughs and Lawrence correctly assumes Rodrigo has told them all about their work exploits. The girl in the delivery outfit pours him a beer. "Sit down and have a drink. I'm Betsy."

Feeling completely out of place in his drug dealing outfit, he uneasily sits down next to her. "Nice to meet you, Betsy. I'm Lawrence."

"Don't listen to Rodrigo, he's a jerk." She smiles and bumps up against him. "I like your outfit. Brings a little gravitas to our table."

"Thanks. But I'd feel more comfortable in my work clothes. I'm not even sure where this shirt came from."

"So that's how you two know each other?"

"He didn't tell you?"

"I was just trying to make conversation. He told us you were his friend from work and that you had the hookup on party favors." Betsy pauses and polishes off the last drop of warm beer before pouring another one. "We're ready to party."

Lawrence takes down his first beer of the night in one swallow. "Same here."

"So… When does the party get started?" She opens up her purse and flashes a hundred and fifty dollars in mixed bills.

"About three hours ago back at my place."

Betsy leans in and puts her hand on his thigh. "Sounds like I'm three hours behind. When can I catch-up?"

"Right now." Lawrence reaches into her purse and, in one smooth motion, deposits an 8-ball while pulling out the cash.

"If you'll excuse me." She rubs her fake fingernails along the back of his neck. "I have to go powder my nose."

Rodrigo looks down from the ballgame. "Where'd she go?"

"Powder her nose."

"Ohhhh. You know? This beer's been running through me like a Kenyan at a marathon. I need to go take care of business too." Rodrigo collects his freebie on the way to the bathroom.

Another of Rodrigo's friends walks over from a nearby table. "Hey, I'm Norm… Are they doing what I think they're doing?" Lawrence arrogantly nods his head. The man is starting to fit the outfit. "Cool. One fifty?"

Lawrence motions for him to come over and Norm stuffs the money under a napkin while he slides the bag in his pocket.

Now that Norm is gone, Lawrence is left at the table with just one other guy. Feeling an uptick in confidence from the three hundred dollars in his pocket, he leans in and goes for the sell. "I'm Lawrence." He sticks his hand out over the table. "I'm the guy Rodrigo told you about."

"I'm Rick. No offense, but I don't do that stuff." Rick grabs a beer and directs his attention back to the ballgame.

Betsy walks back in and catches the tail end of the exchange. "Barking up the wrong tree with Rick. He's the good guy. When we start getting wild and crazy later on, he'll be the one that keeps us out of jail."

Lawrence grabs the empty pitchers from the table. "That's good news. I like Rick." He walks to the bar and refills both pitchers. While waiting, he turns around to make sure Betsy is still hot from a distance. Gaudy neck tattoo and all, she still is.

The cocaine has loosened up the entire table. Even Rick appears to have a contact high. Lawrence makes his way back just as the Braves hit a leadoff homerun in the bottom of the seventh to take a one run lead. Betsy wraps her arms around Lawrence and gives him a kiss on the cheek.

That's not good enough for Lawrence who maneuvers his head around and gives her a kiss square on the lips. "Pour me a beer. It's my turn to powder my nose."

From the other side of the table, Rodrigo gives Betsy a knowing look. She innocently shrugs her shoulders and winks back.

Lawrence returns from the bathroom with a dab of white powder conspicuously dusting his top lip. Betsy pours him a beer and leans in to clean off the cocaine remnants with her tongue. "You had some white stuff under your nose. I got it."

As the night goes on the party keeps getting better. Lawrence has sold the rest of his stash and is drunk off his ass. His original plan to go home as soon as he made his money has changed to getting Betsy back to her place. Close to midnight, a pinch hitter drives a single deep to left field and secures a victory for the home team.

All pretense of innocent flirtation is removed when Betsy jumps in his lap and shoves her tongue down his throat. Lawrence kisses her back and rubs his hands all over her bathing suit areas. The making out continues off-and-on until all of Rodrigo's friends have left to go party at some other bar. After half an hour of fooling around alone at the table, Betsy invites him back to her place.

He pays their tabs and throws her into the backseat of a cab. She slovenly shouts the address to the driver while Lawrence climbs on top of her and nibbles on her ear. Betsy resists and politely shoves him off. "You've waited this long. You can wait a little longer."

The driver takes off down the road. Betsy rolls down the window and sticks her head out to yell at the other partiers who are stumbling from club to club. "Whooooo!!" She vurps into her mouth and swallows it back up like a champ. "That's some good coke."

"I'm glad you like it." Lawrence leans in for a kiss but is denied yet again. The cabbie adjusts the mirror to get a better look at what's going on. Lawrence leans back and straightens himself up like a scolded child. "Have you had better?"

"I don't know. We haven't done anything yet." Betsy laughs like she just told the funniest joke in the world.

"Not that. The blow?"

"I've had better. But not a lot better. I've definitely had worse… a lot worse. I used to work at this college bar where these guys would come in with pretty much straight baby laxative and sell it to all the rich assholes."

"Really?"

"Definitely. They'd come to campus from all over town with shit that's been stepped on more than home plate at Turner Field. Those poor kids didn't know any better."

"Assholes." Lawrence tucks away that little nugget for later. "How far are we from your place?"

"Another fifteen minutes."

Lawrence taps out a taste on the back of his hand and motions for her to take it. When she's done, he taps another one out for himself. "What a night." Betsy leans in and cuddles against his red shirt.

An indeterminate amount of time later, the driver drops them off at the front gate to her apartment complex. Still feeling a bit guilty about stiffing the last cabbie, Lawrence gives this one an extra twenty in hopes of banking some karma.

•   •   •   •   •   •   •   •

Largely because the building rests on the edge of campus, Betsy's seventh story apartment has a college feel to it. The cars in the parking lot are covered with team stickers and Greek letters Lawrence never had any reason to learn.

The furniture on the inside is nice. For thrift store furniture. Framed photos from wild parties and extravagant date nights are crowded on a small table in the entryway. The bay window in the living room provides a nice view of the city skyline.

"Are you taking classes?"

"No, that's my sister. School was never really my thing. The last test I took was a pregnancy test." She laughs. Lawrence doesn't.

"This is awkward." Betsy stressfully massages her temple. "I'm on the pill, so this isn't... I'm not trying to get you to... I mean. I always use condoms." The blank look on Lawrence's face makes it worse. "And that's the last time I took a test."

"You are so fucked up." Lawrence laughs at her with that stoned giggle. "I almost stopped you after the whole *I'm on the pill* thing, but you were on such a roll."

The two share a laugh. He taps out two lines while she goes into the fridge for some beers. "Does your sister get down?" Assuming the other girl in the pictures is her sister, Lawrence is interested in meeting her.

"Sometimes. But she's got lab in the morning."

Lawrence's dream of a coked up threesome has been quashed. "What's it like being a grownup and living with your sister?"

She hands him a beer and picks up the straw. "It's alright. She can be a drama queen. Which is why the room was available in the first place."

"What happened?"

"Her and her roommate got in some big fight." Betsy lowers her voice. "I think my sister might have blown her boyfriend or something. Anyway, she moved out and I needed a place to stay," she takes her line and hands him the five spot. "And apparently help pay her half of the bills."

"That's sucks." Lawrence takes his turn.

"Meh. It's all good. I'd only spend it on more stuff like this." She holds up her half empty beer. "But, when I'm still a broke loser in ten years, she'll have to have my back. It's called long-term financial planning."

"Solid." Lawrence wipes his nose. "I've been investing heavily in quick picks and scratchers."

She walks up behind him and kisses his neck. "Diversification. Impressive."

"You can't put all of your eggs…" Betsy interrupts his financial philosophizing with a kiss. Lawrence pulls her in and lifts her onto the counter. He's overcome with thoughts of the murdered(?) housewife from yesterday.

Lawrence spots a potted bonsai tree on a table in the corner. While he's kissing on her neck, he notices a small woman hanging from the little tree. Her head limped off to the side.

Betsy claws at his back. Lawrence moves her hair to the side and flicks her ear with his tongue. She groans in delight and loosens his belt. The sweet smell of the perfume on her neck is replaced with the odor of road kill. Fighting to keep his sanity, he grabs a handful of her hair and covers his nose with her fruit flavored shampoo.

Her once soft, black hair is greasy and filthy. It reeks of old dirt and rotten foliage. Finally unable to take it any longer, Lawrence pulls away with the tip of her black earlobe stuck to his lip.

By now he has been through this too many times not to realize that this is a figment of his imagination. Lawrence spits her ear out on the counter and wipes his mouth with the back of his sleeve. He drains both of their beers before grabbing the putrid flesh of her rotting wrist and dragging her down the hall for a night of passionate lovemaking.

· · · · · · · ·

Lawrence once again finds himself walking through the forest. He shuffles down the trail to the clearing. The weight of the gold and silver he has wrapped himself in has weakened his legs.

The ground below him turns to mud. A thick layer of pine straw is the only thing keeping him from sinking up to his knees. He reaches the edge of the clearing and climbs over the fallen logs. The weight of the precious metals makes the task that much harder.

The sparse green grass that surrounds him is dry and firm. A circle of bodies hanging overhead looks like trinkets dangling from the mobile over a child's crib. The ground rumbles. A horde of hands reaches up out of the ground. They keep trying, but can't get a hold of him.

Lawrence is being lifted up by a noose around his neck. He tries to loosen its stranglehold, but his hands won't budge. All of the skin and muscle has eroded and his arms are now nothing more than bloody bones. Lawrence looks down at the ground that is stretching away and prays for death.

The ground has disappeared. So have the trees and the rope. He is floating in a sea of black. His arms have regenerated muscle and flesh. Even if he isn't sleeping, this is the best rest he's had since Brett told him about that dumbass plan.

Next thing Lawrence knows, he's standing on the lowest branch of a tree and is lowering a noose around his neck. Once properly secured, it tightens itself and urges him forward. The branch starts creaking and bends under the weight of his ill-begotten riches.

The trees that form the circumference of the clearing are all holding nooses. All but two of which are corpseless. Those two hold the freshly twitching bodies of the couple he and Brett robbed on Friday. They are fresh and intact, yet the gold and silver is missing.

Lawrence carefully leans over the edge and sends them a prayer. A breeze flows through the clearing and knocks him off balance. He manages to keep himself from falling to his death by rolling his arms out to the side.

After the initial shock wears off, he calms down and enjoys some fresh air. If he is going to die tonight, his last moments on earth will at least be tranquil.

He searches the forest for clarity before lifting one foot over the ledge and leaning forward. The other follows and he is released from all of his worries. A broad smile crosses his face.

A fully skinned and partially clothed Betsy taps him on the shoulder and startles him awake. Lawrence turns back from the open bay window in the living room and dives on top of her as if she were the last parachute on a crashing airplane. He gropes at her feet and whispers. "Thank you. Thank you."

CHAPTER SEVEN
Penicillin

Lawrence looks around to find Betsy still sleeping on his right arm. The dryness in his mouth makes him regret not taking the morning off. Looking at the makeup-less butterface next to him makes him regret partying at all. As carefully as possible, he lifts his arm and rests her head back on the pillow.

Then he remembers making love to her animated corpse. Her left boob had mummified while her right one was a drippy blob. Her face looked even worse that it does now. The actual love making felt strangely familiar.

The million watt bulb in the lamp next to her bed lights up the entire northern hemisphere as he scans the floor in search of his underwear. After gathering up his clothes, Lawrence peeks down the hallway and crosses to the bathroom.

"Who the fuck are you?" A surprised female sitting on the toilet yells to a still naked Lawrence. She looks just like her sister, but with a better looking face. Then again, she already has her makeup on.

Lawrence slams the door and covers himself with the pile of clothes in his arms. "Oh my God. I'm so sorry."

"That's nice." She whispers over the sound of the flushing toilet. "But who the fuck are you?"

Lawrence hears the lock click from the other side. "I'm Lawrence. I'm a friend of your sisters." He starts getting dressed in the hallway.

She yanks the door open and examines her sister's most recent conquest. "So she did it?"

"Did what?"

"Umm… nothing."

"Umm… what?" Lawrence moves in closer. His voice asks a simple question while his body demands an answer.

"Well," the girl rustles her hair and sticks out her hand. "I'm Britny by the way."

"Britny and Betsy?"

Britny wraps her hair up in a ponytail. "Our parent's weren't the creative type."

"What did your sister do?"

"After that last guy, Rodrigo or whatever, I told her she just needed to get laid. I said *just find some guy and go to town on him.*"

"Rodrigo?" Lawrence didn't hear anything else she said after his name.

"You know him?"

Lawrence's jealousy rages over a girl that he doesn't even care about. "I think I met him last night."

"I don't get that girl."

"I don't get any of them. What happened between her and that guy?"

"He just treated her like shit for a while. They were never really dating, but she treated it like they were in love. She called and texted him all the time. Then he'd only call or text her back late night when he was hammered. It was a shame watching an independent woman morph into a booty call for some landscaper."

Lawrence does his best not to take offense. "Happens to the best of us."

Britny puts her hand on his forearm. A pulse of energy flows from his body to hers. Caught up in the moment, she moves in. Just when Lawrence starts outlining his letter to Penthouse, Britny remembers what happened with her last roommate and backs away.

Lawrence bites his bottom lip and mentally releases a string of cusswords. "Do you mind if I take a quick shower? I've really got to get to work?"

"Sure. Towels are under the sink."

"Awesome." He steps into the bathroom and closes the door. "Do you think you could do me a favor?"

"Yeah…"

"Could you call me a cab?"

"Sure." She obediently gets to work. Ten minutes later - still hungover as hell but feeling significantly better - Lawrence walks into the kitchen.

"Your cab will be here any minute." Britny surprises him with coffee in a paper cup stolen from a cheap hotel. "It's plain black. I don't know how you take it."

"As hungover as I am, anything less than an IV straight into my arm is too little too late." Lawrence sits down at the counter and rests his head on his fist.

The coffee has cooled to the perfect temperature. Like a good wife-in-training, she had done a fantastic job of anticipating his needs. It only takes him two swallows to down the little cup before she pours him another. After a rather one-sided internal debate, Lawrence pulls out the last of the 8-ball and sets it on the table.

"That explains a lot."

"You get down?"

Britny thinks about it. "Sometimes, but I really shouldn't. I've got a three hour biology lab."

"You sure? It's the least I could do for your hospitality. And scaring the shit out of you earlier."

"It would make my lab a lot more interesting."

Lawrence taps out another line next to his. "Atta girl."

"Whoa, cowboy." Britny grabs his hand. "I just need to sit through a lab, not fly to the moon. If I take that, I'll wind up dry humping the little graduate assistant that teaches the class."

Never one to argue with a potential sex partner, Lawrence grabs a nearby postcard and moves a portion of her line over to his side. He pulls out the still rolled up five dollar bill from last night and hands it to her. Britny takes her line and passes it back. Lawrence takes a sip from his coffee before tackling his.

Britny claps her hands in excitement and grabs her backpack from the counter. "Thanks for the hookup. It was a pleasure meeting you."

"You're just gonna leave me here?"

Her hair swirls in the breeze when she opens the door. "I'm assuming if my sister can trust you with her flower, then I can trust you not to rob or kill her until your cab shows up."

He banks an image of her ass shaking as she walks out the door. As he finishes his second cup, a rumbling noise comes down the hallway. Not wanting Betsy's face to be the last impression from this experience, Lawrence grabs his things and quietly ducks out the door.

•   •   •   •   •   •   •   •

"There he is." Handy points to Lawrence excitedly climbing out of a cab.

Sean sneers as his worst employee swaggers their way. "He looks happy. Wonder what the hell's gotten into him?"

Handy laughs and waves. "He's skipping like a girl."

"What the hell got into you?" Sean asks with suspicion.

"More like what I got into, boss." Lawrence slaps Handy on the shoulder.

Sean laughs at the joke he is about to say. "Reckon that explains why Rodrigo's gonna be late too."

"Har, har, har." Lawrence helps Handy lift the trailer onto the hitch.

Handy thinks for a second and then laughs. "They'd make a cute couple."

"All inter-office romances must be reported, in writing, to management. So I can scan it and post it to Twitter."

"You're on Twitter?"

"Yeah. You surprised?"

"No. I just assumed you and your friends used carrier pigeons. Or maybe a couple of tin cans tied to a string.

Handy notices Lawrence's teeth chattering. "You cold or something?"

"No, why?"

Handy leans in for a better listen. "You're teeth are chattering something fierce. I can hear 'em."

Lawrence consciously stops the chattering. "The *girl* I was with last night left me fully loaded this morning. Between that and the ungodly amount of grounds she put in the coffee, I'm probably a little wired."

"That's Rodrigo for you. He likes his coffee like he likes his men. Strong and bitter."

"You are on fire, boss. Please tell me I get to ride with you today." Lawrence bites his tongue when he realizes the coke will eventually wear off and then he'll be stuck riding around with a boss who doesn't particularly care for him.

"Not a chance in hell. Me and Handy are gonna go knock out that shopping center on Monroe. I left a couple of addresses taped to the steering wheel. You should be able to knock out the first two before lunch. Then you can come back and pick up Rodrigo to finish the rest." Sean toots the horn for Handy to climb aboard.

Lawrence kicks the trailer. "Ya'll aren't gonna help me hook this up?"

"Nope." Sean answers bluntly before taking off. On their way out the gate, they throw their arms out the window and give Lawrence the bird.

"Assholes." Lawrence shuffles into the office and clocks in. He drops the nearly empty 8-ball on the table and takes a seat. There's just enough left for one line. Not nearly enough to carry him through a hungover day of mowing grass.

"Fuck it." If Rodrigo doesn't bring his, he'll run by his place and grab some more. Lawrence taps out half of his remaining stash on the table.

"Alright, Thursday. Let's do this." The chair falls backward as he jumps up and jogs into the garage. He even remembers to lock the door behind himself.

"Shit!" Lawrence turns and looks through the foursquare window pane. Just as he thought, the remnants of his stash are resting in an open white bag in the middle of the table.

Of course his asshole of a boss doesn't trust him with a key, so he can't get back in. There's no sense in calling Rodrigo. Wherever he is and whatever he's doing, he ain't answering a phone call from anybody at work.

"Shit, shit, shit." Lawrence paces around the empty storage unit. Glancing through the window every time he passes by the door. The bag taunts him from the other room. It feels as if the last week of his life has all been leading up to this moment. And the ensuing moments where his boss fires him and calls the cops.

"I ain't going down like this." Lawrence sees his perfect life with Lydia bursting into flames. "This ain't happening." He grabs hold of a pair of pliers and takes back his future. After knocking out the shards of glass surrounding the perimeter, he reaches in and unlocks the door.

The decision to break the window means he has to spend the next hour cleaning up broken glass, running to the hardware store, and reinstalling the window. While he's at it, he might as well stop by his place and pick up some more blow.

•　•　•　•　•　•　•　•

Two hours behind schedule - and high off his ass - Lawrence jumps in the truck and takes off to the first job. Even if the boss somehow notices the window has been broken, he'll at least get credit for fixing it. As far as work goes, he'll just have to powder through the afternoon and get it done. Even if the finished product turns out to be a little sloppy.

The first track that plays on his mp3 player is an introduction to Spanish series that Linda uploaded to his computer. He skips past that and cranks up the riding mower. The only line of Spanish she ever taught him runs on repeat through his head. *Mi hombre es Lawrence. Me encanta a Linda.*

One time she even went so far as to grab his tongue and manually roll his *R*s for him. Not long after that, she gave up on him ever learning Spanish. Within a week, she was speaking conversationally with the waiter at their favorite Mexican restaurant. By the end of the month, Linda was stopping employees at the *tienda* where she started doing her shopping to discuss homemade tortilla recipes.

That was Linda. She put her mind to something and made it happen. There was no lollygagging, just a decision followed by precise execution. All of that learning Spanish business erupted out of a simple conversation they had about their theoretical honeymoon.

The truth is he'd marry her right now if she'd take him back. Not that there's any chance of that. But he can't help but wonder how different his life would be if things had worked out. There's no way in hell he'd still be cutting grass for Sean. Her uncle once told Lawrence he could have a job at the bank if he ever decided to *grow up and start acting like a man.*

Men come in all shapes and sizes. Lawrence regretfully told him at the time.

Not until too late did he realize what her uncle meant. A man loves a woman. And he loves her so much that he does whatever it takes to be with her. Even if that means slowing down all the partying and dressing a little nicer from time-to-time to get a good job.

A man isn't someone whose entire future rests on ill begotten gains from raiding suicide victims. A man controls his destiny. If Linda was still in his life, that's the kind of man he'd be. He'd be a good citizen, father, husband, and faithful believer. He knew it the whole time they were dating; he could see it clear as day.

Linda couldn't. So she gave up on them.

How could something so obvious to him completely escape her? Maybe something is wrong with her. There has to be if she couldn't see the light at the end of their tunnel of love. Sure they had their share of bad times, but the good times were almost good enough to cancel them out.

Had he been fooling himself the whole time? Was the light a figment of his imagination? Maybe there was nothing but darkness. Maybe there *is* nothing but darkness.

His relationship with Linda started off so amazingly natural it was like they had been together since time began. They agreed on all the things that mattered and neither one of them cared much about the things on which they disagreed. Those first two months were amazing.

Then his lease ended and she broke hers so they could get a place together. The apartment was far from fancy, but it was nicer than anything they could afford separately.

Linda spent her days working on a fashion blog and her nights waiting tables at a neighborhood bar and grill. Meanwhile, Lawrence spent his days mowing yards and his nights drinking. More often than not at the same bar and grill where she worked.

Before long, her blog started gaining a loyal following and requiring more of her time. Eventually her success at home spread to work where she started getting managing and bartending shifts. Suddenly, the party girl he met was morphing into the successful woman they both knew she would become.

No more sitting together at the bar getting hammered at the end of her shifts. Now she had to set an example to her employees. Or go straight home and edit her latest blog entry.

Somewhere along the line, Lawrence got left behind. Linda was an overnight success and Rodrigo had just been promoted to his boss. All the while, Brett was a few blocks away. Stuck in an identical rut.

The same friend Lawrence had written off because Linda called him a *bad influence* was the same one that was there to pick him up. *That's great news.* Brett told him when he heard. *She'll be an internet entrepreneur, cagillionaire chick and you'll be her sugar daddy. Then I can be your sugar buddy. You can drop the kids off at school, come pick me up, and we'll go to your fancy ass house and drink til we can't stand each other. Then the next day, we'll wake up and do the same damn thing.*

Maybe Linda wasn't wrong. Instead of leeching off of her, he should have followed her lead and made something of himself. Fuck Brett.

Why did it take him twenty-two years to realize this? That fucking kid has been nothing but an albatross around his neck from day one. Look where it's gotten him. Shitty job, shitty apartment. Not to mention he is now haunted by supernatural demons and a budding cocaine habit. Thanks, friend.

Lawrence's family had warned him about *that Perry kid* since they found out the two were friends. If it wouldn't have been for *that Perry kid*, he would be living in a mansion with his billionaire wife.

"Why didn't I go after that promotion?" Lawrence asks under the whirring of the weed eater.

At one point, Linda told him to start showing more initiative and try to get Sean to take him under his wing. But who wants to spend the rest of their summers cutting grass and their winters living in the back of a pickup truck at tacky ski resorts?

If he had been *chosen* as Sean's understudy, he'd be running this bitch by now. Or at least he would have his own company. Not like Rodrigo.

Rodrigo's got his whole life in front of him. Yet he spends his week nights getting fucked up and hooking up with perfectly good girls and never calling them again. Lawrence wishes he could sit Rodrigo down and tell him to take advantage of everything he has. But he wouldn't listen. Rodrigo's an asshole.

Linda would be so proud of him. His business would advertise on her website and her website would advertise with his business. They would pass the money back-and-forth like the rest of the one-percenters. They would live their financial lives like a fiscal roach motel. The money would check in, but it would never check out.

They would be the young, up-and-coming, rags-to-riches, couple all of the old money in town wants to be associated with. They'd go to all the parties and their pictures would be taken in front of cool backdrops. Once they're established and things have started to take off, they'll end up at parties so fancy even the entertainment media isn't invited.

At the time, the breakup hit him like a ton of bricks. Even though he had seen the writing on the wall for weeks, it still destroyed him. The drinking and the partying with Brett worsened. If he wouldn't have thrown up one night at the bar, it would have been him driving the night Brett got his second DUI.

All of the partying and bad decisions inevitably led to him being two months behind on his rent. Which led him to pillage a dead body in the forest just to keep a roof over his head.

Something has changed in the last week. Women have been seeing him in a different light. As a result he has been getting more quality action. Lydia and Betsy were quality, even given the handicap that Betsy calls a face. If he would have pressed the issue, he could have scored with Britny. She was quality, but something was off about those chicks.

Lawrence imagines what Thanksgiving would be like with Betsy and Britny's family. He pictures their mother sitting around the kitchen table hammered off of whatever wine is closest. She deals another round of Russian Rummy to her daughters and whatever other female relatives have gathered for the occasion.

Meanwhile Lawrence has to spend the entire afternoon in the living room with their father who is constantly looking around before texting his mistress. The rest of the male relatives are outside smoking cigarettes and pounding beers.

Inevitably, some family drama will break out. Just like it does every year. Probably over something like their aunt having hooked up with their father before he met their mother.

Somehow, Lawrence'll get caught up in the middle of it. In a drunken fury he'll say some things he doesn't mean and wind up having to call everyone later to apologize. Then him and whichever one of them he knocked up would go back to their crappy house where things are just as miserable.

All of a sudden, he can't even remember what those two skanks looked like. Lydia's face is the only thing he can see. She might be the second love of his life. More importantly, she could be the one that showed up at the right time. Just when he got his act together. Maybe Elizabeth was right. Maybe Lydia is just Linda 2.0. A better looking version with upgraded firmware.

If everything works out as planned, he'll soon be out of that crap apartment and living in a rented house before the end of the mowing season. Then he can buy some new clothes. Including a couple of fancy suits for the nice dinners they'll go to. Lydia will start going to school and then graduate straight into her career as a housewife who has an accounting degree to fall back on. By the time their first child hits kindergarten, Lawrence will have earned their first million.

• • • • • • • •

Rodrigo is waiting outside for Lawrence and scarfing down the last bite of his cheeseburger. "What the hell happened in there?"

"What gave me away?"

"You left the broken glass in the trash can. You gotta take that shit out."

"You're speaking from experience?"

Rodrigo jumps in the passenger seat. "Half of my job is covering up your screw-ups. For example, I took out the trash."

Lawrence takes off through the gates and lights a cigarette. "Thanks. I fucking left my sack sitting on the table this morning and didn't realize it until after I locked the door."

"You cranked out a line at work?"

"Yeah. We weren't all smart enough to take the morning off."

Rodrigo snatches the lighter and gives him a knowing smile. "You mean like me and Betsy?"

"You hooked up with her, didn't you?"

"Yeah." Rodrigo gloats. "You remember two months ago when we had to stop by the drug store to pick up that prescription?"

"Yeah."

Rodrigo laughs like a bastard. "That was from her. The penicillin cleared it up though. Until one night I got drunk and called her again."

"So..."

"Yep. You have your first STD." Rodrigo pats him on the back. "And we're eskimo brothers now."

Lawrence can't help but be a little pissed. "Why didn't you tell me last night?"

"Would it have mattered?"

Lawrence thinks back to last night and the image of her rotting earlobe in his mouth. "Probably not. But still."

"Was it worth it?"

"Not at all. I didn't realize how blugh her face was until this morning. Now if her sister would have joined in… that would have been worth the trouble."

"Darkness is definitely Betsy's friend. And Britny, she's hotter than hellfire. Boy does she hate my ass." Rodrigo flicks his cigarette out the window. "Probably because she thinks I treated her sister like a booty call." While Rodrigo yaps away, Lawrence can't stop thinking about whatever is growing in his crotch. "Did you get any work done this morning? You know, between doing blow and fixing the window?"

"I finished both yards on my list."

"Nice. Amazing what you can get done after a whiff of inspiration."

"Definitely. I was in this crazy zone. My mind was racing, but my body was steady on task."

"Got any left? We can knock out these last houses real quick and get off early. I could use some more shuteye."

"Sounds good to me." Lawrence pulls a fresh sack out of his front pocket and tosses it to Rodrigo.

Rodrigo looks for something to tap out a couple of lines on. "Right now?"

"You had five more hours of sleep than I did. If it wasn't for that stuff, I'd be sleeping it off in the break room right now."

"Don't gotta tell me twice." Rodrigo finds a loose brochure in the glove compartment and taps out two small lines.

"More." There has been a change in Lawrence's tone. Something about it makes Rodrigo want to please him. He taps out a little more powder and pulls a red straw from an empty coffee cup in the floorboard.

Half an hour later, they pull up to the next job and back the mowers down from the trailer. Lawrence waves Rodrigo to start without him. "I'll catch up in a second. I've got to call my sister."

"You ain't gotta lie to me. You're calling the clinic, ain't you?"

"For your information, I'm calling my sister to check on my sick niece. She was up all night with the flu." Lawrence feels horrible for using Carol in a lie.

"I'm not buying it. But I'm gonna leave you alone because I'm feeling guilty for not telling you. I've still got half a bottle with a refill if you want to save yourself the time. Then again, a girl like that may have picked up something else since then. It's probably best to go ahead and make that call." Rodrigo doesn't bother hiding his laughter as he pulls away.

Lawrence makes the call and sets up an appointment for tomorrow morning. Just thinking about it makes his privates itch. The cocaine and alcohol infused sweat drowning his manhood only makes things worse. He reaches into the bag with his pinky nail and takes a bump before getting to work.

CHAPTER EIGHT
Freak Clinic

After the best night of sleep he's had in years, Lawrence's alarm goes off at 8:00. He is filled with a clarity and conviction not felt since he was five and told his father he wanted to be an astronaut.

He's gonna go to work and get there early. Upon arriving early, he'll be a model employee. Sean will tell him to do something and he'll do it. No attitude and no stupid jokes.

Rodrigo wants fish from a fast food place for lunch? Forget about it. No problem. Eating is just something he has to do to get to the end of the day.

Then he can ask Lydia out on a proper date. It may already be too late, but if he stops by her work with some flowers, she'll say yes.

Not flowers, a single rose. He'll ask her out in front of all of her coworkers and perverted customers. She'll say yes because she sees what he sees. And she knows because he knows. Not like Linda.

"Fuck." Lawrence lifts straight up in bed. His clinic appointment is in thirty minutes. About the same time Sean will be sitting at his desk to find a note informing him that Lawrence is taking a personal day. Sean'll be pissed for a bit. Then Rodrigo - like the ass kisser he is - will tell him the real reason he's skipping work. After explaining everything to Handy, they'll all have a good laugh at his expense before getting on with their day.

The last remnants of sudsy water squeeze down the clogged drain as Lawrence throws on his pants and a shirt before running down the stairwell. Deftly dodging traffic, he jaywalks across the four-lane street before hopping in his car and making a risky U-turn.

Ten minutes later, his red SUV pulls into a shady parking spot on the far side of a white brick building. Lawrence takes his seat in a row of old, orange, plastic seats bolted to the wall.

A miscellany of the unemployed, underemployed, and disabled fill the room. Each person has their own depressing story, but Lawrence can't be thinking like that right now. He's got to keep thinking positive. His mind needs to be clear and his thoughts need to be pointing forward.

He starts singing in his head. Without provocation, his thoughts shift to Betsy and the wild night they had together. The disgusting night of grossness brings his energy down. The brightness surrounding him seconds earlier has descended into decay.

His internal jukebox switches to an old party anthem in hopes of brightening his aura. A pen dangling from a sign up sheet on the counter grabs his attention as it sways to the beat of the rhythm in his head. Lawrence's foot taps in beat with the dangling pen. He uses his index fingers as drumsticks as he taps on his knees.

He tugs on his sweat stained collar. The heat in the waiting room is suddenly stifling. His eyes wander away from the pen. The room around him has darkened and he is overcome with a morbid feeling. The dark wallpaper has ripped to reveal interspersed sections of drywall and cinder blocks. The sick people around him are now on death's doorstep. With every cough and sneeze, luminescent globs of pure death spurt out.

A rat sticks its head out of a hole in the corner and brashly steps out onto the shoulder of a ghastly looking woman. She is either sleeping or dead with her head leaning against the wall. Her general lack of concern over a rat on her person leads Lawrence to assume the latter. Frightened for his life and worried about his waning sanity, he glances out the window.

There is nothing. Not his car. Not the parking lot. No brick sign displaying the name of the clinic.

His pale, bruised reflection in the window now matches that of everyone around him. His clothes are ragged and torn. A spark lights up in the distance. It could have been two feet away. It could have been two miles. A line of fire erupts and blazes toward the building. Of all the shit surrounding him in that waiting room, the flames frighten him the most. Something about them feels so real. So absolute.

Cautiously facing the fire, he backs away from the window and slams against a check-in station. Lawrence starts singing out loud as he scuttles against the wall and takes his seat. The late nineties classic fails to soothe him as he taps his decayed leg on the busted tile floor. He closes his eyes and starts singing louder.

When he bravely opens his eyes again, there is a body hanging from the clipboard. The hellish, whip-wielding, slave-driving receptionist looming over it threatens him with her dead eyes.

She grows weary and bangs against the window before pointing down. She smiles at him with her sharp, tiny teeth. Her nostrils flare and smoke streams out from her nose. The claws connected to her fingers aggravatingly tap against the glass before she once again motions to the clipboard.

After finally realizing what she wants, Lawrence grabs the rotting body and gingerly squeezes it between his thumb and index finger. Even under modest pressure, he can feel the frail body squish between his fingers. He signs the form with the blood oozing out of the woman's tiny head then slides it through the jagged opening. "That all?"

"No." The receptionist growls and points to the right. "You need to go through that door. Ron will meet you on the other side and get you set up to see the doctor."

Lawrence looks around to find himself surrounded by a semi-normal looking crowd of sick people. Relieved the hallucination came and went before he made it back to see a doctor, he drops the pen and struts back to the examination area.

• • • • • • • •

After Ron has checked all of his vitals and not-so-vitals, Lawrence hops onto the examination table. He is wearing the mandatory white gown imprinted with the clinic logo. His pulse rate and blood pressure are both very high. If Nurse Ron had just sat through that diseased purgatory they call a waiting room, his blood would be running a little hot too.

While waiting for the doctor, Lawrence can't help but wonder why yesterday had gone so well. The night before that was pretty bad and today was starting off like a real shitshow. Yet somehow he had gotten one of the best night's sleep of his entire life. Things don't just stop haunting you and then come back out of nowhere to scare the shit out of you in the middle of some waiting room.

The only difference between yesterday and this morning is that there isn't any cocaine running through his system. Surely he's not supposed to go through the rest of his life harboring a coke habit just to keep himself from going crazy.

What if that's the problem with all those celebrities? Maybe they aren't spoiled kids who party too much. It could be that they're all haunted and trying to hold onto their sanity.

"Good morning, Mister…" the doctor has to check her chart. "Lawrence?"

"Yes, ma'am."

"Your name is Lawrence Lawrence?"

"Yes, ma'am."

"You could have just made up a false name and nobody ever would have said anything. This Lawrence Lawrence thing is just lazy writing."

If it was her crotch tingling with fire, she probably wouldn't be so clever either. "Sorry I didn't consult F. Scott Fitzgerald before I made the appointment. I was too busy scratching my balls."

"Sorry." The youngish, overweightish doctor sounds sincere. "One of the few perks of this job is seeing the entertaining names people come up with. This was just the worst. And I've cured more than my share of Luke Skywalkers."

"I'll keep that in mind next time I dip my wick in the wrong candle."

"Thank you." She smiles and grabs a tongue depressor.

• • • • • • • •

"Fucking Rodrigo." Lawrence curses underneath his breath. He's not even sure what gonorrhea is. The doctor holds the clipboard over her face, but she is unable to muffle the sound of her snicker. "I'm glad to see you think this is funny."

The look in his eyes scares her. She backs away. "I'm sorry. There's nothing funny about your situation."

"I shouldn't have snapped. You're just trying to help." Lawrence pulls up his pants. "This put a major kink in some plans I have with a girl tonight."

"Oh, so…? I thought you were cussing some guy named Rodrigo for this?"

"No. No. I'm not gay. He's just a friend of mine who knew the girl was infected with something and didn't tell me."

The doctor bends over in laughter. "Okay, cause I thought… You don't look like the normal gay guys I get in here."

She pauses before feeling the need to further explain herself. "We tend to treat a lot of the transvestite sex workers. When I heard you say Rodrigo, I thought of this one guy… girl? anyway I pictured you as one of those guys who has a wife and kids at home but comes to this part of town for that kind of thing."

"Sooo, penicillin?"

"Yes. Good old penicillin." She rips off a prescription. "Have a good weekend. Do everybody a favor and keep it in your pants for a couple of weeks." The doctor leaves the room.

"Fucking Rodrigo." Lawrence mutters before punching a first aid kit on the wall.

• • • • • • • •

An embarrassing trip to the store for a single rose and his prescription gave Lawrence time to calm down. The drive home was relaxing. Almost meditative. The trip to the clinic had been nothing more than another ripple in the tide. The river still runs. Before long, this too will be washed into the Sea of Forgotten Problems.

The doctor said the medication should have everything cleared up in a week. It's not like girls are the ones dying to get into bed, so Lydia should be willing to wait.

If she isn't, he can always say he needs more time to get over his ex before jumping into the sack. Not only will that save him the embarrassment of admitting he has a dirty crotch, but it will also give him an air of mystery.

The ding of the microwave lets him know his Salisbury steak is ready. After polishing off the plastic dish, he spends an hour straightening up around the apartment. Cleanliness is Godliness. And for whatever reason, Godliness is something to be desired.

·   ·   ·   ·   ·   ·   ·   ·

Despite not planning on drinking tonight, Lawrence decides to take a cab just in case. The pockets lining his cargo pants are packed with 8-balls. Those will soon be replaced with cash. Lydia's rose rests gracefully next to him in the back seat.

The strip club is much busier tonight. The aggravated cabbie pulls into a long, slow-moving line of luxury cars and limousines. Some are loaded with locals out for a bachelor party while others carry select groups of performing artists and Hollywood actors. Lawrence wonders if he'll even be allowed inside on a night like this.

A drunken group of bachelors crawls out of a stretch Hummer and line up at the door with their IDs out. Lawrence sees an opportunity and throws a twenty at the driver. "If I'm lucky, I'll be back before you reach the end of the drive." He snatches up the rose and climbs out. "Thanks for the ride either way."

Lawrence tucks in behind them and tries to blend in. The bouncer waves him through without even checking his ID. He scans the room for Lydia but doesn't see her. A seat opens up next to the brass rail dividing the server's station from the rest of the bar.

A little nervous - and feeling like every other asshole he's ever seen flirting with a stripper - Lawrence posts up as inconspicuously as possible with the rose tucked by his side. A hulking, male bartender walks up. "What can I get you?"

"Nothing. I'm waiting for somebody."

"No you're not." From his demeanor, Lawrence can tell he's not the first guy that's shown up to ask out one of their employees.

"Of course not." Lawrence sets an apologetic fifty on the bar. "Two shots of tequila with a beer back. Please. And keep the change." Just like that, Lawrence's non-drinking policy is out the window.

Lydia taps him on the shoulder and snatches the flower out of his hand. "Please tell me you ordered a drink. Guys coming around here holding roses are generally bad news." She lowers her voice to a whisper. "We call this the stalker station."

"Oh my God. Am I one of those losers?"

She smiles and rubs his forearm. "There are a ton of unwritten rules around here."

"Really?"

"For sure. Like we can't accept presents from customers. You're never supposed to go out on a date with anybody you meet here. And never bring your boyfriends around."

Lawrence turns to face the bar and speaks covertly out of the corner of his mouth. "So what do we do now?"

"I'm assuming you came here to ask me out?" She loads a variety of liquor drinks and bottled beers onto a cocktail tray.

"Yes."

"Since you kept me waiting for almost a whole week, I can't very well let you come in here and win me back just like that." Lawrence's hopes are dashed and the excitement painted on his face melts away. "But, if I'm the first person you think about when you wake up in the morning, call me and ask again." She picks up the tray and Lawrence watches her walk away.

The bartender sets two shots and a beer down in front of him. "How'd it go?"

Lawrence slams the first one. "Not bad." He wipes his mouth with a cocktail napkin and takes down the next. The bartender walks off and Lawrence gets to work on his beer before realizing he still has a chance to catch the cab. Not one to be wasteful, he stuffs the beer in his pocket and hurries out the door.

· · · · · · · ·

The taxi pulls onto a street lined by bars where drunken college students stumble back and forth between clubs. Still giddy over his unofficial yes from Lydia, Lawrence has regained his confidence and is ready to take on the world.

His plan is simple: go to the bar, have a couple of cocktails, sell about three grand worth of coke, then go home and get a good night's sleep.

One day down the road, this will be the night he and Lydia tell their grandchildren about. How grandpa stopped by the diner and asked her out on his way to work the late shift as a bartender. The two of them will look deep into each other's eyes and explain that *It was just meant to be*.

Despite falling within the socially acceptable age range for this particular strip of bars, Lawrence just doesn't fit in with the rest of the crowd. He with his townie gear. They with their collared shirts and pressed pants. Not sure where to start, he strolls up to the bar and orders two shots of tequila with a beer back.

After downing both shots, Lawrence grabs his beer and strolls to the bathroom. Along the way, he keeps an eye out for the guys surrounded by the hottest girls. These guys would have the scratch to throw down on some fresh powder. Along with the influence to get everyone around them to buy some too.

The line outside of the bathroom is long but it moves fast. Once inside, there are still five dudes waiting in front of him for the only stall. After watching dozens of people come and go from the urinal, the last drunken scholar ahead of him staggers out.

Lawrence slides in and latches the door. Now safely hidden from judgmental eyes, he taps out a thick line on top of the tank. He crudely rolls up whatever bill is on top of his stash and snorts away.

On his way out, a young man in the urinal line gives him a hopeful look when he sees Lawrence wipe his nose.

More relaxed, and yet acutely aware of his surroundings, Lawrence sits alone at the bar. The guy from the urinal points Lawrence out to a friend from across the room.

The friend is exactly what Lawrence pictured when he came to this place. A strong-jawed, alpha-male, drunk off of daddy's money, and surrounded by women looking to party. The friend stands up in his seat and motions for Lawrence to join them. Not one to be presumptuous, Lawrence looks around to make sure there isn't some hot undergrad behind him waving back.

Lawrence pokes his finger in his chest and mouths *Me?*

They enthusiastically wave back. Lawrence slams another shot and heads to their booth in the corner where the leader opens up the conversation. "My friend says he saw you partying in the bathroom."

"Guess I shouldn't have had that burrito before I left the house."

"Knock the bullshit, man." The dude flippantly slaps Lawrence's shoulder and laughs. "I'm Alex and this is Charlie. And we're no fucking cops. What kind of party favors you got?"

"What are you looking for?"

"We'll take a couple of whatever you were snorting in the bathroom earlier." Alex lays two hundred dollars down on the table.

"That'll get you one." Lawrence is confident and willing to walk away from the deal right now. Alex looks at Charlie who responds by dropping another two hundred dollars on the table. Lawrence clumsily shoves the crumpled wad of cash in one of the zippered pockets.

While fumbling around for the goods, he drops one on the floor and it rolls under the table. Alex quickly reaches down and snatches it up. "Thanks. You know of anybody else looking to get down?"

Alex stands and pats Lawrence on the shoulder. "Possibly. If we hear anything we'll send them your way." Alex heads to the restroom while Lawrence heads back to his post at the bar.

A few minutes later, some drunk kid walks up to him with cash in hand. Then another. And then another. Before long there is a virtual line of horny college kids coming up to him with two hundred dollars. Lawrence knows to expect a new customer every time he sees somebody walking to the ATM. In a little under three hours, he has sold fifteen out of twenty bags.

Pleased with the work he has put in, Lawrence pays his tab and heads outside to hail a cab. A van stops and picks him up along with some drunken college students.

"Heeey!" A familiar voice yells from the seat behind him. "How'd your night go?"

Lawrence turns to see Alex with a young girl's tongue buried in his ear. "It went alright. Looks like you're doing pretty good."

"I do what I can." Alex leans in. "You got any left?"

"A little. What's up?"

"When I get back to the house the other guys are gonna want some. To be honest I don't feel like sharing."

"I've got five left. If you'll take them all right now… I'll call it eight hundred."

"No." Alex laughs. "Then I'll have to turn around and sell it to my friends and, no offense, I'm not a fucking drug dealer. Just come by the house, have a few beers, and hook a couple of the brothers up. After that, you're more than welcome to hang out and party. Or we can make one of the pledges take you home."

Lawrence weighs going home versus the extra cash Alex is offering. "You sure I can get rid of it all?"

"Definitely." Alex pats him on the shoulder and leans back to allow the young coed to continue having her way with his earlobe.

●　●　●　●　●　●　●　●

"We were wondering when you'd get back." The drunkest, fattest fraternity member says through a mouthful of pizza. Several of them have been sitting around all night watching the ballgame and drinking beer. "Where's that guy at?"

"Jesus, Joel. Calm down. He's coming." Alex reaches into the mini fridge in the common room and doles out beers to the crowd streaming through the door.

Surprised by the arrival of females, Joel jumps up from the couch and brushes the crumbs off of his shirt. "Did you come in a fucking clown car? Where'd all these people come from?"

"I don't know." Alex hands Joel a beer. "This guy says we can get five 8-balls for eight hundred. And a ride home."

Joel is a little wary about bringing a coke dealer into their fraternity house. "He needs a fucking ride home? What's this guy like?"

"I'm pretty sure he's not in school. I'd say he's a townie, but he doesn't sound like a townie. He's alright. Kind of a good ole boy."

"If you say so. Let's get him his money and get it started."

Alex sits down in Joel's spot and is instantaneously surrounded by the two hottest chicks. "Yeah man, you go work on that. We'll be in here."

Lawrence grabs a beer from some girl and sits down on the couch facing Alex and his friends. "Thanks."

"No problem." The sober-seven, drunk-nine girl answers as she takes a seat next to him.

Alex takes another pull from his beer. "Lawrence, right? You taking classes?"

"No, sir." Lawrence has no idea why he called this guy sir, but the girl next to him finds his southern ways charming. "I just moved to town a couple of years ago with my girlfriend. Then we broke up. I've just been working and living ever since."

"Looks like you're doing alright." Alex refers to his drug dealing business as opposed to his side gig as a landscaper.

"It comes and goes."

The room falls awkwardly silent. The girl sitting next to Lawrence yawns. The party killing disease crosses the room where it is contracted by the two girls hanging on Alex.

"Joel will be back in a minute with that money." Alex holds out his hands. "You can trust us. We're good for it."

"You guys've been cool, so I'll front the first one." Lawrence pulls a bag from his pocket and tosses it to Alex.

"Cool." Alex kneels down in front of a glass coffee table and dumps out the entire sack. He pulls a platinum card out and cuts a line for all ten people in the room. "Everybody line up."

The rest of the group obediently kneels down at the table. Not really sure what's going on, Lawrence follows the lead of the girl next to him. Everyone pulls out their crispest bill and rolls it up.

"What's this? The last fucking supper?" Joel walks back in and flashes eight hundred dollars.

"Shut up! I'm about to say the blessing…" He looks around the table. "Go!" Everybody takes their line on Alex's command.

Another group of about ten people follows Joel into the room. "Last time you hooked it up you got some shitty coke, Lambert." An older brother named Lincoln barks at Alex. "This stuff better be good."

"It's real good." The girl sitting next to Lawrence answers. She looks deep into his eyes and runs her fingers through his hair.

"Good to hear. Joel, pay the man."

Alex and his crew stand up to make room for Lincoln and his posse. The ritual they had just completed repeats itself with Lincoln at the helm while Alex doles out beers to his team.

The girl sitting next to Lawrence whispers in his ear before dragging him into the hallway. "Where are we going?"

"I'm not sure." She leads him into a stairwell. With both arms wrapped around him. "I'm Penny by the way." Penny leans in and gives him a kiss. It doesn't take long for Lawrence's motor to rev up. He picks her up and slams her hard against the concrete wall. Her head gets banged up pretty bad, but not hard enough for either of them to stop.

She unzips his pants and whispers in his ear. "We shouldn't be doing this here." Penny grabs his hand and drags him up a flight of stairs and into a lonely hallway. She spots a crack in the door at an intersection of two halls and pulls him inside where she gently shoves him onto the couch and pulls down his pants before treating him to the best three minutes he's had in quite some time.

After he finishes, she straddles him on the sofa and shoves her tongue down his throat. Lawrence instinctually pushes her away before deciding just to deal with it. After kissing on him for a while, she gets bored and falls asleep with her head on his shoulder.

"Really?" Lawrence is still revved up on cocaine. Now this chick has decided to set up basecamp on his shoulder. He doesn't want to leave her there. Not sure what to do, he looks around for something to do.

He spots a video game controller on a nearby desk and gently moves her head. On the desk next to it is a picture of an extremely intoxicated fraternity member wearing a tuxedo and cheesing it up for the camera. An equally drunk girl is hanging on him in a pink sequined gown.

Resting at the base of the silver picture frame is a solid gold, diamond encrusted, high school class ring. Lawrence checks to make sure the girl is still passed out before stuffing it in the zippered pocket with the rest of his profits from the night. While searching the room further, Lawrence runs across five hundred dollars sticking out of a text book and hastily deposits the cash. "In for a penny, in for a pound."

On the chest of drawers behind him, Lawrence finds a wooden box that holds Alex's jewelry. He slides a gold watch around his wrist and stuffs the silver one in his pocket. Just as he gets done wrapping two gold chains around his neck, Lawrence hears an explosion of laughter from the hallway followed by a key sliding into the doorknob. With little time to think, he jumps on the couch and cuddles up next to his paramour.

"Lawrence? Penny? Ohhhh…" Alex smiles and points down at Lawrence's still unzipped pants.

A girl walks in and catches him zipping them up. Alex's girlfriend du jour laughs. "Oh my God, Penny. You are such a skeeze! Did you really just blow this townie drug dealer?"

Lawrence feigns offense and uses the insult as an excuse to leave. "I better get going."

"Let me get a pledge to drive you home."

"No, thanks, I'll just grab a cab. You guys have done too much already."

"Alright." As the two men shake hands, Alex notices his watch wrapped around Lawrence's wrist. "What the fuck man?"

"Susan! Go get Joel and Lincoln! Tell them we've got a low-life, drug dealing thief to deal with."

The girl refuses to budge. "My name's Marsha."

"Who gives a shit?! Go get some fucking help." Alex wrestles Lawrence to the ground and spits in his face. "Piece of shit."

"Where is he?" Lincoln storms in and shoves Alex off of the would-be robber. He picks Lawrence up and punches him in the gut. The beer in Lawrence's stomach rises back into his mouth and overflows onto the carpet.

Alex joins in and awkwardly punches Lawrence in the back of the head before Lincoln shoves him away. "Not here! Get your stuff back."

Alex breaks the clasp on the band when he yanks his watch off of Lawrence's wrist before removing the two necklaces. "I had another watch."

"Well get it. This piece of shit ain't going nowhere." Lincoln pins Lawrence's hands behind his back. Imitating every TV cop he has ever seen, Alex frisks him and finds the silver watch in one of Lawrence's zippered pockets.

"Anything else?"

"That's it."

"He's got to have some cash on him. We just gave him eight hundred bucks." Lincoln takes his turn frisking him. In Lawrence's one stroke of luck for the night, he only finds the larger of the two wads of cash. "Got it."

"That's stealing." Alex argues.

Still loopy from a night of partying and getting his ass kicked, Lawrence watches the two men talk about him like he's a turtle in a terrarium.

Lincoln smacks Alex across the back of the head. "What's he gonna do?" Lincoln stuffs the money in his back pocket. "There's almost two grand here."

"He's a drug dealer. What if he knows people?" Alex pleads as Lincoln shoves Lawrence out the door by his bound wrists.

"Look at this guy. He don't know shit. Do you?" Lincoln shoves Lawrence down a flight of metal exterior stairs. He throws his hands out to cover his face as his body slams against the hard edges of the grated stairwell. When he hits the bottom of that level, Lincoln tosses him down to the next platform. Then one more time until Lawrence lays bloody and beaten in the parking lot.

Lincoln uses the feeble rails to jump down the last few steps and crashes down hard on Lawrence's stomach. Groaning in pain and frightened for his life, Lawrence rolls over on his side.

Joel comes stampeding out of a side door and kicks Lawrence squarely in the back. "I knew there was something wrong with this guy!"

"This is for taking my watch." Alex rears back and kicks Lawrence in the face. The tip of his shoe hits the ridge between Lawrence's upper lip and the base of his nose. Alex holds up his hands and orders the other two guys to back off. Lincoln smiles and lets the younger brother have his vengeance. Alex paces around Lawrence's beaten body and kicks him in the back. "That's for stealing my cross."

Joel gives Alex a high-five before leaning down and punching Lawrence in the face.

"Nice." Lincoln slaps Joel on the back and kicks him in the stomach. "Don't you still owe him for stealing some other stuff?"

Alex is breathless from the adrenaline rush. "Yeah."

"Help me out, Joel!" Lincoln drops to the ground and pins down Lawrence's left side while Joel drops down to pin down the right. "Have at it."

"This is for stealing my grandfather's watch!" Alex drops his knee into Lawrence's groin.

"Holy shit!" Joel exclaims when he sees the blood running out of Lawrence's mouth and pooling up on the concrete driveway. "This guy sure can take a beating."

"Let's see how he takes this." Alex takes a running start and kicks Lawrence in the face with the grace of a place kicker.

Lawrence groans in anguish. His entire face and most of his body are in excruciating pain.

"Great job. Let's go grab some beers and split up this asshole's money." Lincoln punches the code into the door and leads the gladiators back inside. That's probably the closest thing to an honest dollar any of them will ever earn in their lives. But Lawrence dares not point that out.

After his attackers have disappeared, Lawrence rolls over and starts crying. He lays there for a while. It could have been minutes or it could have been an hour.

Even if he remembers to call Lydia in the morning, she won't be able to understand a word he says through what he assumes to be a broken jaw.

At some point, a couple of pledges pick him up and drag him to a corner across the street from their house. One of them stuffs a twenty in his shirt pocket and hails a cab.
The obviously unhappy and mildly drunk cab driver jumps out and helps him into the backseat. Feeling too much pain to speak, Lawrence shows him the address on his license and lies down.

CHAPTER NINE
Game Night

It's still dark out when Lawrence wakes up with his head on the bottom of the stairwell. The cabbie left the twenty dollar fare in his shirt pocket out of pity. He wipes the bloody drool from the corner of his mouth and picks himself up off of the black-and-white tiled floor.

Passing by a mirror on his way up the stairs, Lawrence doesn't notice the worms and insects crawling in and out of his dirty, stringy hair in the reflection.

He touches a swollen lump over his left ear that brings to mind the beating he took. After realizing how lucky he is to be alive, he checks his pockets to find that he still has a stolen ring and about a thousand dollars cash left. Those assholes had been too hyped up on cocaine to do a proper search.

Lawrence tosses the ring and the cash onto his closed laptop as he passes by on his way to the kitchen. He yanks two bottles of water from the fridge and crushes one. Holding the second bottle over his left eye, he walks into his bedroom and crashes on his mattress.

· · · · · · · ·

The first thing Lawrence thinks of when he wakes up shortly after noon is that phone call to Lydia. Unfortunately he doesn't bother to test his jaw's ability to form words before dialing.

"I'm assuming you are just now waking up?" Lawrence can hear the smile on her face. Picturing it brings a painful smile to his.

"Just this minute." His voice is muffled and barely audible.

"You sound terrible. What did you do last night?"

"I'm alright." His jaw rings in pain with each syllable. It's a miracle she can understand him. "A couple of guys jumped me."

"Oh my God." She fumbles the phone. "Want me to come take care of you?"

"Thanks, but I just need to put a little ice on it and get some rest. Not to make it sound like a chore, but I wanted to call and ask you out before I went back to sleep."

Lydia is genuinely touched. "Awww. I would love to."

"Great. Can I call you back tomorrow to set up a time? My face is killing me."

"Definitely," Lydia answers happily. "If you need anything. Soup, bandages… anything at all, please call. I don't want you dying before you've had the chance to buy me dinner."

"I wouldn't dream of it. Call you later?"

"You better."

Lawrence drops the phone and closes his eyes. After falling asleep for a few minutes, he awakens to find his ex-girlfriend Linda entering the room with a bowl of warm water and two white rags on a wooden tray. She is wearing a short, tight nurse's outfit with bright red lipstick.

Lawrence looks around the room. "What are you doing here?"

"I heard what happened to you last night." Linda gently dips the tip of a rag in warm water and uses it to softly wipe the dried blood off of his face. "Fucking assholes. Sometimes there are people in this world that show up just to create obstacles. And it's up to us to overcome them. When we learn to overcome these life obstacles, nothing can stop us."

"You really think so?"

"Definitely, sweetie." Linda's voice is much sweeter and more comforting than he remembers. "Look at us. We've had our ups-and-downs. But here I am. And nothing's gonna stop us now."

Lawrence wraps his arms around her and moves in for a kiss. Linda stops his puckered lips with a seductively tender touch of her fingertip. "I'd love to baby. First we have to get you better. Your destiny awaits." She motions to the shoebox of 8-balls on the dresser.

"Let's toss all of it and start our life right now." He throws his head roughly back on the bed. The impact sends shocks of pain from his face down to his chest.

"See?" She smiles at his determination. "Just think if some other assholes decide to jump you again. You're in no shape to defend yourself."

The scrapes on his knuckles throb as he rubs her knee. "I guess you're right."

"Of course I am. Just lay back and let me take care of you." She runs her fingers through his hair.

"I think I can handle that." His hand runs up her thigh before she stops him at the goal line. "Then I'm gonna take care of you for the rest of our lives."

Linda walks out the bedroom door. The momentary privacy allows him the opportunity to hide his erection before she walks back in with a tube of warming massage oil. "Let's get that shirt off."

"Oh my God! Poor baby." She touches the size twelve purple welt on his back and leans in to kiss the bruise.

The touch of her lips on his back is painfully erotic. Linda leans back and squirts lotion into her right palm. She rubs her hands to kick start the warming elements before putting her hands on his bare shoulders and whispering in his ear. "Don't worry, baby. I'll be gentle."

Lawrence rolls over and lies on his stomach as Linda digs her hands deep in the right places. She straddles his waist and lightly drags her fingers over his bruises. The faintness of her touch sends a pleasant feeling up his spine. She works her way down to his lower back and back up to his shoulders.

Her fingers pass over his collar bone and start working the top of his chest. The oil has dried up and the friction between her fingers and his skin grows coarse. The hands that had been gliding over his body like an Olympic figure skater now drag on his skin like sixty grit sandpaper on a knotty pine. Her sharp fingernails catch a red welt on his chest and rip a hole in the skin.

"Sorry, baby." She leans down and nibbles on his ear.

"It's okay. Just remember I'm still a little sensitive right now."

"I know baby." Her thighs tighten around his waist and she laughs demonically. "Those mean old frat boys found you stealing from them and beat the shit out of you."

"Who told you what happened?" Lawrence can't believe how quickly word can spread in such a large town.

"You know how things get around. People talk and what they've been saying is you've been doing all of this in order to get me back." She buries her right knee into the center of Alex's footprint.

He grunts through the pain as she presses her thumb hard on one of his smaller bruises. "I've never thought about it. But I guess that makes sense."

"Of course you did." Linda leans down and kisses him on the cheek. Lawrence opens his eyes to see her distended brown pupils bulging out of her decaying sockets.

The shock on his face makes her laugh. He shields his eyes from the sight of her decaying teeth and maggot infested gums. "Are you ready for your destiny?" Her voice is evil and her rotten teeth have sharpened. Her hands tighten around his neck.

"Finally…" Lawrence sighs in relief and closes his eyes. Her claws dig into his throat and he starts bleeding from five newly formed holes in his neck. Linda tightens her grip as she chokes the life out of him.

For a brief moment Lawrence feels no pain.

Which is soon followed by a chirping noise from his cell phone. It is a text from Lydia that reads: *Hope ur feeling btr ;)*.

Lawrence rubs his neck. Is the pain he's feeling from Linda murdering him or the beating he took last night? He realizes it doesn't matter. Both instances are part and parcel of the same problem.

Something bad attached itself to him that day in the clearing and, until he can get to the bottom of what it is, his only future is his present.

And his present can go fuck itself.

• • • • • • • •

Lawrence steps out the front door of his building into the bright sun. He lowers the baseball cap over his eyes and retrieves his sunglasses from the front seat of his car. After that craptastic daymare, a strong cup of coffee seems like just the thing to snap him out of this funk.

Strangers on the street try not to stare as they pass. A cool breeze picks up to soothe the bruises and cuts on his face. While the wind helps, his jaw still hurts something awful.

He steps up to the counter and orders a cup of black coffee and a newspaper. On his way over to a seat near the window, he notices the young man behind the counter pointing and laughing with his coworkers. At first he gets offended before remembering he used to be a smartass teenager. Lawrence puts his sunglasses back on and stares out the window at the pedestrians strolling by.

He unfolds the paper and flips straight to the local crime report. The first thing that catches his eye - right underneath the picture of a grounded jet surrounded by emergency vehicles - is an article entitled *The Woman Who Cried Ghost*.

According to the article, six days ago, a woman named Elena George locked herself in the airplane bathroom soon after takeoff. After finally unlocking the door an hour later, she backed out and threw a ring at the mirror and shattered it to pieces. Any steward or stewardess with the nerve to approach her was either kicked or punched.

After speaking with her husband and taking a seat in the back of the plane, Mrs. George opened up about what she claimed to have seen. Soon after take-off, the ring on her finger started giving her pain. She thought maybe she was experiencing swelling from the altitude so she tried taking it off. Even with her husband's help, the ring wouldn't budge and the swelling continued.

Mrs. George went to the bathroom to lubricate her finger with soap when she says the swelling started to subside and the ring eventually slid right off. After relieving herself, she noticed the finger had begun to wither. She claims it had gotten so bad she could distinguish the outline of the bone under her skin.

According to Mrs. George, she put the ring back on to see if the change was as drastic as it appeared. She said the moment the gold touched her withering finger it melted through the skin and bone so hot that it cauterized the wound as it fell. This, she told the flight attendants, is when the screaming started.

Frightened by the loss of her finger, Mrs. George said all she wanted to do was find her husband and go home. After several unsuccessful attempts at unlocking the door, she picked up her finger to examine the damage. The decomposing face of a dead woman revealed itself in the mirror. Mrs. George fell back on the toilet and cried while she prayed for her husband to come save her.

In her prayer, she found herself walking through a forest. *It was so beautiful I thought I'd died and gone to heaven*! It was then that she looked up and saw a figure dropping toward her. The noose around its neck snapped tight and left the victim's feet dangling mere inches from her face.

This is when the screaming started again. Mrs. George says she lost it when she recognized the limp body as her own. When she snapped out of it and looked in the mirror, she could see the decaying face laughing at her. Finally she was able to unlatch the door and run into the waiting crowd of aggravated airline employees and full-bladdered passengers.

Not long after Mrs. George finally calmed down, the plane landed back at Hartsfield-Jackson International. The Georges and the other passengers were met on the runway by a staircase truck, several police cars, three ambulances, and two fire trucks. Mrs. George was taken away by authorities for a psychiatric evaluation.

The tests found her to be highly unstable. The next day she was sent to an unidentified mental institution for further testing.

After what officials described as three *tumultuous* days under the constant care and supervision of doctors at the facility, Mrs. Baker asphyxiated herself by tying her bed sheets around the metal railings of her bed and leaning forward. When a nurse found her, she was still standing upright at a thirty degree angle.

One hospital administrator determined that *She must have been very troubled to have successfully killed herself in such an extraordinary manner.* While another doctor indicated that he assumed it humanly impossible to kill oneself like that before witnessing it with his own two eyes.

"Holy shit." Lawrence flips to the next page in hopes of finding a picture of the couple. With no visual verification, he has no choice but to assume Mr. & Mrs. George are the same couple he met at *Dale's Discount Pawn.*

After taking another sip from his coffee, Lawrence looks down at a police report from the Chattahoochee National Forest that provides little relief.

Responding to an anonymous phone call, investigators traveled deep into the forest in search of two sets of remains reportedly decomposing in the woods. Tests to determine how long the bodies have been there were inconclusive, but family members reported Mr. and Mrs. Fincher missing nearly a month ago.

Authorities used this information to create their timeline. They believe the couple hung themselves in the lofty pines and that natural decomposition led to them falling from their nooses.

Family members, who did not wish to be named, said the couple had been dealing with financial hardships due to a sharp decline in profits at their dry cleaning business. Mr. Fincher was getting less-and-less sleep. His work life and marriage deteriorated around him.

The couple was fighting constantly. Local police were called to their business twice in one week when customers reported yelling and other odd noises coming from the back room. No charges were filed in either instance.

A friend says Mrs. Fincher mentioned something to her about a *bad decision* the couple made on an investment in precious metals. According to the friend, Mrs. Fincher said she and her husband felt trapped by fear that they would never be able to repay the debt. As rumors spread across the neighborhood, business dried up almost completely.

The Finchers dug deeper-and-deeper into their savings to cover their personal and business losses. As the money disappeared, the rift in their marriage widened. They then started asking friends and family for loans. What little money they received was soon invested in more precious metals. After the Finchers maxed out their credit with loved ones, they started stealing from them.

Instead of reporting them to the cops, their friends and relatives planned an intervention to confront them on their spending habits and offer moral support. This meeting never occurred.

Mrs. Fincher called one of her friends minutes before the planned intervention with an excuse everyone deemed implausible. Following their disappearance, a friend discovered they had gone to a psychic who had promised she could fix everything.

Through a series of e-mails, the psychic told the *Informer* that she and the couple agreed on a price for a service that she provided in full. The psychic did say she felt sympathy for the friends and family of what she deemed *the unlucky couple*. She was unaware that after their meeting, the Finchers robbed a nearby jewelry store. A crime for which they were arrested while making their escape.

Officials at the separate facilities where they were held, described similar occurrences during their detention. In between psychotic breaks, both of them spent the night crying uncontrollably.

Mr. Fincher spent a great deal of his night screaming for help. When none arrived, he tried to squeeze through the cell bars. When that didn't work, authorities say he tried to kill himself by banging his head against the cell walls.

Upon being released from prison, police believe the Finchers went straight home where they spent a nice evening together. The clues left in their home indicate that they cooked dinner and dined together over a nice bottle of wine. After dinner, evidence indicates they drove their car to the Laundromat and set the building on fire. By the time the fire department arrived, the building had almost burnt to the ground.

That was the last anyone had seen or heard of the Finchers until an anonymous phone call was received earlier in the week. Authorities are asking that anyone with any information call the police.

•　•　•　•　•　•　•　•

There's no reason to show up at Brett's place without any booze unless you don't mind malt liquor. Lawrence wanders the whiskey aisle in search of the cheapest bottle in the store before settling on some black label brand from Tennessee. Next he makes his way to the beer cooler to pick out a domestic case.

"Hey!" Brett is holding an armful of malt liquor with a loosely filled backpack strapped around his shoulders. "I was grabbing some beer before coming over to your place."

Between running into Brett and the two articles in the paper, Lawrence is a little freaked out. "Why are you coming to see me?"

"I don't want to talk about it now." Brett flinches at a reflection in the beer cooler. "Let's get out of here."

Aside from a few comments about women passing by, the two of them are relatively quiet on the walk home. Brett doesn't say one word about Lawrence's busted face. The rattling of the plastic in Brett's backpack haunts them all the way to Lawrence's apartment.

Lawrence leads the way up the dim, steep stairwell. Studying the folk art on the wall, Brett notices a scenic print depicting a plantation home at the end of a long row of moss covered oaks.

An elderly couple is sitting in matching rocking chairs chatting over a glass of lemonade. One-by-one, right before Brett's eyes, bodies start throwing themselves out of the trees.

Their necks snap in a chorus line like a satanic xylophone. The aged couple sitting on the front porch morph into dark specters before floating down the dirt path to reap their victims' souls.

"So how have you been?" Brett tries to sound casual as he sets his stuff down on Lawrence's desk.

"Great. Plastic surgery went a little awry, but the doctor thinks it'll look better after the swelling goes down."

Brett takes a pull from the handle of whiskey before popping the top on a beer. "I didn't want to say anything. But what the fuck happened?"

"I went to a bar to soak these college kids on the price of that coke." Lawrence takes his first pull from the whiskey. "This one guy invited me back to their frat house. He said his buddies would buy up the rest of what I had at a discount."

Brett is amazed and a little envious. "You've gotten rid of all of it?"

"No. Not even close. I had five balls on me that I sold him for eight hundred."

"Dude, don't call them balls. That's just weird." Brett still finds himself impressed by Lawrence's drug selling prowess. "But eight hundred? How much were you charging before the discount?"

"Two. And they were happy to do it." He adds gleefully. "Then they found me doing something stupid and rightfully beat the shit out of me."

"What were you doing?"

"Some girl pulled me into this guy's room and went down on me."
Lawrence pauses to remember how the beating went down. "This
guy, his name was Alex, left his class ring sitting out on his desk so I
pocketed it. Then I saw some money sticking out of a book so I took
that. Next thing I remember, he sees me with his watch on my wrist
and two of his necklaces around my neck.

He tackled me and sent his girlfriend to get a couple of his buddies.
Then they took me outside and did this." Lawrence motions to his
face and the bruises on his arms. "Later on, somebody picked me up.
Next morning I woke up at the bottom of the stairs using the bottom
step for a pillow."

Brett lights a cigarette. "How many guys?"

"Three." Lawrence grabs the lighter. "How are things with you?"

"I've been selling a little here-and-there. I've been doing a lot
actually." Brett pulls three 8-balls out of his backpack and sets them
on the table before dumping half of one out on a nearby magazine.
"I've sold like ten sacks for a total of a grand."

Brett's hand shakes uncontrollably as he divvies the pile into two
thick lines. "Haven't been sleeping much." Lawrence can tell he has
been waiting to spew out his secrets to someone who might
understand. "Not that I want to sleep. My life has been one long
nightmare since we went out to the clearing." The fact that one of
them said it out loud lightens the dark tension that has been filling
the room. "Just when I think whatever it is has gone away, it comes
back and knocks me right back into a world of shit."

"I've been going through something similar."

"That makes me feel better." Brett rips his rail. "The other night, me and a friend of mine went to the basketball game. Close to the end of the second quarter, me and him snuck down to some empty seats near the court. We were only two rows up. Right underneath the basket. It was awesome. Right before halftime, two players got in a scuffle.

The ref called a jump ball, but they kept going at it. Then the bigger dude goes ape shit and lets out a yell that echoes across the whole arena and rips the ball out of the other guy's hands. While he's at it he smacks the guy in the nose with his elbow. Blood went everywhere. My head started spinning and I started getting nauseous. And I usually don't get like that around blood."

Lawrence picks up the magazine and takes his line while Brett continues. "As luck would have it, there was an empty popcorn bag under my chair that I was able to throw up in. Not a lot, but enough that people around me noticed. Then a medic comes running onto the court." Brett snatches the bottle from Lawrence and takes a long pull.

"He's holding a rag up to the guy's nose. Out of nowhere his wedding ring blinds the shit out of me. Like it was the fucking sun. Then," Brett snaps his fingers, "I went blind. Couldn't see a damn thing."

"What did your buddy say?"

"Nothing. I didn't tell him. By this time, so much crazy shit has gone on I just assumed it would pass. Then all of a sudden, as quickly as it went away, my sight came back."

Lawrence hands him another beer. "That's good."

"Not really. They held one of those slam dunk contests at halftime. The one where the different versions of the same mascot dunk against each other. The muscular one floats down from the ceiling on a harness and I flip my shit. All of a sudden it was like I was back in the clearing and the mascot turned into the guy from the forest. I don't know how long I was out of it, but when I came to, I was sweating like crazy and Sonny had gone to get help."

"What happened after that?"

"The paramedics gave me some oxygen then we took the train home." Brett lights another cigarette. "That's not even the worst of the shit I've been dealing with." He takes a deep drag from his smoke and impatiently waits for Lawrence to jump in with a story of his own. "Anything fucked up like that happen to you?"

Lawrence takes a seat on the couch next to him. "I've had my share."

"Feel free to elaborate?"

"Not really. Is this why you were coming over?"

"No, I just wanted to stop by and catch up on old times." The sarcasm oozes out of his mouth.

"Sorry. I was thinking maybe you had a plan or something. Personally, I was hoping everything would fix itself after I reported the bodies to the cops. That obviously didn't work."

"I thought that might have been you." Brett holds the cigarette in his mouth while he reaches into the backpack and pulls out the board game. "This is what I've come up with."

"Really dude? A Ouija board?" Lawrence sounds as if he's too good for the cheap piece of cardboard and cheaper piece of plastic. "Shouldn't we trust this to a professional or something?"

"What's the purpose of this game?"

"To help people communicate with the dead?"

"Exactly. And what would some hippie charging us a hundred dollars an hour do?"

"Help us communicate with the dead."

"I don't know about you, but I think we've been doing pretty good communicating with the dead lately. I think what we need is a translator."

"Have you tried it?"

"I wanted to wait until we could get together and do it."

Even under these circumstances, Lawrence finds it hard to believe Brett's intentions are pure. "Why's that?"

"I thought we'd have a stronger energy field or whatever."

"If you'll admit you're at least a little scared, I'll do it."

Brett shakes his head with a big smile on his face. "There's no way in hell I was doing this alone."

Lawrence picks up the cardboard box and examines the picture of the smiling family on the back cover. "Do we need anything else? Or is this all inclusive?"

"I was thinking we'd cut off the lights and light a few candles. At least try to set the mood. After that, if they want to talk to us, they know where we are."

• • • • • • • •

After emptying their bladders and refreshing their beers, the guys sit cross-legged from one another at Lawrence's coffee table. The overhead lights are off and the sky outside is darkened by cloud cover. The oversized candle from the back of his toilet provides the only light for their little séance.

Lawrence is careful not to touch the pointer while his hands linger over it. "What do you want to ask it first?"

"It's called a planchette. That's what the directions said anyway."

"So what should we ask the planchette?"

"First we need to make sure they're here." They lower their hands and make contact at the same time. The nerves in their muscles twitch uncontrollably when an electric charge zings up their arms. They look to each other to verify they both felt it.

"I guess they know we're here. Now what?"

Brett starts things off. "Are you here because we stole from those people in the forest?" The pointer abruptly jerks their hands over the word *YES*. Brett gives Lawrence a look that orders him to ask the next question.

"Okay." Lawrence wants to tell Brett that this was his idea and he should ask his own fucking questions. "What do you want?"

The planchette doesn't flinch. The flickering flame from the candle shines on the magnifying glass and reflects blinding white light straight into their eyes. The plastic edges of the pointer heat under their fingers. Lawrence yanks his hands away but the plastic sticks to his fingers and stretches out like hot cheese from a pizza. Brett experiences similar results.

"Holy shit, dude." Brett looks up at Lawrence. "What does that mean?" Below them, the distinct scraping of the planchette moves across the board in a circle. The melted strands of plastic stuck to their fingers have disappeared. The guys watch in horror as the magnifying glass takes noticeable pauses over the letters *B-U-R-N*.

Lawrence's lips quiver. "It wants us to burn?" He bravely puts his hands back on the magnifying glass. The slider pulls his hand over the word *YES*.

Brett hesitantly places his hands back on. "What can we do to stop this?"

The lack of a response almost brings Lawrence to tears. "Please. There's got to be something. We'll do anything."

Another pulse of energy shoots out of the pointer and sends a vision racing through Lawrence's mind of him jumping off of the cliff. His arms are spread out wide. As Lawrence nears the ground, he sees Brett's dead body folded over a tree branch.

"There's got to be some other way?" Brett pleads with tears running down his face.

The magnifying glass shifts to *NO*.

• • • • • • • •

Ten minutes after the last electric shock, Brett finally gives up asking the Ouija board questions.

"I think we have our answer." Lawrence picks up the planchette and hurls it over Brett's head shattering it against the wall.

"So that's it? We're going to hell because we stole a bunch of crappy jewelry from a couple that committed suicide. You saw all that jewelry! And that's just what they wore to kill themselves."

"It was stolen." Lawrence tells him bluntly. "They were being haunted... tortured it sounded like." Lawrence hands him the newspaper and then dumps out two lines on the coffee table. He stares at the cocaine with drool in his eyes as he impatiently waits for Brett to finish reading.

Brett sits down next to him. "So you're just gonna give up?"

"I don't see much of a point. Those two were like the perfect married couple. Always went to church. Owned a house. Their own business. Lots of normal friends. It drove them to commit all those crimes and they still killed themselves because of it. I'd hate to see what it'll do to two low-life assholes like ourselves."

"We're not low-life assholes." Brett mutters even though he knows his friend is probably right. "We don't deserve this."

"Nobody does. But look at us." Lawrence motions around to the empty alcohol containers and drug paraphernalia surrounding them. "This shit's been going on for a week. What have you done to solve the problem?"

Brett feels compelled to defend himself. "I've been doing what I can just to grab a few hours of sleep every night."

"I'm not saying there's anything wrong with it. Look at my fucking place. The only thing I did that you didn't was go out and buy a newspaper. That and get my ass kicked. And that didn't help much at all."

"I'm not gonna lie, looking at your busted face makes me feel a little better."

"At least you'll leave a prettier corpse." Lawrence leans down to take his line before exhaling in laughter and blowing the powder all over the place. Seeing the aggravation growing in his buddy's eyes, Brett straightens up the dust with a loose business card.

"Fuck it." Lawrence leans in and blows the powder all over the room. "No sense in being cheap now. You can't take it where we're going." Lawrence rips open a fresh 8-ball and empties the whole thing out. Then he dumps the Ouija board back on the table and starts using the plastic baggie as the planchette. "Can you suck my dick?" Lawrence drags the crumpled bag across the board and slams it down on the *YES*. "Goddamn right."

He uses his index finger to roughly bisect the pile into two smaller piles. He jams his snortation device into the nearest one and takes in half of it before pulling up for air. After a couple of deep breaths, he leans in for a second round but Brett slaps the straw out of his hand. "What the fuck are you doing?"

"Did you see what I saw? We're gonna end up dying in the woods like the rest of them. That's what it wants. Might as well get fucked up until it happens." A tear lands in the pile of powder as he leans in and takes another hit. "So if I happen to overdose between now and then, at least it was under my terms."

"Not on my watch." Brett picks up the board and tosses it across the room. "You just need to calm down. If anybody can beat this, it's gonna be a couple of low-life assholes like us." Brett sees a fleeting smile cross Lawrence's face.

"What was it that old man said when we bumped into his shopping cart with your mom's van?" Brett lowers his voice and does his best old man impression. "Damn white trash! Them and cockroaches will be …"

"…the only thing that survives the apocalypse." As Lawrence finishes Brett's thought, calmness fills his body.

The two of them sit around and shoot the shit for a little while, mostly so Brett can rest assured Lawrence won't kill himself after he leaves. When he's finally convinced that Lawrence has backed away from the ledge, Brett pats him on the back. "This is our apocalypse buddy, I hope you like cockroach meat."

●　　●　　●　　●　　●　　●　　●　　●

Brett slides through the closing doors of the bus and takes a seat right next to the entrance. The driver pulls the squeaky lever and takes off down the street. From somewhere in the back, an old woman strenuously coughs into a tattered handkerchief. The track lighting that lines the windows fades to darkness.

The rising temperature only amplifies the sweaty stench coming from the other passengers. Waves of heat pour in through the windows. An intense wall of flame bursts to life on the other side of the Plexiglas. Brett's heart fills with an equally intense sense of hopelessness.

The decrepit bus driver stumbles down the aisle while the bus careens back and forth. Slamming against cars is the only thing that keeps them on the road. The woman behind him lets out another sickening cough. Brett watches as her body deteriorates to nothing more than a loose collection of leathery skin swatches.

The heat from the flames continues filling the bus. Sweat pours down his face and has started soaking through his shirt. A second passenger spills down the aisle and stops directly in front of him. Piss dribbles down Brett's thigh and forms a puddle in the poorly cushioned seat.

The homeless man lifts a bony finger and touches the tip of Brett's nose. The thin layer of skin covering the stranger's finger melts away, uncovering his metacarpals. The flesh erosion spreads to Brett's nose and his skin quickly fades to black.

A gaping hole opens up displaying his coke abused nasal cavity. The decay spreads across his face and his upper lip is the next thing to disappear. He looks up to see the old man is now hiding under a black hood. The widening sockets around Brett's eyes crumble and his eyeballs drop into his lap. He tries to scream but his vocal chords and most of his neck have disintegrated.

"Listen son, I can't take you through that fence. If you don't get off, I've got no other choice but to call security." The bus driver shakes Brett awake and points to the guard shack on the other side of the fence. "End of the line, son!"

Brett finds himself disappointed to snap out of the dream. It was so close to being over. Even such a shitty ending as fading to ashes in a pile of your own piss is preferable to living through another nightmare.

He climbs down the metal stairs and steps out onto the dimly lit sidewalk. As luck would have it, the route's last stop is only four blocks from his apartment. Unfortunately those four blocks traverse through some of the rougher neighborhoods in the city.

"Did you take a piss in my bus!?" Brett doesn't even bother to turn and see the driver sticking his head out the window. "You're banned for life! Don't think I don't remember what you look like! They've got cameras all over these things you know?!"

The flickering of the few street lights that haven't been shot out provides just enough light to cast freakish shadows everywhere. Every one is either a demonic specter or a thug with a gun. Every alley he walks by and every corner he turns feels like passing an open pit of venomous snakes. The alleys that are not occupied by working girls are lit up like fireflies with lighters torching glass pipes.

Daring to glance down one particularly well moonlit alley, Brett makes out the figures of a man and a woman having sex against a dumpster. For some reason he stops to watch what he assumes to be an exchange of goods for a service.

"Help!" The woman yells.

The presumed rapist looks up at Brett and punches her in the back of the head. "This ain't none of your business!" Brett pulls the phone out of his pocket and hastily walks away. "I told you this ain't none of your fucking business!" The attacker zips up his pants as he runs to the end of the alley while the woman yanks down her dress, straightens her hair, and calmly follows him.

Without hanging up, Brett jams the phone in his front pocket and curses himself for not taking up track in high school. Instead, he chose to party and is about to pay the price. The criminal tackles him from behind and wrestles the phone out of his pocket.

"Is everything okay? What's going on?" The operator asks before Brett's assailant hangs up.

"I told you to mind your own damn business." The man kicks him in the face and knocks Brett out cold. The rapist removes the battery cover from the phone and tosses out the SIM card before running away.

After watching her attacker beat and rob the Good Samaritan, the victim sneaks up to Brett's unconscious body and takes the thirty or so dollars cash in his pocket.

Anywhere from a few minutes to a half hour later, Brett wakes up on the sidewalk. His nose is broken and his right eye is swollen shut. Other than that, he's in relatively good shape. He dusts himself off and limps the last block to his place, all the while hoping another predator doesn't see him in his weakened condition. Upon arriving home, Brett spends the rest of his evening drinking malt liquor and banging out rails until he passes out watching a replay of the Braves game.

· · · · · · · ·

Not long after Brett left, Lawrence took a strong pull from the half full bottle of whiskey and lay down on the floor in his living room. Watching the ceiling fan only worsened the spinning in his head. Then came the dumbass decision to close his eyes.

Someone told him a while back that lying on the couch with one hand on the wall and one foot on the floor would fix his equilibrium. But it turns out that is complete and total bullshit. The Lord is looking out for him and has placed a dirty piece of Tupperware nearby that is large enough to hold most of the vomit. The rest overflows onto the floor. He tries to lie back down before realizing the disgusting odor from the Tupperware is eventually going to make him throw up again.

He carefully scoops up the bile filled plastic container and carries it into the kitchen where he pours the contents down the garbage disposal. The trembling in his arms and legs demonstrate how weak he has become.

Lawrence fills his hands up with water from the faucet and slurps it down. A half-gallon or so later, he's had his fill and splashes some on his face to ease the throbbing in his skull. He plugs the drain and dips his head in water until it covers his mouth and he is no longer able to hold his breath. He slumps down to the floor and rests with his back against the wooden cabinets.

After resting for a bit, he picks himself up and walks back into the living room. "I have to know." He gathers up the Ouija board and puts the planchette back together. Once again, he plants himself cross-legged on the floor in front of his coffee table. Without Brett's company, he chooses utter darkness over a pale candle.

"Did I pass this evil on to that woman from the airplane?" The feebly constructed pointer wobbles over to *YES*.

Lawrence thinks back to that day and visualizes selling the rest of his booty. He sees himself talking to the stranger at the fast food restaurant, Dale, and all three of the Cash4Gold attendants.

Without Lawrence even vocalizing the question, the planchette emits an electric pulse that he takes as his answer.

"What about the people they sold it to?" Lawrence thinks aloud as he walks away.

Behind him, the pointer collapses into several pieces over the *YES* and a new image is zapped into his mind.

Every tree lining the first row of the clearing has at least one dead body hanging from its branches. The same with the second row. And the third row. And the fourth row. And the fifth row…

CHAPTER TEN
In Every Bet There Is A Fool & A Thief

Lawrence rubs the sleep out of his eyes. "Holy shit." Somehow he had forgotten the bruises covering his head. Hungover as hell, he tromps to the bathroom and rinses his face off. The reflection in the mirror has morphed into something completely different than what was there a week earlier.

The cuts and bruises covering his face are exacerbated by the significant amount of weight that has melted off. His cheeks are sunken-in and his lips are dry & cracked. His hair has lost all of its body and has started to recede.

On top of that, there are specks of gray sprouting out of his three day beard. The fingernails attached to the end of his bony fingers are yellow and dry. "I need a shower and some breakfast."

The hot water spews from the showerhead and fogs up the mirror. The baking soda in his toothpaste grinds against the beer, whiskey, and cocaine staining his teeth. The light touch of the shaving cream and ensuing razor on his face is nothing less than a necessary evil.

Upon climbing into the shower he is slapped in the face by a stream of freezing cold water. Despite the room around him being filled with steam. He forces himself to stay under the icy water long enough to lather up his hair before jumping out and rinsing off in the sink. After wiping down with a soapy rag, Lawrence takes a step back to check out his post-shower reflection.

Little droplets of water run down the length of the mirror. The steam covering his reflection darkens and the drops of condensation thicken to a runny mixture of blood and mud.

A worm crawls out of his distended right eye. Lawrence can feel his nasal septum eroding to a dark, flaky powder that swirls up his nose and down into his lungs. His gums start to erode and bleed profusely.

He hears a clattering noise rolling around in the porcelain sink. His bottom row of teeth has grouped together near the drain. The blood spurting from his mouth dribbles down his chin and flows down to his withering chest and along the curved ridge created by his protruding ribs.

He watches muscle mass erode from all over his body. In a matter of seconds, his thighs are too weak to support his weight and he collapses. As he crumples to the ground, the back of his head slams against the ridge of the ceramic tub and knocks him out cold.

•　•　•　•　•　•　•　•

Lawrence comes to with fresh bumps and bruises on the back of his head. Feeling a little woozy – and possibly concussed – he reaffirms his decision to head out for a hearty breakfast. He throws on a t-shirt and his best smelling pair of jeans and gently climbs down the intimidatingly high stairwell.

Possibly suffering from some sort of daymare dummy effect, his legs struggle to carry him the two blocks to the nearest diner. Without so much as glancing at a menu, he orders a stack of pancakes, eggs, toast, grits, and bacon. With an orange juice and water to drink.

From the look on her face, he can tell the waitress is wondering who beat his ass.

This causes him to feel self-conscious so he lowers his hat and turns his chair to face out the window. He scoffs at the foolish people walking up the steps to church.

Little do they know that when you actually need God, He's nowhere to be found. When your very life and soul are at stake He disappears completely. Even if you walk straight up to Him with hat-in-hand and plead for forgiveness, He forsakes you. As far as Lawrence can tell, *The Good Lord* they are there to worship, is at least complicit in everything bad that happens to his flock.

The waitress sets three full plates down in front of him. The religious people across the street can keep their stale crackers and cheap wine. Happiness is a steaming stack of pancakes, melted butter, and warm maple syrup. The first bite of that crisp bacon is all the religion he'll need for the rest of the week. As if the sheer deliciousness isn't enough, all of that tasty grease soaks up the cocaine in his system.

Like all other great things in life, there's a catch. In this particular instance, the catch is that the horrible things he's been putting into his system have to go somewhere. Several bites into those pancakes and a rumbling in his stomach reminds him that it has been two days since he has experienced a bowel movement.

He covers his food with a napkin and shuffles - with cheeks clinched - to the unisex bathroom. He can feel the judgmental eyes of other diners watching him as he slides into the bathroom and conspicuously pops the deadbolt shut.

The familiar potpourri smell in the bathroom is very pleasant for a brief moment before Lawrence plasters over it with the putrid smell of diarrhea that is infused with over forty-eight hours' of cocaine and alcohol. He rightfully assumes the tables in the back of the restaurant can hear everything, but there is very little he can do about it at this time.

After washing up, he straightens his posture and works up the courage to walk outside. There were two tugs on the door while he was inside, so it's safe to assume there will be at least one person watching the door. Lawrence can only imagine what they may have heard on the other side, but he knows what they're gonna smell.

Determined not to let the staring take away his power, Lawrence puts on a brave face and strolls across the dining hall. From the looks on their faces, they had heard everything. Several of the younger diners laugh-out-loud when they are finally able to put a beaten face to the noises they had heard.

The syrup had soaked all the way through the stack and turned his pancakes into a loosely held together pile of deliciousness. The grease filling the crevices in his bacon has congealed to form white pools of hangover cure. Meanwhile the toast has hardened and is no longer fit for human consumption. The only thing that can fix those grits is to take them to another restaurant and ask their chef to recook them.

Five minutes after his bathroom misadventure, Lawrence has finished and is motioning to the waitress for the check. A little girl in a red dress bounces out of her parents' minivan and thinks that the bruised stranger is waving at her. Eager to make a new friend, she runs to the restaurant and bangs on the window.

The loud rattling of the glass literally almost scares the shit out of him. Even in his pissed off state, he can't deny her cuteness. He smiles and waves back.

"Are you coming to church, mister?"

Lawrence half hears her and half reads her lips. "No."

Even the little girl can tell he's been through a lot. "You should. There are a lot of nice people there. It'll make you feel better."

Lawrence leans in like he's in confession and whispers through the glass. "I think God's mad at me."

"For what?"

"I'm not a very good person."

"Are you a being a good person now?"

"I reckon so."

"Are you gonna be good from now on?"

Lawrence allows a smile to cross his face. "You bet your sweet bippy."

"Then God forgives you and you should come to church." The little girl's mother grabs her hand and pulls her away. She looks back and waves for him to follow.

She made it sound so easy. Maybe it is. Maybe now that his victims have had a proper burial, all he has to do is ask again. Then again he'd have to be an idiot to walk back into a church after what happened last week.

The little girl crosses the street with her family. Halfway across she turns back and looks at her new friend. This time there is an angelic glow about her. It is almost physically impossible for him not to follow when she gives him a wink and a nod.

Meanwhile, the waitress is busy trying to figure out how to split the check on a ten top in the corner. Lawrence guesstimates the cost plus twenty percent and leaves cash on the table. He tucks his t-shirt into his pants while he Frogger's his way across three lanes of traffic.

The little girl waves to him from the top of the stairs as he limps his way over. The aura around her has strengthened since he first saw it. He can't tell if it's because she is getting closer to the church or farther away from him.

First thing he does when he enters the congregation hall is scan the audience for the her. He doesn't see her or her family anywhere. The glaring eyes of impatient parishioners waiting in line for a seat are burning holes in his back. Lawrence cracks under the pressure and truffles down the aisle to take the closest seat he can find.

Compared to the rest of the crowd, Lawrence looks like a hot mess with his busted face and smelly t-shirt. The frayed ends of his blue jeans and holes in his tennis shoes are the cherry on top.

The music director takes his place as the choir lines up behind him. Once everyone in the sanctuary is seated, he regales them with news from the church business breakfast that was held earlier in the morning.

The baptismal pool above the choir is half hidden by black curtains with gold fringe. The little girl steps out from behind them and looks down into the water.

From the crowd's reaction – or lack thereof – Lawrence assumes he is the only one who sees her. Her head is wrapped in a crown of thorns and blood is pouring from her sides. She has been beaten and appears weak. The pink dye created by the mixture of blood coming from her forehead and the sweat dripping off of her brow crawls down the front of her white dress. She scans the crowd for Lawrence. Her cold, dead eyes see straight through him. She lifts up her right hand and points at the ceiling.

Below her, the choir director is still making his announcements as flames shoot up out of the baptismal waters.

The audience laughs politely at one of the speaker's jokes while Lawrence desperately gasps.

A leather noose is lowered around the neck of the giggling little girl. She continues smiling as she is lifted up into the air and slowly drug out over the choir. She stops in midair while the choir leads the congregation in a rousing rendition of *Shall We Gather at the River*?

Her parents climb out of the fire filled baptismal pool. Their bodies are charred from the flames yet dripping wet from the blessed water. They reach out for their daughter, but she doesn't reach back for them. She is resigned to her fate. A bright light erupts from the ceiling overhead and bathes her in the warmth of God's mercy.

The music director silences the room. A young mother with the voice of an angel steps out front to belt out the last verse.

Soon we'll reach the silver river,
Soon our pilgrimage will cease;
Soon our happy hearts will quiver
With the melody of peace.

A look of calm spreads across the little girl's face. It's as if she has reached nirvana while listening to the last song she will ever hear. The leather noose yanks tight and snaps her neck.

The music minister takes the podium and compliments the congregants on their singing. All the while, the young girl's tongue is hanging out of the smile forever frozen to her face. Her head collapses to the side sending the crown of thorns crashing into the choir pit below. Blood drips from her scalp and lands on the soloist's still empty seat.

"Today, we'd like to set aside a moment, as we are prone to do from time-to-time, to take a second and greet our neighbors. Shake their hands. Maybe even pat 'em on the back. If you don't know them, make sure to introduce yourself. A stranger's just a friend you haven't met yet."

An elderly woman offers Lawrence a pocket sized packet of tissues. "You don't look so well, son."

"I just... I've been going through some..."

"Don't worry honey. You're right where you need to be." Lawrence thanks her and turns to greet the next stranger in line. The elderly woman persists by grabbing his shoulders and pulling him down to her level. "Just look at me and my husband. Three years into our marriage, Anthony here…" she lowers her voice. "He had himself a little indiscretion and I left his sorry you-know-what. We hardly even talked for six months. When we did, it wasn't pretty. We'd fuss and fight and curse each other to high heaven.

But every Sunday, we'd both be in church. We'd be out til God knows when doing Lord knows what with God knows who on Saturday night. But we'd both be in church come Sunday morning."

"Forgive me, ma'am, but why are you telling me this?"

"Faith." Her answer elicits but a blank stare from Lawrence. "It's that simple. Don't listen to these blowhards. Jesus knows life is tough. He expects us to make mistakes. Life is a test that nobody gets an A on. God bless us, He grades on a curve.

"So you can go out all week and do whatever you have to do to deal with the hand you're dealt. But at the end of the week, when the bars are closed and the whores have put on their Sunday best, you come back to church and you tell Him about it… and be honest. Keep the faith and listen when the Lord talks. He'll make sure you get there."

"Get where?"

"Your destiny."

Lawrence wants so bad to believe her. "How do you know?"

"I don't." The choir director takes his place behind the podium and introduces the pastor. "But our son does. Maybe his message can change your mind."

Lawrence turns to face the front and a smile crosses his face. The old woman gives her husband a peck on the cheek. He wraps his arm around her as they watch their son deliver his message on *Forgiveness*.

• • • • • • • •

Happier than a pig in shit to be home, Lawrence falls back on his couch and calls Lydia who picks up on the first ring. "How are you feeling?"

It's a little annoying how she jumps right into the conversation. But it's whatever. "Hey, beautiful."

"Oh my God! You sound so much better." Her voice is filled with genuine excitement. "I hope this means we're getting closer to our date."

"The sooner the better." The smile running across his face causes a pain in his jaw.

"Turns out I've got a pretty busy week. Lisa's on vacation. Don't tell anybody, but I'm pretty sure she's finally getting her boobs done. Then I've got to get ready for an investment meeting with this guy. It sounds shady as hell, but he's really rich and says he can help me build up my college fund."

Lawrence has been looking forward to this for so long that he can't help but feel disappointed. "What about later in the week?"

"I can try to get somebody to pick up one of my shifts, even then… I'll have to find a sitter for my two girls." You could have heard a pin drop on the moon. "Hello?"

"Two…" Lawrence clears his throat, "two girls? How old are they?"

"Nine and twelve."

"You look really good for having had two kids." He pauses for a moment hoping she might say something. "How old are you?"

"I'm twenty-three."

Lawrence checks the math in his head "No way!"

Lydia laughs hysterically. "I totally could have had you."

"I knew you were joking the whole time."

"If I would have said I was like… twenty-seven, you totally would have believed me."

"That may be true. But let that be a lesson to you." His smile vibrates across the distance.

"What lesson is that?"

"That I'm gullible and you shouldn't take advantage of that."

The flirtation continues on like that for well over an hour before her battery starts dying. Once again, they hang up without setting an official time for their first date.

For all he cares, they just had their first date and it went wonderful. He and Lydia are now boyfriend/girlfriend.

Still floating in a bubble of romanticism, Lawrence is disappointed to find that his apartment is an atrocious mess from the night before. No responsible husband and father lives like this.

It takes him an hour or so to clean up, but when it's finished he feels like a new man. All of the bad mojo filling the place went out with the rest of the garbage.

As his excitement over the future with Lydia grows, Lawrence grows more convinced than before that it's time to get rid of the cocaine. But there's no way he can just throw it all away. Just because drugs are illegal doesn't mean there's anything immoral about offering someone a great product at a fair price.

At worst, it can't hurt to do a little line while he thinks about it. He withdraws a sack from the shoebox, grabs a cold beer, and sits down at the little table in his kitchen. He taps out a moderate amount of powder and takes the first line straight off of the table.

He dumps out another line and looks around the room. The shoebox of cocaine and cash calls to him from the counter. As much as he wants to grab it and take control of his future, he wants to run away and save his ass more.

Why does it have to be that way? Life isn't fair. His mind, body, and soul have been beaten to shit over the past several days and he deserves to get something out of it. He dives in and snaps up another line.

When you really think about it, he hasn't really gained that much from the whole ordeal. After catching up on bills and getting jacked by those douchebag frat guys, he only has about a thousand dollars left. That would *maybe* cover the medical bills from the doctor he should have seen.

Look at all the horrible shit people get away with all over the world. Dictators, drug kingpins, bankers, weapons dealers, politicians. These people all make hundreds of millions of dollars through their evil endeavors and get away with it. Yet you don't see them freaking out in the middle of a church or running away from private dances.

Maybe you don't hear about it. Maybe their daily lives are just like his, except with better food and more elegant surroundings. It may very well be that all of their yachts and private jets are haunted. Or maybe for every family they kick out on their ass, the bankers get a huge boil on their nuts or something.

Yet, here Lawrence is, coked out and haunted over a measly grand. He pops a top on another beer and starts flipping the cap in the air. Light from the ceiling fan bounces off of the gold on Alex's class ring. Lawrence has never really noticed how nice of a ring it is. Judging by the size of the diamond in the center, Westwood must be one nice school.

Of course he went to a nice school. One where you don't get your diploma until you've properly demonstrated what a rich asshole you've learned to be. Soon he finds himself filled with jealous rage. The next line is the fattest one of the day.

When you think about it, it's really not that bad. The whole being haunted thing. It's only a little loss of sleep and having the shit scared out of you a couple of times a day.

If he can walk away with ten thousand dollars after all of this, he'll be alright. He'll take some time off to clean his soul then get to work. Maybe invest the money in some sort of business. Something low maintenance like vending machines or a DVD rental machine. Then the good Lord will realize that his was a special set of circumstances and he deserves another chance at a better life.

"Fuck it!" Whatever he can't sell between now and his first date with Lydia will get flushed down the toilet. In the meantime, he'll sell as much as possible and spend his free time researching businesses with low startup costs.

Lawrence isn't an idiot. He is well aware that this means he is extending the barrage of hallucinations and nightmares. Assuming he doesn't go insane first, by next Sunday morning he'll be walking hand-in-hand with Lydia up the stairs to the church. Then on Monday he'll wake up and start his new life.

• • • • • • • •

Meanwhile Brett is at home in his crappy apartment getting ready to have a fire sale of his own. He calls up his friend Carlos in hopes that he knows a few people looking to party. Not to mention, you can have an absolute blast getting fucked up with Carlos and his friends.

"Hey!!" Carlos yells happily into the phone. "You come down on the price yet?"

Brett can already feel the good times flowing. "Just now."

"Ha! I knew you couldn't say no to me!" Carlos covers the phone and tells the news to his friends. "They want to know how much."

"Tell them we'll figure something out when I get there. There's only one thing."

"What's that?"

Brett knows this isn't going to come easy. "I'm gonna need a ride."

Without bothering to cover the phone, Carlos yells to his friends. "His broke ass needs a ride, ya'll!" In the background, Brett hears the crowd howl in laughter before somebody says "Tell him to take a cab!"

"I'm not taking a cab all the way out there! I'm gonna cut you guys a huge discount, it's the least you can do."

"I don't know." Carlos honestly sounds stuck. "Let me see what I can do. You know how we like to get fucked up on Sundays. I wouldn't let anybody in this building drive a golf cart right now. I'll call you back in a minute."

"Sure." Brett tells the dial tone.

Before he has time to adjust the television antenna, Carlos calls him back. "Johnny said his sister is heading out this way in a little bit, she can pick you up."

"Great when will…"

Carlos sounds absolutely hammered. "She just got off on your exit. We sent her the directions. She'll honk the horn when she gets there."

"I hear honking all the time."

"Dixie!" Carlos yells over the growing crowd noise behind him.

"What's that?"

Carlos runs outside. "Her horn plays Dixie. She used to date some old redneck that gave it to her for her birthday one year. Dumbass broke up with her a month later and she hasn't had time to replace it."

"Is she hot?"

"Yeah. And she's a slut too."

•   •   •   •   •   •   •   •

The hour drive out to the country is long and tedious… for Haley. Brett on the other hand has a great time building a solid foundation for what he hopes will be hookup later. She parks the old truck in front of a tractor shed in the middle of a recently plowed field. A tool shed off to the right houses a variety of green & yellow farm equipment.

Brett holds open the door to the smoke filled office and let's Haley make an entrance. The wood paneled walls are lined with large bags of seed and fertilizer. She is greeted with a variety of woots and cattle calls from the five men sitting at the poker table when she struts through the door. The celebration abruptly ends when Brett walks in.

"Who's this guy?" Haley's cousin Adam asks through the bottom of his glass.

"I don't know, Brett or something. You guys told me to pick him up."

"This is the guy with the cocaine." Carlos adds.

"Ohhh." Adam licks his lips. "How much?"

Brett takes a seat. "How much you got?"

"Twenty an 8-ball?" Haley's brother Johnny laughs and drops the cash on the table.

"That's insane." Brett grabs the open beer in front of him and takes a pull. A cigarette butt hits his tonsils and he spews the warm, ashy suds all over the cards and poker chips. Everybody in the room bursts into laughter. "I'm glad you think that's funny."

The embarrassment is written all over his face. He nervously dries his now sweaty palms off on his pants. Why is he putting up with this shit? He's the one with all the power. He's the one with a pocketful of cocaine.

"I'll tell you assholes what." Brett wipes the drool off of his chin with the back of his hand. "The first one of you assholes to get me a beer can have the first one for eighty." Desperate to get rid of the white monkey on his back, Brett is almost willing to pay them to take it.

Carlos runs and grabs Brett a beer. "This better be some good shit."

"A friend of mine in the city's been getting two hundred."

Johnny fears he may have just missed out on a great deal. "How much for everybody else?"

"Whoever wants a sack can have one now for a hundred. But since we're all here to gamble… you can wait and see how the market fluctuates. If I start winning big, the price goes down. But if I start losing my ass, the price goes up."

"Gamble my ass, I'm ready to get fucked up right now." Johnny is the first to drop five twenties on it. Pretty soon the table is covered with cash.

Pedro is the only holdout. "Come on, Pedro." Carlos pats him on the back. "I thought you said we were gonna get down tonight."

"After seeing how he played you fools, I'm counting on him cleaning up. When he does, I'm gonna swoop in and catch a bargain on that shit."

Haley didn't bother to throw in and has pulled her chair up right next to Brett with her hand on his shoulder. "What are you gonna do until then?"

"Until then... I'm bumming off of you kind folks." Pedro nudges Carlos to bum a line. The rest of the gang joins in the fun while Brett taps out an extra for Haley.

After everyone has settled down from the rush of their first line, the cards are dealt and the gaming begins. It takes Brett less than an hour to double his initial cache of chips.

Pedro deals the next hand. "Hey, hoss! Price dropped yet?"

Brett eyes his stack and confidently shows Haley his cards. "Talk to me after I win this hand."

After the cards are dropped, Pedro celebrates with Brett as he rakes in the pot. "Two for one." Brett announces to Pedro as he tosses the bags across the room.

When Pedro reaches up to catch the second bag, the fluorescent light overhead glistens in the gold cross wrapped around his neck. Brett quickly covers his eyes, but a headache swells to life anyway.

Pedro taps out a fat line and yanks it right up.

Carlos reminds him that it's time to settle his debt. "I almost forgot." Pedro dumps out two for Carlos and himself.

The games continue. Brett keeps winning while Pedro has all but checked out for the rest of the evening.

"You might wanna slow down, Pedro," Scott warns. "We've gotta work tomorrow."

"You can tell the boss to kiss my ass." Pedro laughs. "On second thought tell him I have a stomach virus." He takes another line. The cross dangles out of his shirt and flashes in Brett's eyes.

An ominous, black energy surrounds Pedro. It darkens as it gains strength and blankets itself around his head.

Pedro snorts another line. "Where you boys at? I thought we came here to party!" His friends answer with a series of blank stares. He is unaware of the blood flowing from his nose until it hits the tip of his lip.

Haley screams. "Holy shit! You need to lay off of that stuff." Everyone at the table nods in agreement.

Except for Brett. He's too busy freaking out at the dark energy working itself around Pedro's shoulder and down to his chest where it bores through his sternum and into his heart.

Pedro starts convulsing and collapses to the floor. Carlos drops to the ground. "Pedro!" Carlos slaps his face. "Come on Pedro! Don't do this!"

Adam looks at Brett. "What the fuck's going on?"

"I don't know!" Brett knows this is his fault in more ways than one.

Haley runs over to check on Pedro and looks back at Brett with hatred in her eyes. "What do we do?"

Brett has no idea.

"I'll call an ambulance." Scott pulls out his phone.

Pedro stops shaking and his arms fall to his side. His eyes remain open.

Carlos slaps the phone out of Scott's hands. "There's no point." Carlos fights through the tears. "He's gone."

The room goes quiet. Nobody says anything because nobody knows what to say.

Scott picks his phone back up. "Somebody's got to come get him. They'll take him to the morgue." Scott looks around to see he's the only one wanting to do the right thing. "He's got to have a funeral."

"He'll have a funeral. But if we call the ambulance we all go to jail. And us going to jail ain't gonna bring him back."

Haley chugs her beer. "This isn't right."

"You're right." Carlos wraps his arm around her. "Nobody is arguing with you. But it wasn't our fault. There's no reason we should all end up in jail over an accident."

Brett knows it was no accident.

"What do we do?" Adam asks no one in particular.

Carlos is the only one in the room who has kept his cool. "We clean up and then we leave. Somebody'll show up tomorrow and find him."

Johnny can't believe this is happening. "They'll know he wasn't alone."

"Okay." Carlos gathers his things. "You guys stay here and deal with the authorities. I'm leaving." He walks out the door and tosses a sack of garbage in the back of his pickup.

One-by-one, the rest of the crew follows his lead. Pretty soon it's just Pedro lying alone on the cold floor. The office in the shed is cleaner than it has been in years.

·   ·   ·   ·   ·   ·   ·   ·

After a long drive back to the city, Haley parks her truck in front of Brett's apartment building. "It's late, you should probably just stay here." This is the first time either of them has spoken since they left the farm.

"A friend of mine lives around here. I'm gonna stay with her."

"You sure? It's been a long night and I imagine we could both use a little company." Brett reaches over and clumsily runs his fingers through her knotted hair.

She politely moves her head away. "I really need to get some sleep."

Taught by his father to be persistent, Brett slides across the vinyl bench seat and sidles up next to her. His right hand lands on her left knee as he whispers in her ear. "After everything that happened tonight, I could really use the company." Brett presses his lips against hers. When she doesn't reciprocate, he tries to pry her mouth open with his tongue.

She gruffly shoves him away. "I'm not interested in you like that!"

Brett wraps his arms tight around her. "You don't need to be. We can just be friends tonight. Comfort each other after a traumatic experience."

She feels him tighten his grip and is repulsed by his warm breath blowing on her neck. "Sounds tempting. But I don't want to get a reputation."

Haley fights him off for a little longer. Brett fights back harder. He pins her against the door and holds her down. Not sure how far he is willing to take this, she goes limp and prays for him to stop. When he doesn't stop, she closes her eyes and prays for him to finish.

CHAPTER ELEVEN
Swangin'

Lawrence wakes up five minutes before he is supposed to be at work and calls the office. He has never been so happy to hear Rodrigo's voice. "Hello."

He doesn't even try to sound sick. "Hey, tell Sean I'm not feeling good and I can't make it to work today."

"Alright." Rodrigo pauses. "What do you want me to tell him?"

"Just tell him I'm sick."

"Sick how? Throw up sick? Diarrhea sick? Flu sick? I'm not gonna make up your lie for you."

"Diarrhea sick." Lawrence answers flippantly. "And throw up sick. Tell him I ate some bad oysters or something."

"Alright, man. You need to keep your nose out of your own shit."

Lawrence hangs up. "Where was that advice when I was about to hook-up with Betsy?" He takes a line off of a magazine and lies back down on the sofa. He turns the television on to a twenty-four hour sports channel just as the announcer is introducing the highlights from yesterday's collegiate diving competition. After watching several athletes perform high-flying acrobatic feats, he remembers his sister's invitation to go swimming.

According to the clock on the wall, he has an hour to make it to her place. He packs up his swimming trunks, a towel, a couple of 8-balls, and two hundred dollars before jogging out the front door. On the way over, Lawrence stops to buy two cases of beer, a new cooler, three bags of ice, and a half gallon of vodka. If her friends don't like to party, they'll have to get used to the idea.

A little while later, he pulls up and parks in front of Elizabeth's driveway as she is loading up her compact car. He toots the horn and she waves excitedly. "I guess calling seemed too easy?"

Lawrence jogs up her mountain of a driveway with the satchel slung over his left shoulder. "You used to love surprises." He peeks his head into the backseat of her car. "Is my cooler gonna fit in here?"

"I've got this little old car and you've got that nice, new, SUV." Elizabeth pulls her beach bag out of the passenger seat. "We're taking your ride, Clyde."

"Alright." He grabs his stuff and heads back down the hill. "Just remember how much you dislike my driving."

"Correction," she locks up her car and chases after him. "I hate your driving. But if I get pulled over for a DUI, the announcement in the paper will read *Single Mother Gets DUI: World Hates Her*. But if you get one, it'll read *Lawn Jockey Gets DUI: World Surprised It Took This Long*."

"I don't necessarily disagree with what you said." Lawrence grabs each of them a beer and hops behind the wheel. "But you could have said it a little more nicely."

"Sorry. *Grass Maintenance Employee Gets DUI: Takes World's Ugliest Mug Shot.*" She laughs at her own joke before taking a long look at his face. "Seriously little brother, who fucked you up?" Lawrence ignores the question and takes off down the street. "I know you heard me."

"It all started when Brett…"

"It all started," Elizabeth interrupts angrily, "when you didn't learn your lesson when you were little."

"This is why I didn't want to tell you."

"He's always been a bad influence. The only reason the two of you didn't wind up in jail after you shot up the town's water tower is because mama used to date the cop."

"Can we please just drop it? Some guys beat me up, okay? I just wanna have a nice day with my sister and hammer down a few beers."

"Tell me why they beat you up and then I'll leave you alone."

"One of them caught me stealing their watch."

"You were stealing a guy's…" She stops herself and takes several deep breathes. "I love you and I hope you're okay. If I have any criticism, it would be that your decision making has been suspect since you and Linda broke up."

The lone tear sliding down his face lets her know he heard her. Like really heard her. Lawrence pulls onto the interstate and takes them out of the city. Not a word is spoken while each of them tries to pinpoint the moment when Lawrence's life took an inexplicable turn.

Elizabeth reaches into the backseat and opens the cooler. "I need another beer."

"I thought you'd never ask." Lawrence snatches the can from her and lights up a cigarette. Almost three beers later, he pulls into a line of cars parked just off of an old bridge. They shuffle down a rocky, muddy path to the river bank. Her friends are already in the water and appear to have been drinking for quite some time.

Richard, the tallest of the guys, yells up to them. "Look who brought her baby bro."

"It was either this or hire a sitter." She opens up the cooler and tosses beers to everyone who holds up their hand. "You guys haven't gone up to the waterfall yet, have you?"

"Nope." Richard answers. "We figured we'd hang out down here until the sun breaks and then head up yonder."

"Good deal." Elizabeth slips off her t-shirt and cutoff denim shorts before wading into the water and wrapping her arms around a tire tube.

Lawrence runs down to the red clay beach and cannon balls into the water right next to her. Richard splashes her and the rabble rousing continues. Everybody is laughing and having a good time. Somebody even brings out a football. After throwing that around a bit, they decide it's time to give the rope swing a try.

Lawrence takes his place in the back of the line so he can watch the others go ahead.

Richard walks up behind him and puts a hand on his shoulder. "What happened to your face?"

Lawrence is embarrassed by the truth, but not concerned enough about the opinion of the stranger to lie about it. "Found myself on the wrong side of a boot. Well, they weren't all wearing boots."

"They all feel the same when they're slamming against your face." Richards laughs a knowing laugh and lifts his can up for a toast.

Lawrence taps his new friend's beer and Richard sits down next to him on a patch of dirt. There's an air of calm surrounding them as if a bond was formed from the shared experience of surviving a proper beat down. "How do you know my sister?" Richard looks back at Lawrence and smiles. "What's that mean?"

"That's your sister for you. She knows everything about everybody, but don't nobody know nothing about her."

"Ohhhh." Lawrence puts it together. "You two have been... dating?"

"Two months now." Richard sounds disappointed. "She hasn't introduced me to Carol. Which I get. But I figured she at least mentioned me to you."

"Don't take it personal." Lawrence takes a swig from his beer. "That's just how she is."

Elizabeth notices the two men in her life speaking to one another and races up to them. "So..."

"Busted." Lawrence warns.

"He mad?" She asks as if Richard isn't there.

"Perturbed?" Lawrence looks to Richard for approval of his wording.

"That works."

Elizabeth squeezes in the small space between them. "Geez," Lawrence stands to leave. "I can take a hint."

"Took you long enough." Elizabeth wraps her arm around Richard. Richard caresses Elizabeth's face with his hand before pulling her in for a passionate, close lipped kiss. Lawrence's heart is warmed by the tender moment and all of his concerns are momentarily washed over by happiness for his sister.

Richard's watch glistens in the sun and reflects the light right into Lawrence's eyes. He shields his face, but he has already lost his balance and falls over backward. Richard runs down to help him up. As painful as it is, Lawrence can't look away from his watch.

The fall only worsens Elizabeth's concerns. "You alright?" Something about the look on his face tells her something is very wrong. He doesn't answer. Now even more concerned than before, Elizabeth wipes the dirt off of his clothes while Richard gives him an amateur eye exam. "Do you think he has a concussion?"

"I don't think so. But I'm not sure." Richard tries to manually close Lawrence's eyelids. His pupils dilate as the watch grows nearer to his face. It is only when Richard's finger touches his eyelid that Lawrence finally snaps out of it. His eyes flutter to life, but he doesn't say a word.

"You okay?"

"I'm… I'm okay." Lawrence looks around. His eyes inevitably fall back on Richard's silver watch. "I guess I tripped over something."

"Alright." Richard claps his hands together. "I'm gonna show these guys how to jump off of a bridge."

"What about your watch?" Lawrence's question confuses him. "Your watch? Is it waterproof?"

"Uh, I don't know." To be safe, Richard takes it off and hands it to Elizabeth.

"He recently started his first office job." Elizabeth explains to Lawrence without being asked. "He thinks the watch will help him fit in. Maybe it would if he didn't look so ridiculous wearing a tie."

"Two months, huh? You know how pissed off you'd be if I had been dating somebody for that long without telling you?"

"That'll never happen."

"How's that?"

"First, I have my ways. Second, you call me with a heart erection every time you kiss a girl." On the cliff below, Richard is fumbling with the rope and planning out his dive.

"Then how come you haven't heard about Betsy?"

"There's a Betsy *and* a Lydia now? How long has this been going on?"

"About a week or so."

"I told you. The first chance you had, you brought her up." Elizabeth laughs before she notices Lawrence has taken the joke personally. "There's not anything wrong with it. You wear your heart on your sleeve. I just don't want your sleeve getting get ripped off like mine did. That's all."

Lawrence decides to ignore all of her previous statements and focus on that last line. "Thanks, sis. Looks like your man's finally about to jump."

"Hey, babe! You watching?" Elizabeth is a little put off by Richard's use of a term-of-endearment in public.

"Yeah, babe." Elizabeth watches Richard grab the loop at the end of the line and lift himself up. He obviously has some intricate dive planned as he wraps his feet around the rope.

"Did you used to be a stripper!?" Lawrence yells before grabbing another beer from the cooler.

"No!" The rest of the guys pull an upside-down Richard back in preparation of launching him over the cliff. "I just learned a few things from your mom!" Richard says before he realizes that he has just said that to his girlfriend's brother. "Sorry, babe. Force of habit."

Elizabeth waves him off and takes a beer from Lawrence. "Be safe doing the Triple Lindy or whatever you're up to!"

"Now!" Richard orders his friends and they shove him out over the ledge. After he is a few feet over the water, he unwraps his legs. "Holy shit!!"

But it's too late. His friends watch helplessly from the ledge while Richard soars through the air with his hands bound together by the loop at the end of the rope.

Richard violently struggles back and forth in a futile attempt to wiggle out of the trap. He's still facing away from the cliff when he reaches the far arch of the pendulum and swings back for the return trip.

From the look on his girlfriend's face, Richard can tell this isn't going to end pretty. He is about to slam against the cliff face with no way of protecting himself. Elizabeth closes her eyes and wraps her arms around Lawrence.

The rope twists in the wind and rotates his dangling body several times before finally leaving him face-to-face with the red wall. The timing of the rotation leaves him just long enough to thrust his legs forward to slow the force of impact.

His shin bones shatter and break through the skin of both legs before his head and torso slam furiously against the cliff face. One of the guys yells to the paralyzed onlookers. "Let's pull him up!"

"Baby?! Can you hear me?" Elizabeth yells helplessly from the back of the pack. Lawrence gently pushes her aside and helps the rest of the group pull him up. Richard doesn't make a sound and there is no movement coming from the end of the line. "Is he okay?"

Too emotional to help, the only thing Elizabeth can do is scream and cry harder. The guys finally pull Richard up and roll him over on his back.

Elizabeth's screams worsen when she sees the terrified, bloodied, look on his face. Then she almost passes out when she looks down and sees the bones poking out from his shins. Both of his feet have been smashed to smithereens and his thighs have swollen to the size of watermelons.

"Is he okay?" Elizabeth asks through the tears rolling over her mouth.

Lawrence bends down and checks his pulse. "I can't feel anything."

Elizabeth kneels down to check Richard's pulse for herself. "I felt something. Let's get him out of here." Elizabeth grabs both of his arms and tries to pull him up the hill. Richard lets out a painful moan. "He must have separated his shoulders. We'll have to be careful. Lawrence, help me with his head. Amanda, you and Matt grab his midsection. David, Eloise, you two grab his legs. And be careful!" While everyone is taking their positions, Elizabeth looks down at her boyfriend and prays for him to open his eyes. "It'll be okay baby. Just hang on!"

After a tedious climb up to the side of the road, Lawrence pulls his SUV up to the crowd surrounding Richard. When he climbs out of the car, the first thing Lawrence sees is his sister in the middle of the circle. She has just stood up from checking Richard's non-existent pulse and is crying heavily.

The rest of their friends don't really know what to do, but the general consensus appears to be that everyone will wait on the authorities to come pick up the body. When the police and ambulance finally arrive, everyone satisfactorily tells the same story. Give or take a few small details.

Everybody except for Elizabeth agrees that she should be the one who gives Richard's parents the news about his death. Before the group departs, David pulls out his pocket knife, reaches up as high as he can, and removes the rope. Rendering it useless.

Lawrence and Elizabeth are the last to leave the scene of the accident. He kicks a quick U-turn while Elizabeth stares blankly out the window. Her eyes steady fixed on the blood stained spot of soil on the side of the road.

· · · · · · · ·

A few miles down the road, Lawrence comes around a corner and runs up on a pickup truck carrying a load of late season cabbage. Lawrence honks the horn and flicks the guy off. The son-of-a-bitch has the nerve to stick his hand out the window to return the favor.

"Just slow down." Elizabeth scolds him through the lump in her throat. "It's not worth it. Think of what we've already been through." For one of the rare times in his life, Lawrence heeds his sister's advice and gives the truck a little breathing room.

"Thank you." Elizabeth leans her head against the window and stares out onto the revolving vista of forests and open fields.

Then the asshole in front of them swerves onto the shoulder before overcorrecting into the other lane and narrowly missing an alert driver in a compact car. The driver of the truck jerks back into his lane and the load of cabbage spills all over the highway.

Elizabeth looks up just in time to see the truck crash through an old barbed wire fence and slam into a pine tree near the edge of the road.

Lawrence jumps out and rushes through the minefield of cabbage to check on the driver. "Hey man, you okay?"

The man lifts his bloody head up from the steering wheel and stares up at Lawrence. "I think so."

Elizabeth yells from the bed of the truck. "Lawrence!"

"He's alright! Just call the cops!"

She breaks down in tears. "It's not that."

Lawrence runs to the back of the truck to see what has his sister so worked up. "You've got to be fucking kidding me." He can't believe that the pile of cabbage had been covering up the body of what appears to be a dead migrant worker.

The driver stumbles to the back and stares at them before darting back to the cab. Lawrence dives after him and tackles the man by his ankles. He briefly kicks and fights before succumbing to defeat.

"Calm down!" Lawrence straddles him and shoves his face into the ground. "Elizabeth, get the keys out of the ignition."

Elizabeth removes the keys and runs them back to her brother. Lawrence lets go of his captive, walks to the back of the truck, and examines the corpse. An image of Brett sitting around a poker table with a bunch of farm workers manifests in his mind. Lawrence looks down at the old man as he picks himself up. "What happened to this guy?"

"I don't know." The driver dusts himself off. "Boss said they walked in this morning and found him like that."

Elizabeth pokes her finger in his chest and gnarls her teeth like a mother bear. "Where are you taking him?"

"We dug a grave with the others." The stranger sits down next to the body and lights a cigarette. "Fucking place is cursed. The whole world is cursed."

"What do you mean others?" Elizabeth starts crying, but the man still doesn't answer. At this point, answering questions from anybody could only lead to more legal trouble down the road.

"What's this about a curse?" The man looks up at him but doesn't answer. "The cops aren't gonna believe anything you say about a curse anyway."

The driver takes a long drag from his cigarette and shrugs his shoulders. "Lot of accidents have been happening. Avoidable things. Stuff that shouldn't happen keeps happening all around. Boss thinks it's just part of their culture to believe in voodoo and curses. Entire crew's about to run off I think. Shit, I don't blame 'em. Something fucked up's happening."

"What kind of accidents?"

"Accidents." The man takes a long drag from his cigarette. "Uhhh... a hydraulic lift collapsed the other day when one of the guys was changing the brakes on a truck. Wheel well dropped right on his face. Crazy shit like that."

Elizabeth becomes infuriated at his blasé attitude toward America's migrant population. "So you just take them out and bury them in the woods because they're here illegally?"

"It's not like that at all. We have a little graveyard." He can tell his answer has not addressed Elizabeth's concerns. "His friends and family are all waiting there. They all know it was an accident. All the authorities will do is ship his body to Mexico. Along with most of his friends and family."

The logic sounds reasonable. No sense in ruining all of their lives. The three of them stand around the tailgate and wait for the sound of emergency sirens to break the silence.

"Is it alright with you guys if I give the boss a call? Give him a heads up? It don't make sense for him to lose his farm cause this kid can't handle his dope."

Elizabeth can't believe he would even ask. "No you cannot call..."

"Yeah." Lawrence offers the stranger his phone but he waves him off and pulls one out of his pocket. Elizabeth taps Lawrence on the shoulder to give him an angry look.

"Just one of those things, boss? I'll be fine with anything under three months. With everything that's been happening there, I've been thinking about leaving anyway." He picks at his front teeth with the long fingernail on his pinky finger. Lawrence sees the fiery depths of hell in the shiny reflection of the diamondless ring wrapped around the stranger's finger.

After making the necessary arrangements for his impending arrest and incarceration - including half pay for every day he's locked up – the driver hangs up the phone. "Thank you."

Lawrence nods his head. He can't help but feel bad for the guy. The signs are all there. His appearance is generally disheveled. He has bruises of various sizes all over his body. And it looks like he hasn't slept in days.

After ten more minutes of awkward silence around a dead body, the authorities arrive. Different ones from the last time. The driver of the truck is cuffed, Mirandized, and shoved in the back of a squad car. Elizabeth and Lawrence again give statements to the cops and even help them move the cabbages off the road.

∙ ∙ ∙ ∙ ∙ ∙ ∙ ∙

A giant, red paddle wheel pushes the *Delta Queen* down the mighty Mississippi in a latex-on-canvass painting lining the stairwell. His land lady procured this jewel from a pile of garbage on the side of the road one rainy afternoon. She thought the water splotches gave it more of an *authentic look.*

A ghastly seabed of dead bodies floats down the river. The corpses crash against the side of the *Delta Queen* as it cuts through the human seaweed like an icebreaker forging through the Arctic. The bodies being crushed by the paddle wheel leave the water behind the ship blood red and speckled with limbs.

Lawrence reaches the top of the stairwell to find Lydia hunched over a tiny spiral notebook. She is writing him a note in eyeliner. "Aren't you a sight for sore eyes?"

Lydia looks up with a huge smile on her face. Her teeth gleam in the dim hall light. She jumps up and wraps her legs around his waist before remembering his injuries. "Oh my God… I completely forgot about your bruises." She bends over and picks up a plastic grocery sack with two cans of chicken noodle soup, cheese crackers, and apple juice. "I know it doesn't look like much, but it's really good.

My mama used to fix this for me when I felt sick. She'd crush these cheese squares up in the soup. Cause chicken noodle soup is boring but these things make it awesome. After you get finished with your hot soup, you drink the cold apple juice and take a nap. Three hours later, you're as good as new."

Her concern and generosity touches his heart. It turns out she isn't just another incarnation of Linda. Lydia is a better incarnation of Linda. One that gets him.

Linda would never show up unannounced to care for him after he'd done something so stupid. She'd judge him for being a drug dealer and cut him off for a couple of weeks. "That sounds delicious." He reaches around and unlocks the door. "Did you bring enough for two?"

"Two cans. The stars are really just little noodles. So don't be nervous." Lydia struts to the kitchen, slams a pot on the eye of the stove, and pops the top on both cans of soup. Lawrence reaches into the fridge for a couple of beers but comes out with two bottles of water.

"Will you put the apple juice in the freezer? The cold really brings out its natural healing powers."

"Yes, ma'am. You know you could have just brought over a pizza or something. You didn't have to go to all this trouble."

"Mama said guys like a woman that can cook." She turns and smiles. "But this is as good as it gets, so don't go getting your hopes up."

"I prefer take-out anyway." He wraps his arm around her and kisses her neck just under the ear.

She turns and lays one on him. "If I burn the soup, it's all your fault."

Lawrence's excitement takes shape in his pants while his contentment with the heretofore chasteness of their relationship fades away. As much as he hates to do it, he has to pull away. *Fucking Rodrigo.*

"Sorry. I think my bruises are still too sensitive to do anything physical. And if you keep kissing me like that, things are gonna get physical."

Lydia purses her lips and slithers up against him. "Not even a little physical."

"I don't think so. But that doesn't mean you can't stay the night."

"I can't leave you all alone like this." She kisses the bruise under his right eye and turns back to tend the pot.

CHAPTER TWELVE
Dale's Demons

An alarm clock blares from the bedside table. Lawrence stretches his bare armpit over Lydia's nose and slaps the snooze button. "Nice pit hair." She gently blows into his underarm. He giggles like a little school girl and yanks his arm back. "Ticklish? That's good to know."

"Not ticklish. Just armpit sensitive." Lawrence lies back down and she rests her head on his shoulder. She drags her fingernail along the ridge between his third and fourth ribs. Lawrence fights as hard as he can before finally breaking down into another childlike giggle. "Okay, okay. I'm ticklish."

Lydia climbs out of bed and scans the floor for her dress. "You're lucky that I have to leave."

"You don't want to hang out?"

"You don't have to go to work?" Lydia slips on her dress then lays back down.

"Yeah, but you don't have to leave. Just lock the door when you go." Lawrence is starting to sound desperate, but what he really wants is for her to stay and never leave.

"Please. I showed up at your door last night. Uninvited. I am not just gonna hang out at your apartment when you're not here. I mean, stalk much?"

"If this is stalking, it should not only be legalized, but it should come with a reward of some kind."

Lawrence gives her a kiss on the forehead and goes off to take a shower where he kills the time by whistling the theme to a cartoon he can't remember the name of.

After drying off and getting dressed, Lawrence is ecstatic when he walks out into a nearly spotless apartment and a hot girl in the kitchen. He kisses her on the back of her neck. "I really need to get to work."

"You're not gonna let me finish cleaning your kitchen?"

"I offered." Lawrence places his hand on the small of her back and leads her out the door. They walk down the stairs with twin smiles plastered across their faces. Standing outside of the front entrance, she waits for him to offer her a ride while he waits for her to head to the bus stop. Finally, Lawrence squeezes her hand and gives her a peck on the cheek before hopping in his car.

He fumbles around in the glove compartment for a minute before he sees the bus pass by. Once it is out of sight, he jumps out and runs back up the stairs. He gathers up all of the cocaine he can find and piles it up on the coffee table before giving Brett a call.

"Brett!" Lawrence yells to the dead air on the other end.

"Lawrence?" Brett breathes into the line. "Is that really you?"

"Yeah it's me. Quit fucking around."

206

"If it's really you, remember that time we went downtown looking for hookers?"

"Yeah I remember. We promised to never talk about it again."

"Good. Did you just have a dream about me?"

"Nope. I'm actually having a pretty good morning. Yesterday was a clusterfuck. But today's started off a lot better. I've decided I'm getting rid of all this dope." From the silence on the other end of the phone, Lawrence assumes things haven't been going so well for Brett.

"That's cool. So nothing at all about the clearing? Or a smelting pot?"

"Nope. Slept like a baby last night and I don't think I've ever dreamt anything about a smelting pot."

"Maybe it's just me."

"I've had my share of bad dreams though. Don't you worry."

Brett loses it. "If you had a dream like the one I had you'd be the one freaking out right now!"

"Sorry. Calm down. I'm sure everything'll be alright. Can you get me Keith's number?"

"I thought you said you were going to get rid of that stuff? Why you wanna call Keith?"

"I figure we can work something out. I want to get rid of it all at once."

"Alright. But if he asks, you have to tell him I told you it was a bad idea." Brett looks up the number in his phone and texts it to him.

"Thanks buddy. What have you got going on today?"

"Trying to stay awake. That means drinking a bunch of coffee and doing a bunch of cocaine." Brett has obviously fallen further into the rabbit hole than Lawrence.

"Alright. I might stop by later to check on you."

"You do that." Brett abruptly hangs up the phone.

Lawrence considers Brett's dilemma and decides it can't be much worse than anything he has been going through. He calls the office and Rodrigo once again answers the phone. "What is it this time?"

"How did you know it was me?"

"It's about that time. Don't tell me you're going with the *I've got the shits* lie again?"

"Is that what I said yesterday?"

"Yeah. And Sean wasn't buying it. He said if you call in sick today, to tell you to show up tomorrow or never again."

"He wants to fire me for being sick?"

"But you're not sick."

"He doesn't know that."

"I'm just telling you what he said. If I was you, I'd just suck up whatever it is and come in today. I'll tell him you had a flat tire and are on the way. It'll save everybody a lot of trouble."

"Tell him I have the runs." Lawrence tells him before slamming his thumb down on the *END* button. "What a dick!" He takes several deep breaths and floods his mind with positive images. Mostly snapshots from his romantic evening with Lydia.

The next person he calls is Keith. "Hello." An especially non-excited voice picks up.

208

Lawrence can tell that he is playing a video game in the background. "Hello? Is this Keith?"

"Yeah. Who's this?"

"This is Lawrence... Brett's friend. I was hoping we can do a little business."

"Yeah, yeah, store's open. Just come by and see what we got." Keith drops his phone on the floor without hanging up.

"Actually..." Lawrence yells before realizing there is no chance Keith is picking that phone back up. Now he has to drive all the way to Keith's place with twenty-five years' worth of cocaine on the slight possibility that he is willing to buy up his inventory.

One-by-one, he counts the 8-balls and drops them into his leather satchel. After all is said and done, he has one hundred and twenty bags left. By conservative estimates, that comes out to at least fourteen thousand dollars' worth of cocaine. If he can get anything close to that, this whole endeavor has been worth the trouble.

• • • • • • • •

After stopping by an ATM to empty out his checking account, Lawrence knocks on the door to Keith's apartment. "Oh, hi Steph. What are you doing?" She is covered in stolen jewelry. Lawrence feels the beginning of a headache pound to life and stares up at the ceiling to avoid looking at her.

"Oh my God! I haven't seen you in forever."

"It has been a while." Even after all these years, Lawrence still can't believe how Brett ever pulled such a fine specimen of womanhood.

"So what are you doing here?" Of all the dumb shit the three of them have done together, she had never known Lawrence to do cocaine.

"I talked to Keith earlier about doing a little business. He said the store was open."

Steph smiles a curious smile. "Ohhh, I didn't know you were in the industry. What does Linda think about all this?"

"Linda doesn't think about it. We broke up a while back."

Steph is absolutely shocked. "Wow! I thought the two of you would be together forever."

Lawrence can't help but take offense. "Thanks for bringing up my heartache. Is Keith here or not?"

"Sure." Steph answers with an attitude and points up the stairs. "Watch yourself. He's been acting strange lately. Even for him."

Lawrence stops halfway up and backtracks a few steps. "Strange how?"

"Just strange." She looks up from her cold cup of coffee and conjures up an example. "Weird shit keeps happening. The weirder it gets, the worse he handles it. The other day, we were hanging out in his room upstairs and out of nowhere this vulture slams into his window. Motherfucker died right there on the deck. For the next couple of days he kept going outside and looking at it. Sometimes he'd poke it with a stick. Sometimes he'd just stare at it for hours."

"Is that it?"

"The other day I finally got one of his dealers to take it to the dumpster and now he's been holed up in his room for the past three days. I keep telling him he needs to get some sleep. No matter how bad the nightmares are, it can't be worth staying up three days straight." She picks up a jar of purple polish and starts painting her toenails.

"How about you? Have you seen anything crazy or had any dreams?"

210

"I've been having night terrors since I was a kid, so I wouldn't know the difference. It is weird how some of our nightmares have synced up though. I told him it's just because we're soul mates."

"What'd he think?"

"He said *I hope you're right*. Then he went upstairs and locked himself in his room." She laughs and motions for him to leave her alone. "You have fun up there. I'm sure it smells fantastic."

• • • • • • • •

Lawrence knocks on the door but Keith doesn't answer. After waiting for a solid minute, the door opens and Keith welcomes him into the dank dungeon. The only thing separating Lawrence and *all* of Keith's glory is a worn-out pair of titey whiteys loosely wrapped around his waist.

"What's up man?" He turns around and falls back into his bean bag chair. "What do you need?"

He puts his hand out. "I'm Lawrence. It's been a while."

Keith grabs the controller and unpauses his game. "Hi, Lawrence. I'm Keith. What do you need?"

"Well," Lawrence's voice trembles. "Remember how Brett came by the other week and traded with you for that kilo?"

"Remember? Worst business decision of my life. Probably the stroke of bad luck that started all of this shit." Keith doesn't realize how much Lawrence understands what he's talking about. "The stuff I could sell barely made up for the cost of the ki. What I couldn't get rid of you probably saw wrapped around Cleopatra's neck downstairs."

"About that." He drops the open leather satchel in front of Keith. "I was hoping you would want to buy some of it back."

Keith looks down from his video game to see a couple of 8-balls pouring out from the opening. "What's that?"

"Cocaine."

Keith pauses his video game. "I got that part. Why did you bring it here?"

"I was thinking we could work something out. Turns out I'm not a very good drug dealer."

"It's tough when you're nickel and diming it. Stick with it. You'll get the hang of it." Keith picks up the satchel, stuffs the two loose 8-balls inside, and hands it back to Lawrence.

"I don't want to get used to it. I want to liquidate everything and get on with my life. This shit has brought me nothing but bad luck."

"There's a reason I sell quantity. And that's because I don't like dealing with cokehead assholes."

Lawrence snaps. "I'm not a cokehead!" Then he remembers why he's here. "I just got in over my head and I'm hoping you can help me out."

"What do you got?"

"A hundred and twenty balls. That's over ten grand."

"Street value." Keith makes sure to point out. "I think I could get one of my guys to take it. But if you're expecting ten grand, you best get out on the street and start hustling."

"Alright, throw out a number." Lawrence is damn near willing to take anything just to get rid of the white devil.

"A thousand bucks."

"Eight thousand."

"Hit the streets, dude. I've already been screwed over by you and your buddy once on this coke."

"Six?" Lawrence pleads. "Five?"

"I'll give you twenty five to shut up and leave right now."

"Deal!" Lawrence accepts. Keith unlocks a safe in his closet and tosses him five stacks of twenties. Lawrence dumps out the satchel's contents and fills it back up with the cash. "Do you keep any around? You know, small quantities?"

"Yeah." Keith unpauses his game and starts back collecting gold coins. "I keep a few around."

"How much do you charge for an 8-ball?"

"Since I usually sell to close friends, I don't go higher than a hundred."

"Can I get five?" Lawrence is not at all surprised by the eatshit look Keith gives him when he pauses the game and reaches into the pile he had just returned. "Can I get them from your stash?"

"You're a real pain in the ass." Keith makes his way back to the closet safe and withdraws five sacks from his private stash. "I can see why you and Brett are such good friends."

•　•　•　•　•　•　•　•

Lawrence scans the crowd of street vendors and beggars crowding the sidewalk at the Five Points train station. The stranger in the leather duster has to be somewhere in the mix, peddling his wares. After a few minutes, he gives up and makes his way down to *Dale's Discount Pawn Shop*.

He squeezes past a middle aged woman looking at a collection of ceramic cats in aisle two and steps up to the window. Surprisingly, there is a woman behind the counter. "Where's Dale?"

"He hasn't been feeling well lately. He's taking a break. But I'm Mrs. Dale and he has entrusted me to make all business decisions while he's on sabbatical."

"I came in a few weeks ago and sold him a cache of my grandmother's old jewelry."

"And you started feeling guilty and now you want to buy it back?"

"Something like that."

"I'd love to help you, but he is the world's worst record keeper. I have no idea what or when anything here was bought. You're more than welcome to browse the jewelry selection and pick out anything that looks familiar."

Scanning the random selection of rings crammed into the display cases, Lawrence wishes he had studied the details of the jewelry more carefully. With all that's been going on, he expected the stuff from the forest to beckon him or at least give him a headache.

The display case next to the rings is filled with a variety of watches and necklaces hung from metal tree stands. He notices a pendant hanging from one necklace that is missing its jewel. "Excuse me, Mrs. Dale?"

"Yes, honey."

"Do you have any more pieces like this one? Ones with the jewels pried out?"

"Your that guy?"

Lawrence leans in closer to the window and whispers. "What do you mean *that guy*?"

"You came by last week. Said your grandma died and sold my husband a bunch of her old jewelry with all of the jewels pried out?"

"Yes, ma'am. But what of it?"

"Dale doesn't like to hold onto stolen merchandise for too long…"

"It wasn't stolen."

Mrs. Dale pauses for a moment to church up her accusations. "When he has a large influx of inventory from questionable origins, he has what he calls a *Dead Grandma Sale*. It's a tongue-in-cheek way of letting the neighborhood know they can come buy up some stuff on the cheap.

One day, some voodoo witch woman that lives around here came by and made a big deal about the stuff being cursed. After that, he couldn't give it away. Then he started getting those headaches. From there things kept getting worse and worse."

"Headaches?"

"Bad ones. Like a migraine he says, but worse. Said he started getting them the day he put that stuff out on the shelf. Then after it wouldn't sell, he took it down to one of those Cash4Gold places and sold it at a loss." She pauses and smiles before joking. "I think that nearly killed him."

"So if I want to get back any of my jewelry, I need to go ask them?"

"You can try. They send their gold to corporate headquarters once a week where it gets melted down and made into bars."

"So there's no chance?"

"There's never no chance. But yes, there's very little chance."

"Thank you." With his head hung low, Lawrence walks out the door.

Once he steps out into the sunshine, he feels a renewed sense of hope and looks down the street at the three Cash4Gold businesses he visited a week earlier.

Halfway through a crosswalk, Lawrence stops when he hears the sound of squealing brakes. He turns around to see a pedestrian *Froggering* his way across five lanes of traffic. "Heyman!" It's the jewelry merchant in the leather duster. Traffic on both sides slows down but doesn't stop for what they assume to be a very disturbed individual. "HEY!"

Lawrence hurries across the street to meet him. "I was just looking for you."

"Looking for me?" The stranger sounds insulted. "I did everything but put an APB out for your ass. What the fuck did you do to me?"

"I don't know. That's what I'm trying to find out."

"Find out? You need to fix this shit. I'm damn near going crazy. That train down there... It turns into hell's waiting room every time I go across town. I tried walking everywhere. Now my feet are torn to shit. And don't even get me started on that fucking bus."

The two of them sit down at a bench on the edge of the park. "Do you still have anything I sold you?"

"Got rid of the last piece the other day. Damn near had to give it away. I was hoping all of this shit would end when I got rid of it, but things just keep getting worse."

"I'm trying to get it back to see if that reverses everything. Do you think there's any way you can get any of it back?"

"Not a chance in hell! My business is largely tourist based." Not having time to mess around, Lawrence stands to leave. "Heyman! What are we gonna do about this?!"

• • • • • • • •

"Knock, knock." Lawrence vocalizes knocking on the unlocked door to Brett's apartment. "You on the john?!"

Of all the filthy components of Brett's apartment, the old wooden desk in the corner warrants the most attention. From the look of things, Brett has become quite the expert on the occult.

The desk is covered with books about witchcraft and notebooks filled with page after page of notes, drawings, and disturbing ramblings. Lawrence flips through the library books and notices the same meandering pattern in their pages. While Lawrence spent his days and nights worrying about appeasing the curse, Brett has kept himself busy trying to understand what has been going on.

Lawrence shoves aside the sports magazine covered with uncut powder and opens up the notebook. The first ten pages are filled with Brett's retelling of their adventure in the forest. The story backtracks to when his cousin first told him about the scheme before circling back to Brett selling his share of the jewelry.

The next page is covered with a crude drawing of the Chattahoochee National Forest with a line tracing their path from the moment they entered grounds to where they parked the truck at the edge of the forest. From that point, Brett has drawn little footprints marking their trek from the truck to the clearing.

The clearing is depicted by a circle of trees filled with people hanging from low hanging limbs. Others are climbing up. While even more people are standing on the ground waiting their turn. On the ground below, two young men are standing over a couple of dead bodies fighting over who gets to take what jewelry.

The next page is a list of all the people he fenced the stuff to. Some of the names Lawrence recognizes as friends and family of Brett's. Others were strangers or the names of local pawn shops. Alongside each of the names are check marks representing whether or not he had talked to them and if they mentioned anything about being haunted. So far, everyone Brett had been in contact with has experienced at least some degree of paranormal activity.

Next in the notebook are several pages of drawings featuring characters with gaunt faces and decaying corpses hanging from trees. Lawrence finds Brett's theory on the curse written in a discordant array of boxed text. He has drawn a confusing mix of lines and arrows connecting them to one another. Lawrence studies the diagram and eventually puts together Brett's narrative as best he can.

The long and short of it is that Brett believes they undertook a debt by stealing from the people in the clearing. The price they had to pay is to spread misery and pain by distributing the gold and silver. The only thing for them to do after completing their job is to suffer until they succumb to one of its many death traps. The only way for them to receive any mercy is to commit suicide in the forest.

The following three pages are covered with the phrases *GET GOLD* and *GET SILVER* scribbled in a thousand different designs. In the center of one of these pages is an elaborate drawing of a seventeenth century goldsmith. He is leaning over a smelting pot and pouring the liquid gold into brick molds.

On the last page with any ink on it, it looks like Brett's pen busted and ran all over the place. Undeterred by the situation, it appears Brett dipped his finger in the ink and wrote one more GET GOLD on the back cover of the notebook.

Lawrence flips through the library books for a while before deciding to trust Brett's evaluation of the literature. On his way out the door, Lawrence leaves a note letting him know he stopped by.

At the bottom of the wooden stairwell a little girl in a black dress is sitting cross-legged playing jacks. She cuts her eyes at Lawrence and gives him an angry look. The left side of her lip curls up in a snarl before she smiles and gets back to playing her game.

Lawrence stares in amazement as the little girl slams down little human heads on the concrete walkway while she gathers up solid gold and silver jacks. After collecting all of them, she jumps up, sprints down the breezeway, and disappears around the corner.

•　　•　　•　　•　　•　　•　　•　　•

Later that night, Lawrence is making his way through a dark forest. He stumbles along an invisible path by feeling around for trees. Every time he touches one, the fear arises that it will grab him back.

Eventually he staggers out of the forest and into a moonlit corn field. On the other side he sees the faint image of Brett standing in front of an old, wooden toolshed. Lawrence jogs through the field, carelessly stomping on immature stalks and slowing to a stop as he nears his immobile friend.

His hand tremors as he reaches out and taps Brett on the shoulder. The skin on the back of his neck fades to black. His entire body collapses into a pile of bloody, gooey skin in front of Lawrence's very eyes. The squishing noise of Brett's body splashing to the ground makes him nauseous.

The ground below him starts trembling. The toolshed collapses to reveal a miscellany of homemade crosses just on the other side of the tree line. The ground swells under the only traditional headstone in the makeshift cemetery sending it crashing to the ground and shattering into a thousand pieces. One-by-one, hands poke out of the burial plots. Soon Lawrence is surrounded by Pedro and other zombified migrant workers.

The reanimated bodies close in around him. They lift him over their heads to carry him deeper into the forest where Pedro wraps a noose around his neck. Somewhere in the crowd, another body tugs on the rope and lifts him into the sky. Soon he is hanging in the air and is left dangling while the crowd below him parts.

Expecting to drop any second, Lawrence watches his tormentors light the base of the tree on fire. The flames sprint up the circumference and the golden ring it forms feels like it's burning a hole in his brain. For some reason, he is unable to close his eyes and they dry out. As the fire climbs higher, his skin starts burning and his eyes wither to prunes in their sunken sockets.

Lawrence's skin starts melting and stretches down his body. The ring of fire is now parallel with his head and is about to turn the corner onto the branch supporting his noose. His clothes combust into flames. The pain becomes too intense and he lets out a horrible scream into the forest.

The bodies of the risen are licking their lips in anticipation of his broiling flesh. A fight breaks out over a fiery piece of skin that has fallen to the ground like a flaming marshmallow into a camp fire.

The fire catches the base of the rope and releases Lawrence to the crowd below. Pedro is the first to get his hands on him and take a bite out of his abdomen.

CHAPTER THIRTEEN
Worst Uncle Ever

Not once in his entire life has Lawrence ever been so happy to hear his alarm go off. Bypassing his usual procrastination, he jumps in the shower and drives over to his sister's place. "Fuck that job."

Dressed in his only suit and tie, Lawrence parks his car in front of her neighbor's yard because the pothole patrol is parked in front of her house. The sun reflecting off of the flowing pavement makes the asphalt look like gold. His eyes start burning from the light and heat. Lawrence follows the trail of gold up to the spout at the end of the truck.

A steady stream of rings, necklaces, earrings, bracelets, and watches pours out of the cylindrical mixer. The precious metals melt into one seamless stream as they fall into the bottomless smelting pit. The workers coveralls have been replaced by dark brown robes and they are stirring the pot with long, iron rods.

Lawrence races past the crew up his sister's driveway and raps on the door. He can feel their eyes burning a hole in his back when he finally sees her approaching from the other side. "…and don't get up from that chair. If you behave yourself, you can have a cookie."

Lawrence gives her a hug. "You're bringing her to the funeral?"

"Richard always wanted to meet her. This seemed like the least I could do."

"I hope you don't mind if I tag along."

"Not at all. We've got a while before we need to go anywhere. I'm trying to get a head start on cutting her hair." Lawrence follows Elizabeth into the linoleum covered kitchen floor.

Carol is waiting patiently on a wooden stool wrapped up in a white sheet. "Hi, Uncle Lawrence."

"Hey, sweetie. How's the haircut coming?"

"It's never good when mommy cusses."

"Does she usually cut your hair?"

"Not usually." Carol's head is yanked back forcefully by her mother.

"Do you know what's so special about today?"

"A friend of mommy's died," she answers plainly. "And we have to go to his funeral."

"Have you ever been to a funeral?" Lawrence looks out the window to see the pothole patrol driving off. The tension that was built up in his body dissipates while Carol continues to describe the funeral she saw on television a couple of days ago. Lawrence notices an unusual set of circumstances playing out around him.

Their cat is sitting underneath the television stand playing with the head of one of Carol's dolls. Elizabeth's dog is lying on the couch chewing on a rawhide bone connected to the end of a cotton rope. The chew toy has been torn to shreds from months of abuse. The dog throws it down from the couch while the cat chases after the head as it rolls under the sofa.

He sees himself and Brett in the clearing. In an attempt to distract himself, he tries to think of something to say about Carol's haircut. He watches as a long lock of hair drifts to the ground.

His thoughts drift back to the clearing where his niece is falling to her death. With only a split second to make a decision, Lawrence dives to catch her before she splats on the forest floor. After catching her, he rolls over onto a small sapling near the edge of the clearing. Its tiny root system is torn from the soil. The young tree lets out a violent, pain filled scream.

"Owww!" Carol hollers like only a seven year old can. In his zest to catch his niece's hair, Lawrence had bumped into her stool.

"Oh my God, honey! Are you okay!?" Carol screams louder when her mother puts a wet paper towel on the cropped top of her ear. The blood runs down her neck and soaks into the white sheet.

Still clutching onto Carol's hair, Lawrence lifts up to his knees. Under the shadow of the kitchen counter, he sees a hunk of his niece's flesh. Thanks to his dumbassery, Elizabeth has cut off a full half-an-inch of Carol's ear.

"Get off your ass and do something!" Lawrence stands up and surveys the situation. A pile of bloody paper towels are gathered at Elizabeth's feet and Carol is still freaking out. Lawrence picks up the piece of ear, puts it in a cup, and then covers it with ice. "What are you doing?"

"I don't know. Maybe they can sew it back on. Should I call an ambulance?"

"Grab my keys. By the time they get here we could have her in the emergency room." Lawrence grabs her keys from the counter and runs out the door. He starts the engine and puts the ice cold cup of ear in the cup holder. Then he waits.

For one beautiful moment he relaxes alone in silence before Elizabeth busts out the front door with an injured seven year old and brings him back to his private hell.

•   •   •   •   •   •   •   •

Elizabeth kneels down to give a pep talk to her now merely sobbing daughter before the nurses wheel her to the examination area. "Honey, I love you. Stay strong and do what the doctor says."

"They won't let you come with me?"

"No, honey. It's best if I stay out here. It'll be easier for them to do their job if I'm not back there." She sits down in a plastic chair bolted to the wall as they wheel her daughter to the back. "I need a cigarette."

Lawrence takes the seat next to her. "I'm sorry about… everything. I don't know what happened."

"She'll be fine. One day she'll figure out just to cover it up with her hair. With any luck, she'll grow up to find it gave her some character."

"So they can't sew it back on?"

"Insurance only covers it if it's a *functional* body part. Plus, the nurse said the tissue looked *iffy*."

"Really? I thought you were supposed to put it on ice?"

"But not touching the ice. Don't worry. I didn't even think to try. I would've just left it on the floor if you hadn't picked it up."

"How can I not worry? I'm the reason my niece is going to have a deformity for the rest of her life."

"Trust me, there are worse uncles. That's not to say you shouldn't buy her a car on her sixteenth birthday to make up for it."

"What about Richard's funeral?"

"You still have to go. Either that or you have to stay here with Carol."

"You sure? He was your boyfriend."

"I'll do my best to make it to the cemetery, but I want somebody representing me at the service." Tears well up in her eyes. Lawrence pats her on the knee and walks out to her car.

● ● ● ● ● ● ● ●

As he walks into the small chapel attached to the funeral home, Lawrence is still discombobulated from the events of that morning. The people crowding the pews turn and stare at the disheveled, young man strutting through the doors.

He takes his place at the end of the line and notices the group from the bridge hanging out near an exit behind the casket. One of them looks over at him before adding his two cents to their conversation.

For a moment he considers taking off his sunglasses before concluding that his shades weren't the issue with this crowd. An older woman standing over the casket starts weeping. Her husband steps up and gently guides her away from the casket. Lawrence rehearses the words he wants to say to Richard in his mind. *Hey, sorry that curse killed you. My sister really liked you.*

A little boy is now standing before the casket with his mother. He keeps poking at Richard's broken legs while his mother tearfully says a last goodbye to her dear friend. When she finally realizes what he is doing, the boy is scolded harshly and pulled away from the altar.

Soon enough, Lawrence is next in line. He looks around for someone to give cuts to, but there are no takers.

"Ummm…" he whispers and looks around, "you probably already know what I'm about to tell you. This is all my fault. Not that I did anything to directly cause it, but it was a mistake that I made a few weeks ago that started it. And I'm pretty sure you got caught up in it. And for that, I'm sorry. I just hope that when you got to the other side, the escalator went up instead of down." Tears pour down his cheeks.

"My sister really likes… *liked* you. She was even gonna bring Carol today. If that means anything now. Not that she thought it would fix anything, but she just wanted to show her respect. Then something happened and Elizabeth cut off a big chunk of Carol's ear.

"Anyway, that's why they couldn't be here… but they're gonna try to make it for the…" Lawrence snaps his fingers to help think of the word. His tears have dried up and the conversation has turned more casual. "… the burial."

Lawrence puts his hand on Richard's and almost shits himself when he notices the family has decided to bury him with the watch that caused his untimely demise. The next thing Lawrence knows, he's back in the forest. The perimeter of the clearing is surrounded by a wall of flame. Richard is scaling up the side of a tree dressed in his burial attire. The wall of fire is licking at his feet and forcing him to scramble faster.

There is no way in hell he can let them bury Richard with that watch. He grabs Richard's cold, stiff hand and starts crying. "I'll always remember the good times." He makes a real show of it as he craftily slides the watch off of his wrist and slips it over his own hand. Not everything he learned from Brett is completely useless. "Sorry I had to do that, but I'm pretty sure it was the right thing. Maybe now you won't burn."

It's fairly obvious to Lawrence that Richard's friends in the first two rows are talking about him. After reminding himself that he is there representing his sister, Lawrence smiles and waves to them as he passes by on his way to a seat in the back corner. After the rest of the congregation has taken their seats, the preacher steps up to the podium and gives a moving soliloquy espousing all of Richard's positive attributes.

"Without a doubt, Richard is looking down on us from heaven. His heart overflowing with love… God's love." The pastor's message of hope was having an inverse effect on Lawrence's state of mind.

His heart darkens with guilt. The overhead lights start flickering. The podium starts to tremble and the stained glass windows are rattling. Richard's watch starts heating up and burning his wrist.

The group of judgmental assholes up front stares back at him and rise as one. They dramatically march down the aisle toward the back of the chapel. Their teeth are sharp like fangs and their eyes are glowing with rage. The leader smiles at him and unfurls his forked tongue. Lawrence closes his eyes.

One Mississippi… Two Mississippi… Three Mississippi… He opens his eyes to find they are still coming after him. As calmly as possible, he jumps out of his seat and scurries through the double doors onto the sidewalk in front of a busy street.

After checking to make sure the funeral jerks are no longer following him, Lawrence sits down on a retaining wall and watches the traffic go by while the pastor finishes delivering his message.

About twenty minutes later, the audience disperses out the front doors. He makes a beeline for his sister's car and jumps in line for the caravan to the cemetery. Somewhere along the way he receives a text from Elizabeth letting him know that she would meet him at the burial with his car.

At first he's excited that he'll have some company before realizing that Elizabeth will probably hang out with Richard's friends. That means he'll be stuck babysitting a seven year old with a significant injury. Of course, there's always the possibility the doctor gave her some pills to ease the pain. Maybe she'll share.

As usual, he has no choice but to take it as it comes. He turns the air conditioning on full blast, lowers his windows, and enjoys cruising through the city with a police chaperone. The caravan pulls up to a cemetery in one of the suburbs. Elizabeth and Carol are already sitting under the funeral tent waving paper fans to help cool one another.

Just as he expects, Elizabeth completely ignores him in favor of Richard's friends when he goes to greet her. Without having to be told, Uncle Lawrence sits down next to Carol for babysitting duty. "How's the ear?"

She cups her hand over the bandage. "It hurts."

"I'm sorry. What did the doctor tell you?"

"He said mommy cut off the tip of my ear and it'll never grow back."

"Did he give you anything to make it not hurt?"

"The nurse gave me some Tylenol. It tastes yucky." Elizabeth breaks down in tears and Richard's friends give her a group hug. "Is mommy gonna be okay?"

"She'll be fine. Your mom's a tough girl." The preacher takes his place in front of the tomb to say a few words before lowering the casket. Carol lets out a giant yawn and leans against her uncle for a short nap.

In an act of mercy Lawrence had only heard of in *The Bible*, the preacher wraps up his comments and releases him from the sweaty, sugar stained clutches of his sleeping niece. He takes Carol by the hand and cautiously walks her over to his sister and Richard's friends.

Just up a hill behind Elizabeth's crew, Lawrence notices Brett skulking around the edges of a crowd gathered for a separate funeral. He grabs Elizabeth's hand and links her to Carol. Without asking, he reaches into her purse and exchanges his keys for hers before jogging over to the other burial.

The sermon at this funeral is in Spanish. Lawrence recognizes every tenth word. Even without a strict understanding of the context, he can feel the passion in the minister's voice and a lump rises in his throat.

There is an older woman in the front row who is feeling the passion too. She busts into tears and falls forward onto the ground. Her right arm stretches out for the casket while she clutches a handful of grass in her left hand. Two younger, male members of the family pick her up and put her back in her seat. Brett peeks his head out from the crowd on the other side of the tent and quickly ducks back down to blend in.

Lawrence almost jumps out of his skin when he feels Brett's bony fingers wrap around his shoulder. At first he is overcome with joy when he realizes Brett is still alive.

Then he's overcome with concern for his friend's health. Brett has lost so much weight that he is using homemade holes in his belt. The white shirt and black pants he is wearing look four sizes too big. He looks like a boy who has put on his father's clothes. Lawrence signals for Brett to follow him away from the sermon.

"What are you doing here?" Brett asks through chattering teeth.

"A friend of my sister's passed two days ago. What about you?"

Brett glances nervously around the cemetery. "Friend of a friend. Overdosed." He looks around as if he expects snakes to start falling out of the sky.

"On our stuff?"

"Yeah. But he did a lot. He was showing off to a bunch of his friends after a long day of drinking." Brett's voice grows louder prompting Lawrence to cover his mouth and pull him behind a mausoleum.

"But that's not what killed him." Brett continues through a fear induced stutter. "That's what killed him, but that's not why it happened." Aggravated that he can't put the right words together, Brett punches a slab of marble.

"Then why did it happen?"

Brett looks at Lawrence with anger in his eyes. "You fucking know why."

"Of course I do. But I've managed to hold myself together better than you have. If it's all that bad, shouldn't I be strung out like you? Get it to-fucking-gether, man."

Brett takes a moment to consider Lawrence's point. "Maybe you're right. But if you've been seeing the same shit I have, then you wouldn't be walking around a fucking cemetery all willy nilly."

"It's the middle of the day."

"Do you think they give a shit if it's daytime?" Brett motions to the headstones around them. "Maybe I'm just overreacting. Maybe it's this damn cocaine." Brett pulls a fresh 8-ball out of his pocket and rips it open to fertilize the grass.

Lawrence grabs Brett and pries the sack away for safe keeping.

"It's probably not a bad idea to do that. But now's not the time." Lawrence stuffs the bag in his pocket and looks around the cemetery. "How did you know this guy?"

"A friend of mine said he knew some guys looking to get down. He told me they were playing cards out at a tractor shed in the middle of nowhere. I caught a ride with his cousin and went out to BFE where we were all playing cards. Everybody's having a good time. We're all partying or whatever. Then this kid starts doing line after line after line. He was showing off to his friends is what he was doing. Then the cross on his neck..."

"My guy had a watch."

"What happened to him?"

"Got caught up on a rope swing under a bridge?"

"Hang himself?"

"If only. His arms got caught up in the rope and he broke almost every bone in his body when he slammed up against the cliff. Worst part is, him and Elizabeth had just started going out. "

"Bummer. I'll take overdosing any day of the week."

"No shit." Lawrence leads them back to Pedro's funeral and the two of them listen intently to a sermon they will never understand.

Once they have blended back in with the crowd, Lawrence notices a striking young woman standing under the rear of the tent. She has a pair of bright silver earrings dangling from her earlobes. Lawrence glances over at Brett who is also staring at her.

They wait impatiently for the sermon to end so they can ask the woman where she got her jewelry. When the preacher finally wraps things up, Lawrence has to stop Brett's strung out ass from being the one that introduces them to her.

"Excuse me, miss." Lawrence's words stumble so feebly from his mouth that the woman doesn't hear him. He clears his throat and tries again. "Excuse me, ma'am." She finally turns around. "Are you his girlfriend?"

"Yes."

"Did he give you those earrings?"

"Yes… and this ring too." She holds out her hand and proudly displays a golden ring with an empty setting. "We're engaged. He told me one day, when our time comes, he'd buy me a diamond to go with it."

Lawrence briefly considers taking the jewelry from her and running away, but decides it's best for everyone involved if they just leave her alone for now. "That's very nice." He taps Brett on the shoulder and turns to leave.

"Did you two know Pedro?" She asks with a handkerchief clutched in her hand.

Brett manages to pull himself together, if only for a second. "I did. He was a good guy. Every time I saw him, he made me laugh."

"That sounds like Pedro. Thank you for coming." She shakes their hands and, with a proud smile, walks back to give Pedro's mother a hug.

Lawrence correctly assumes he is giving Brett a ride and they walk to his SUV. "We both saw people die and they both got buried on the same day at the same cemetery?" Brett asks just to see how crazy it sounds to say out loud.

"I think I might have influenced the timing of the funerals a bit. The other day I was driving behind this guy hauling a load of cabbages when all of a sudden he ran off the road and slammed into a tree. The cabbages went all over the highway and it turns out he had what I assume was Pedro's body in the back. Apparently the migrant workers keep some secret burial place out in the woods he was taking him to."

232

They hop in Lawrence's car and light up a couple of cigarettes. "What about your notebooks? Is there anything there that could help us out?"

Brett takes a drag. "Not really. I've seen similar elements spread across several cultures in different eras, but nothing that unites everything."

"So what do we do? There's got to be some reason it doesn't just kill us like it has everybody else."

"I think it wants to torture us. It's pretty obvious that it wants us dead, one way or the other. It don't give a shit. The longer we hang around the more fun it gets to have with us."

Lawrence flicks his cigarette out the window. "So this is it? We just keep letting it fuck with us. Until it kills us or we hang ourselves?"

"Maybe not. Maybe it's just that nobody's ever had the nerve to make it all the way through. Maybe it only lasts for a finite amount of time. Maybe we're the ones that have to hold out for it to disappear. But you've been handling this a lot better than I have. You've got a good chance of seeing this thing through."

"You're a strong guy. Maybe this thing is hitting you harder because it knows you're tougher. Would you rather be getting your ass kicked by your old man or scared shitless by some ghost?"

"That's a good point. That old bastard did always say he was just trying to toughen me up. I'll tell you what, a better man would have just named me Sue and gotten on with it."

CHAPTER FOURTEEN
Crime Spree

After another night of nightmare induced tossing-and-turning, Lawrence wakes up in a pure panic. A few short months ago, he had the perfect life with Linda laid out in front of him. Through persistent inaction, he managed to fuck that up.

Then he fucked his whole life up when he followed Brett into that clearing. For better or worse, he's got to do something before he finds himself locked up in an insane asylum.

It's just past ten in the morning when Lawrence races across town to the bank. His new plan is to buy up as much gold as possible and take it back to the clearing.

His first step is to wait in this long-ass line. There are only two tellers for the twelve people. As his aggravation worsens, a darkness scttles in around him.

The people around him wither to little more than skin and bones. The overloaded deposit bag being held by the manager of a sandwich shop has pulled his arm out of socket. Leaving it dangling uselessly next to him. A young boy is chained hopelessly to his young mother's ankle while she waits to drop off a donation to his college fund. An old man has emptied a small, burlap satchel of gold and silver jewelry onto the counter and is adding up the total on his deposit slip. He notices Lawrence watching and quickly sneaks the valuables back into the sack.

The temperature rises. Lawrence rolls up his sleeves and unbuttons his shirt. Customer after customer walks up to the demon tellers and hands over their loot then are given a form to sign before being pointed to a door at the end of the counter. Every time the door opens, a flame erupts and screams of terror rip through the building.

Lawrence steps up to the counter and the angelically pale woman with dark circles around her eyes and a frown on her face drops a heavy noose on the counter. Her voice is sad and filled with a sense of doom.

"There's no use." She stares down at him with a look of love without hope. "You have to join them." Lawrence glares blankly at the EXIT sign as he fights the urge to walk through the fiery entrance. Others behind him grow impatient, as if the bank is going to run out of hell at any moment.

"Do you have an account with us?" She asks for the third time before Lawrence finally snaps out of his hallucination.

"Yes, ma'am." He pulls himself together and offers her his savings book. "I'd like to empty and close this account."

"You'd like the full amount? Almost three thousand dollars?"

"Yes, ma'am." Through all of his financial troubles, he has never touched the savings account his parents started when he was a child. Lawrence's future crumbles as she counts out his life savings.

No more drug kingpin. No more father of the year. No more life of luxury with Lydia. The only future he has now is fending off the darkness.

•   •   •   •   •   •   •   •

Next on his to-do-list, is another visit to *Dale's Discount Pawn Shop*. Even if he can't buy back the jewelry he stole, he'll buy up as much as he can to sacrifice to the clearing. Upon arriving, he finds a red *CLOSED* sign with a tear-stained note taped underneath.

The typed note eloquently explains how the store had been open every day since Dale opened up shop ten years ago. How much he has meant to the community and how he appreciated being part of such a robust, exciting neighborhood. It goes on to say that tomorrow the doors will be open and business will go on as usual, but today the doors are closed in honor of Dale. May he rest in peace.

After crossing the street, he walks down to a Cash4Gold location three stores down. They've got gold. It's not like they're just hoarding all of it. Maybe they'll sell him some.

This time there is a young man sitting behind the glass window. "What can I do for you?" The guy, who appears to be a recent college graduate, wears a nametag that reads *John*.

"Stupid question, but do you guys *sell* gold & silver?"

John looks around for his manager and whispers "I'm not supposed to tell anybody this, but if the items were sold on the same business day, we are allowed to give you a refund under special circumstances. Were you here earlier today?"

"What if it was late yesterday?"

"Doesn't matter. After we close for the day, everything we take-in is tossed in containers and shoved in a safe. After that nobody touches the stuff. At least not from our end."

"Is there anything you can sell me? You could say you had to give out a refund."

"I'd love to help you, but I could lose my job. I can't have it on my record that I got fired from this crappy place."

"What if I gave you a hundred bucks?"

John does another boss check and leans in even closer. "Here's how we have to do this. Go over there and find a receipt." He points to a trash can in a corner by the door. "I'll give you whatever's on that list. But do it quick. My boss could be back any minute."

"Thanks." Lawrence digs through the trash and finds two receipts. He picks the one with a refund totaling nearly seven hundred dollars. He jogs up to the window and hands the guy the receipt with the cash. Plus tip.

John comes back with three plastic bags. The weight and value of each item is written on a white strip of tape.

"That's it?" Lawrence compares the amount in his hands with all of the gold wrapped around the bodies in the clearing.

"It *is* gold."

"This must be better gold than what I'm used to."

"I guess. You gave me the receipt for transaction number one-four-zero-zero-eight-seven-four. I pulled those three items out of the box numbered one-four-zero-zero-eight-seven-four. The prices match and everything. Anything else?"

"No, thanks." Lawrence wraps the chain around his neck and jams the ring on his finger. He keeps the earrings in their plastic bag and shoves it in his back pocket.

Emboldened by his moderate (though expensive) success, Lawrence heads to a different part of town to another pawn shop. He picks out thirty five hundred dollars' worth of assorted gold and silver then looks the guy straight in the eye and offers him twenty one hundred. Lawrence counts the cash out on the glass counter to whet the men's appetite.

"Alright." The man sets a velvet pillow on the counter and lays out Lawrence's purchases

Growing more desperate by the minute, and down to his last hundred dollars, Lawrence heads to the next shop where he picks out twenty two hundred dollars' worth of jewelry and offers the man face value. Distracted by the golden goose God has put in front of him, the shop owner inadvertently places the jewelry within reach on the other side of the glass window.

While the man turns to find a plastic bag, Lawrence scoops up the valuables and hauls ass out the front door into his still running vehicle. By the time the owner catches on and makes it outside, Lawrence is already speeding down the highway.

. . . .

After stopping off at his place for a quick bite and a thick line, Lawrence searches for the newspaper article about the married couple from the clearing. He looks up the name and address of their psychic and heads across town to give her a visit.

"Sit down. Sit down." The earthy woman points to a chair on the other side of a small table. "You look troubled."

"No shit." Lawrence flops down in the cozy armchair and notices a shift in the woman's eyes. Like she has just caught a glimpse of whatever is haunting him. "You don't look so good yourself."

She stands and motions for him to leave. "I'm sorry. I can't help you."

"I know." Lawrence slams the newspaper down on the red table cloth. "But you told these people you knew somebody that could."

"I think that article speaks for itself."

"Why didn't it work?"

"There was supposed to be a séance culminating in an animal sacrifice. Something went wrong. I wasn't there, but my associate told me something happened with the chicken.

"The wife was holding it and the husband walked up to it with the dagger and it started going crazy. It was flapping its wings and pecking at her arm. All of a sudden, it took off and died in midair. After that, the husband jumped on it and stabbed it mercilessly. But it was useless. Nobody I've talked to has ever seen anything like it. So, since animal sacrifice is our last viable option, there's nothing I can do."

"That doesn't mean it won't work for me."

"Same curse, same result. It's not worth another chicken. You're no good."

"You said animal sacrifice is your *last viable option*. What's the non-viable option?"

"That's none of your business and I won't be any part of it. I won't even point you in the right direction." She calmly sits back down in her chair. "Go home and accept your fate. You did something to rile up this spirit. It's up to you alone to pay the price."

Lawrence grabs his newspaper from the table. "Did the couple say anything at all that could help me?"

"Not really. I did hear them whispering about being scared to death of a smelting pot and the flames. I have no idea what they were talking about."

•　　•　　•　　•　　•　　•　　•　　•

"Can I help you?" The middle aged man working behind the counter at the suburban pawn shop has an impressive black and gray Fu Manchu. Other than him, the store is empty.

Lawrence unclasps the chain from around his neck, slides a ring off of his finger, and sets them down on the counter. "I'll give you this for that Ruger and a box of bullets." The man gives the jewelry a quick once over and takes them back to his grading equipment. It could be paranoia, but Lawrence is pretty sure he hears the guy whispering into the phone.

He hears the distant noise of sirens growing closer and sees the blue lights reflecting in the convex mirror hiding the security camera. Lawrence lifts his hands over his head and readies himself for arrest. The blue lights disappear.

The stranger comes back and sets Lawrence's jewelry on the business side of the counter. "You got a deal." The man unlocks the wooden cabinet and sets the gun and bullets out on the counter. Without examining his purchases, Lawrence grabs the items and strolls out the front door.

He walks out onto the wooden walkway, loads the clip, and leaves the box of bullets sitting on the lid of a plastic trashcan. Following a brief meditation, he kicks the door open and storms through the entrance.

The clerk is holding onto his stomach as he runs to the bathroom. "I'll be with you in a minute."

Lawrence considers ordering the man to freeze, but decides a covert robbery is a better play. He pockets the gun, sneaks behind the unlatched swing door, and searches for the keys. Lawrence gives in and slams a nearby bookend into the glass countertop.

"You break it you brought it!"

"It was just a snow globe!"

"Don't matter! It's yours!" Lawrence finds a little boys backpack under the counter and fills it with as much gold and silver as he can before hearing the toilet flush.

After blending in with traffic, Lawrence adjusts the rearview mirror to find the store clerk standing on the stairwell staring blankly at the passing cars. While waiting at a red light in front of the interstate onramp, a cruiser in the back of the line switches on its blue lights and pulls onto the shoulder. As the patrol car nears, he realizes he will be boxed in if the cop notices him.

Lawrence hits the bumper of the car in front of him as he jumps onto the shoulder and races toward the onramp. When he reaches it, he narrowly misses being hit by a car making a right turn. Luckily, Lawrence is able to scooch by, but the cop has to wait before he can squeeze through. Lawrence takes the opportunity to stuff the gun into the backpack and toss it over the metal railing into a thicket of bushes.

He's hauling ass down the high occupancy lane of the interstate when he notices the officer pull onto the highway. He craftily tucks his SUV next to a semi-truck and watches with a shit-eating grin painted across his face as the cop speeds past.

The euphoria only lasts for a moment before he notices the blue lights have slowed down. A squad car parked on an overpass switches on its lights and speeds down the onramp. Meanwhile, the original patrol car is in the lane right next to him.

Lawrence can see the son-of-a-bitch radioing his partner. No doubt they are working on a strategy to slam him against the guardrail or something. It's probably best to give up and pull over right now.

Then he considers how horrible life in prison would be. Especially with the curse. He slams the accelerator to the floorboard and pulls a few car lengths ahead. The engine of his SUV rattles under the pressure.

The brand new squad car easily catches up to him. Lawrence flips on his hazard lights and pulls over into the emergency lane. Completely embarrassed - and scared as hell about going to prison - he steps out and lifts his arms in the air.

"Sir, I need you to remain in the vehicle!" The officer uses his most authoritative voice when he yells into the bullhorn. Lawrence ignores his demands and leans up against the warm hood and waits to be frisked. He blocks out the sounds of the people honking their horns and tries to enjoy his last taste of freedom.

With gun drawn, the overly cautious officer runs up and cuffs him. "Sir!"

While the uniform is busy frisking him, three other cop cars pull up and block two more lanes of traffic. The other officers lean against their cruisers and watch as the young officer Mirandizes his first solo collar. Not until after Lawrence has been safely put away do they break out into a round of applause.

Somehow, even under this intense set of circumstances, Lawrence is overcome with a sense of calm. He finds himself reveling in joy for the young officer and feels as though he has done his good deed for the day. The warm feeling it gives him remains through the ride to the booking station.

. . . .

Lawrence politely answers "Yes, ma'am" or "No, sir" every time he is asked a question. The whole process – being booked, fingerprinted, and leaving his sister a message – happens in a such a blur he is shocked when he finds himself locked in his cell for the night.

So far, jail really isn't all that bad. While not ideal, he starts to understand how a guy can get used to this. Maybe not used to it, but he understands why Brett's family doesn't consider it to be such a big deal.

Who couldn't go for a couple of months without worrying about rent or bills? You've got a well-oiled system of people here to prepare your meals and clean your clothes. His sexual concerns might change, but there's always the chance that's just an urban legend.

Down the hall, he can hear the cops celebrating the rookie's first big bust. The last clock he saw before being deposited in his cell told him it was just after midnight. This means it will be at least late morning before his sister can get a bail bondsman to come free him. Unable to sleep, he lays quietly on the bed and stares at the ceiling.

The sound of the party at the end of the cell block takes an ominous turn. One of the voices says something about coming and teaching him a lesson. The husky woman who booked him in hurls insults at the *rook* for not slamming Lawrence's car into the wall.

The patrolling guard passes by his cell and slams his nightstick against the metal bars. He mischievously stops right in front of Lawrence's bed and pulls a rope out from behind his back. He dangles it back-and-forth and taunts him with it. "Save us all the trouble." He tosses the noose into his cell.

Lawrence waits until the officer is out of sight before grabbing the rope. From the opposite side of the hall, a prisoner with glowing eyes and a grizzly voice urges him to "Do it!"

Lawrence climbs out of bed, reverently rests the noose on his pillow, and lays the rope down the length of the mattress. He takes a seat on the metal toilet and stares at the depressing scene.

A prisoner in the cell next door holds out a mirror whose reflection shows a fire stretching out from the booking station. "Do it!" The man urges him before the original agitator joins in. "Do it! Do it!" It's not long before the inhabitants of the other cells have joined in and are urging Lawrence to kill himself.

The patrolling guard is briskly making his way down Lawrence's side of the block. The flames grow bigger and brighter with each step he takes. The prisoners chant louder when he stops in front of Lawrence's cell and knocks on his cell bars. He spits tobacco juice through the gap in his front teeth. "Just fucking do it." The guard snarls and then goes back to his rounds.

There's a familiar looking figure slumped over in the cell adjacent to the original protestor. "Brett! Is that you?" The laughter of the guards from the booking station has grown so loud that it rattles the entire cell block. The heat intensifies and ignites a line of fire down the center of the hallway. Sirens sound and the sprinklers switch on. Nothing but a few drops and a bunch of steam flows from the nozzles.

The flames in the middle of the walkway subside. The patrolling guard shakes with laughter as he shines his flashlight across the room. Brett's corpse is folded over on the floor with his back pressed up against the bars of his cell. It looks like he had thrown his noose across the hall and gotten another prisoner to choke him to death. From the look of his mangled hands gripping the rope, Brett changed his mind somewhere along the line.

The man in the cell directly across from his motions for Lawrence to toss him the rope. "Do it!" Lawrence looks at the noose in his hand and then back at Brett. He drops to his knees and starts praying.

The noise in the jail fades away and is replaced with an eerie calm. Lawrence opens one eye and checks out the hallway. The whole building is as dark as it is quiet. He opens the other eye and the only shape he can discern is Brett's dead body on the other side of the cell block. If the dream is over, then his friend really is dead.

A giant flame explodes from the booking station and sends another line of fire shooting down the yellow line on the floor.

As the fire nears the center of the room, it illuminates a stack of human logs piled up like kindling. A spark hits the mound and sends flames shooting into the air. The upper reaches of the blaze lick the bottom of a giant crucible. Bubbles of molten liquid send splatters of metallic lava pouring over the side.

From the invisible heights of an unseen ceiling, a woman is being lowered. The shoes on her feet start melting as she nears the bubbling pool of gold. Her clothes catch fire and welts form on the soles of her feet as she grows closer. Her screams echo across the cell block while the uncaged animals circle the bonfire and cheer on her death.

Lawrence covers his ears and closes his eyes. He can hear her screams even better now and the image of her melting skin is even clearer. While she's screaming for mercy, Lawrence is begging for God to give her a quick death.

The screaming stops. Lawrence uncovers his head. The bars on his cell have been replaced by two giant trees. The stack of flaming bodies and the smelting pot are now the centerpiece of the clearing floor.

One of the freed prisoners fervently waves to him from behind a tree on the other side of the forest. Once he has Lawrence's attention, the man motions for him to put the noose around his neck and pass the other end to him. From there, the stranger indicates that he will toss the rope around a branch and lower Lawrence into the smelting pot.

Other prisoners poke their heads out. The guard is standing between him and the clearing. "Just fucking do it!" The chant gains new life. "Do it! Do it!"

The prisoner again motions for Lawrence to throw him the rope. "Fuck it." Lawrence relents and tosses the line just short of its intended target.

The hunched over stranger sneaks out from behind the trees. His eyes are glowing red. He looks left, then right, then left again before lowering to all fours and scampering across the ground to retrieve the rope. Meanwhile, Lawrence has put the other end around his neck and is tightening the noose. Once his neck is secured, his tree cell disappears.

With his back to the flames, Lawrence once again drops to his knees in prayer. His only concerns at this point are for a quick death and catching the UP elevator after it's all over. The stranger tugs on his end of the rope and painstakingly drags Lawrence across the clearing floor.

The noose tightens as he is lifted into the air. Not enough to break his neck and kill him, but just enough to choke the shit out of him and make breathing very uncomfortable.

Now easily a hundred feet in the air, the ride comes to an abrupt end. The crowd of hellish guards and prisoners close in around the bonfire. Each of them is staring at Lawrence with their own malicious intent.

The hoard erupts into a chorus of screams as he starts his rapid descent toward the golden lava below. At peace with his fate, Lawrence closes his eyes and looks up at the sky with his hands folded in prayer.

CHAPTER FIFTEEN
The Way Out

"Mr. Stubbs," a portly, middle aged prison nurse grabs Lawrence's shoulder. He hears her but doesn't react, preferring to hold onto the hope that he may actually be dead. "Feel free to rest as long as you need to, but I thought you'd like to know that your sister has posted your bail."

Lawrence opens his eyes onto the blossoming moustache gracing the woman's upper lip just in time to see her shove a thermometer in his mouth. "I'm still alive?"

"It was looking iffy there for a minute, but we were able to get you stabilized."

"Stabilized? What happened?"

"We were calling it a stroke until the CT scan came back. Now it's technically listed as a *stroke like event*. But, if you were to ask my opinion?"

"Yes, I would appreciate your insight."

"You need to cut out the cocaine." She looks at him with a knowing eye and a disappointed grimace. "You've still got your whole life ahead of you. Get off that shit and serve your time. Maybe take some classes while you're locked up. There are a lot of ways to better yourself while you're in prison."

Lawrence sits up and motions for the nurse to fetch him a cup of water. "What do I need to do to get out of here?"

"As long as you can walk without assistance, you're free to go." Lawrence downs the room temperature water and climbs out of bed. The nurse keeps a watchful eye on him while he feebly puts on his clothes.

After Lawrence signs his name on a series of release forms, the officer behind the counter rings a buzzer and another guard leads him to the waiting room. Elizabeth is sleeping in a corner chair with her head resting against the white and gray cinder block walls.

Lawrence takes a seat next to her and gently rubs her forearm. "Thanks, sis."

"Thanks my ass. You owe me that money. Plus interest." Elizabeth opens her eyes and stands to leave. "And I'm not kidding. I've been saving up to surprise Carol with a two week drama camp. Your secret coke habit just cost your niece summer camp. I hope you're happy."

Elizabeth shoves through the double doors and mumbles the rest of her insults under her breath as she walks across the parking lot. While he understands her anger, Lawrence is a little surprised he didn't receive at least some pity for his *stroke like event*.

Before he can even buckle his seatbelt, she has put the car in reverse and is backing out of the parking spot. "You know they thought I had a stroke?"

"Really? That nurse told me it was an adverse reaction from all the cocaine you've been doing."

"I haven't been doing that much…"

"Come off it already. They found one of those little baggies in your car. Which I now realize you bought with drug money."

Lawrence refuses to let her drag him into an argument so he closes his eyes and takes a nap for the rest of the ride. This doesn't prevent her from chiming in from time-to-time with some judgmental bullshit.

When Elizabeth finally wakes him up, she has already parked at the top of her driveway. Somebody has left his car parked at the bottom of the hill. "My neighbor rode with me to pick up your car. When you get the opportunity, you should write her a thank you note."

With his head hung like a scolded child, Lawrence follows her inside and takes a seat on the sofa next to his niece. "Shouldn't you be in school?"

"Shouldn't you be in jail?"

Her question cuts deep. Lawrence walks into the kitchen to confront his sister. "You told her I was in jail?"

"She overheard me telling Bernice. After that, what am I gonna do? Lie to her? Tell her she can't go to school today because I've got to pick up her loser uncle from curing cancer?"

"Sorry." A tear runs down his left cheek. He covers his face with his hands. "I don't want this to be all that she remembers me for."

Elizabeth gives him a hug. "She's not gonna remember you for this. You're gonna serve your time. Then come out and be a good role model. You can be the guy that shows her that no matter how bad things get, you can always turn them around."

"Thanks, sis." He cries on her shoulder for a moment before drying off the tears. "I need to use your bathroom. If that's cool?"

"Better than using the laundry room." Her futile attempt at humor fails to lighten the mood.

Lawrence tiptoes through the clothes and accessories scattered around his sister's bedroom floor and onto the stained tile floor in her bathroom. While relieving himself, he sees her class ring and a silver necklace mixed in with a dish full of loose change. Only a real piece of shit would steal from his sister. Especially after she just bailed him out of jail.

Lawrence stuffs the jewelry in his front pocket and washes his hands. On his way back through her room, a jewelry box on the dresser catches his eyes. After picking out only the high quality pieces, he gives in and cleans out every little drawer of the bureau.

Carol is sitting at the kitchen counter nibbling on a slice of cheese toast while Elizabeth is searching for orange juice. Lawrence kisses Carol on the back of the head. "I love you guys. I'm gonna go home and take a nap."

Elizabeth looks up from the refrigerator and runs to catch him at the doorway. "We really need to talk."

"No. We don't. I made a mistake and it won't happen again."

"Are you sure?" She is as angry as she is concerned. "I know things haven't been going that well lately. For any of us. And you seem to be caught up in the middle of everything."

"You're right." Lawrence looks at the bandage covering his niece's ear. "And I aim to fix that today."

The look in his eyes makes her a believer. "Okay. Just be safe. And don't get into any trouble. I can't afford to bail you out again."

Lawrence leans in and kisses her on the cheek before jogging down the hill to his car. The first thing he does after jumping in the driver's seat is unload Elizabeth's jewelry into his console.

· · · · · · · ·

After a quick trip to collect the gun and stolen jewelry from the bushes by the onramp, Lawrence parks his SUV in front of a suburban church. He runs up the stairs, bursts through the tall doors, and makes a B-line for the confession booths.

"Hey. How are you doing?" Lawrence has no idea how to go about this.

"Just like you've seen in the movies, son." The father advises with a smile in his voice.

"Really? Alright. Bless me, Father, for I have sinned. It's been… well I've never confessed before. Not officially. Like to a priest or anything."

"What brings you here today?"

"A few weeks ago, me and a friend of mine robbed these people. These dead people. Then we turned around and sold the stuff we stole. We also traded some for drugs, which we also sold. And we used a pretty good bit of it ourselves. To be perfectly honest, I'm pretty fucked up right now."

"How long have you been going on like this?"

"I've never really done much thievery. The only trouble I ever really got in was for hanging out with Brett while he did bad things. Then this opportunity came up. It was this one time deal. Steal their stuff. Sell some dope. Use that money to catch up on bills. Maybe get a little ahead. End of story."

"It always sounds so easy. Doesn't it?"

"No shit." Lawrence covers his mouth. "Sorry. Right after we pulled the job, things started going to hell. And that's not me using a bad word. I literally mean hell. Like the place in *The Bible*."

"I understand. Continue."

"Things started happening. Bad things got worse. And just when something good happens, something even worse comes along. Then of course you've got the visions and the nightmares. Which led to me doing more and more cocaine.

"I quit my job. I managed to indirectly cause my niece to get a big chunk of her ear cut off. I saw my sister's boyfriend die the other day. Like, right in front of me. Then, about two hours later, I saw the body of a guy who my buddy Brett watched die the night before. All of this crazy shhhhh... tuff keeps happening. I'm on this nightmarish path and I'm pretty sure it's only going one place."

"What place is that?"

"Hell."

"You're still alive. Aren't you?"

"Yeah."

"As long as that's true, there's no way you can be in hell. Because in this world, the only hell that exists is the one you create. It's up to you to choose."

"What if the only choice you have is between hell on earth or just regular old hell?"

"That's still a choice. And in cases like this, we in the church defer to life. You need to continue choosing to live. Choose to see what's on the other side of this hell you keep talking about. If you do, I think you'll find yourself pleasantly surprised. That which doesn't kill you only makes you stronger."

"I don't know, Father. I think something far greater than myself is at work here."

"I know it is."

"Then can't we do something about it? An exorcism or something?"

"There isn't much of a chance that would work. Exorcisms are much more effective when the demon has attached itself to an innocent being. When the inflicted person has earned its punishment – at least from the vantage point of the spirit – time is the only real cure."

"How much time?"

"That depends."

"Depends on what?"

"It's toying with you. What it knows that you don't is that one day it's going to stop. The sooner you realize this and stop making it so much fun for it to play with your head, the sooner it'll leave you alone. You just have to stay on this side and keep moving forward."

This oversimplified answer pisses Lawrence off. "Life must be easy when you duck into God's castle and hide for your entire existence. It's gotta be easy to judge from that little box. Out here in the real world. Shit isn't that easy." With that said, Lawrence storms out of the box and slams the red curtain behind him.

The priest lowers his head in disappointment and mournfully answers to the empty box. "But it is."

• • • • • • • •

The brakes on Lawrence's red SUV squeal to a stop inches shy of the *LOADING ZONE* sign in front of the first Cash4Gold store. After dumping the contents of the little girl's backpack into the floorboard, he pulls his Ruger from the glove compartment. The brim of his ball cap hangs low over his sunglasses and covers most of his face when he marches through the glass door. His cool guy strut is slowed by the weight of the gun in his right pocket.

Once again, John is working behind the bulletproof glass. "Hey man, we can't do that shit again. My boss went back and watched the tape. I almost got fired."

Lawrence walks boldly up to the counter. "It's not like that." He shoves the gun through the hole in the window and shoves the barrel into John's chest. "It's like this."

"Are you kidding me? You know we've got you on video?"

"Just give me everything you've got."

"This job is so not worth it." John frustratingly unlocks the drawers holding the day's haul and dumps all of the contents into a plastic bag. He slides the bag through the opening and Lawrence tucks it into his backpack. "You know I'm just gonna call the cops when you leave here?"

"Why'd you have to say that?" Lawrence pulls the trigger.

The clerk's mouth gapes open and blood spreads all over his white shirt. John stumbles backward and falls into an office chair. He has just enough time to cover the hole in his chest before taking his last breathe.

Feeling no remorse - only fear of getting caught - Lawrence shoves the gun in his backpack and calmly heads out the door. After checking his rearview mirror, he waits patiently for a nearby patrol car to pass before flipping on his turn signal and pulling into traffic.

Things are looking up. If he hadn't killed John, he would be getting busted right now.

* * * * * * * *

It is early in the afternoon when Lawrence parks his car and runs up the stairs to his apartment. In the background of a framed poster for a children's movie, workers are hiking up an ancient pyramid. The Egyptian slaves have Brett and Lawrence strapped to stretchers and hoisted over their heads. More slaves line the perimeter and are hurling rocks at them.

Upon entering his apartment, the first thing Lawrence does is a fat rail. He grabs a cold beer and searches for something to pry the jewels out of his stolen merchandise. The only serviceable tools he can find are a pair of pliers, a hammer, and a flathead screwdriver.

After grabbing another beer and snorting up another rail, Lawrence sits down at his desk and hurriedly sets to work removing all sorts of diamonds, rubies, cubic zirconia, onyx, pearls, and other precious stones that he doesn't recognize.

It's a lot harder job than he originally imagined. After several failed attempts, Lawrence gives up and starts pounding the shit out of the jewelry with the hammer and screwdriver until they fall out.

Sweat pours down his arms and rolls down his hands. While holding the screwdriver in his left hand, Lawrence readies himself to loosen the topaz rock from a silver ring.

As he swings the hammer, the screwdriver slips in his sweaty palms and stops over his pinky. The hammer strikes the handle and rips off his smallest finger. But not clean off, there is still one thin swatch of skin connecting it to the rest of his hand. After a split second of debate, Lawrence picks up the pliers and yanks the finger to disconnect it from the rest of his hand.

Howling in pain, he spills into the kitchen and wraps his nub in the damp cloth hanging over the faucet and uses duct tape to hold it in place. In pain, pissed off, and motivated beyond belief, he boldly marches back into the living room where he snorts a line and gets right back to work.

The loss of his little finger – and the ensuing pain – made a difficult job nearly impossible. The fact that the curse now felt the need to take his finger only proves how close he is getting to the end. That stupid curse can do whatever it wants to him, he has taken back control of his destiny and he is no longer its bitch. Without a doubt, he *will* see the good things that await him on the other side.

The sun is setting over the city skyline when he packs all the precious metals in his backpack and dumps the stones into a purple liquor bag.

Off to his right, just poking her head out from behind the corner of an alley, Lawrence passes by the little girl in a white dress. Her legs are folded underneath her dress which forms a hammock where her doll is taking a nap.

She looks up to him and smiles. Her smile – while sweet in appearance – scares the living daylights out of him. Without either of them saying a word, he drops the liquor bag of jewels in front of her. She discreetly reaches out and tucks it under her dress. The smile on her face flattens and turns into a judgmental sneer. "You're going to a bad place."

"Tell me something I don't know."

"God doesn't forgive you." The conviction behind her condemnation sends chills down his spine. After a momentary loss of resolve, he climbs into his car. The little girl waves to him in his rearview mirror before picking up her doll and brushing its hair.

* * * * * * * *

Two hours later, Lawrence parks his car at the head of the trail to the clearing. He straps on the backpack full of gold and silver and heads deep into the pitch black forest. The walk along the darkened trail is dangerous and time consuming. If he wasn't so afraid of actually finding his destination, he'd be worried that he is lost

In a moment that can best be described as bittersweet, he walks up to the fallen trees that form a makeshift gate to the clearing. He never realized how much of a difference a pinkie can make when it comes to helping one climb over things. But the proof is in the pudding.

When he finally makes it to the other side of the obstacle, the moonlight overhead has just broken through the clouds. The pale glow provides just enough light to help him make out the tree line circling him in varying shades of gray and black. Strands of police tape encircling the clearing flap loosely in the wind. The dirt and grass underneath are covered with footprints – both dog and human.

A whipping wind blows high overhead before shooting down the opening and bathing Lawrence in a foul stench. He looks up into the trees to find Brett dangling in the wind. His body is covered in an abundance of gold and silver. The tears flow down Lawrence's face as he offers up a silent prayer for his fallen friend.

Piece-by-piece, Lawrence removes the jewelry from his backpack and places them at the base of the tree next to Brett's. With every piece he places on the ground, Lawrence's body grows physically weaker. Each piece of jewelry he touches brings to mind the various sins he committed to procure them. This weighs heavy on his soul and causes him to feel even more hopeless and full of despair.

If he can just make it through this last obstacle, this should be the end of it. It has to be the end of it. Any minute now, he'll have emptied out the backpack and fulfilled his obligation to the clearing.

"Holy shit!" Not only is the last piece of jewelry – frat guy Alex's ring – heavy as hell, but it is also burning hot. Determined to end this right now, he wraps the four remaining fingers of his left hand around the ring and tosses it onto the pile.

Still feeble from a two-week long physical and spiritual journey, Lawrence stumbles back into the center of the clearing and examines his work. The clouds shift overhead and release the full power of the moon to rain down on the forest. The glow from the yellow orb bounces off of the precious metals and reflects a rainbow of colors across the clearing.

He smiles and is overcome with a calm he hasn't felt in ages. "I hope this makes us even." The breeze overhead kicks back in and again brings with it the smell of Brett's rotting corpse. Lawrence looks up to say a final goodbye to his childhood friend. "Sorry, bud. I really wish we could have finished this thing together."

Lawrence turns to leave and trips over a root that he knows wasn't there before. Despite his greatest efforts, he is unable to pick himself up. Confident this is little more than a last gasp by a desperate adversary, Lawrence claws his way across the ground toward the trail. The horizontal climb across the forest floor grows harder and more difficult with each move he makes.

Now weaker than before, Lawrence reaches the bottom log separating the path from the clearing and tries to pick himself up. Something greater than himself keeps him down. He reaches up and grabs hold of a rounded numb where a limb used to be and pulls himself up onto the side. His frail legs provide just enough support to help propel him to the top of the next one.

After struggling his way onto the second log, Lawrence is ecstatic to find the gravity has released its hold on him and he can finally stand. He dusts himself off and looks out over the clearing. The light spewing from the pile of precious metals under the tree still fills the circle with colors.

"It's finally over." His debt has been repaid and he can go home to start his life with Lydia.

Then again, maybe not. Who knows? It's a whole new world. The air smells purer and sweeter. His entire life is purer and sweeter. The dead man hanging from the tree overhead is just one more albatross that is no longer weighing him down.

Maybe Lydia is another one that needs to be cut loose. Figuratively speaking.

Lawrence readies himself for the return journey through the forest. With any luck, the clouds will stay away and let the moon guide him down the path. He turns his back to the clearing to start the journey back to his car.

He looks down at the trail to find that he is much higher up than he thought. He sits down to lower himself and finds the ground below stretching even farther away. The other log beneath him has disappeared altogether. The only thing he can make out below is darkness and a rope dangling from the log.

At least it was a log. Now it's a giant branch. The other end of the rope is wrapped around his neck.

The weight he had felt while emptying the backpack had actually been the weight of the gold and silver he was placing on himself. The pushing-and-pulling he had done when crawling across the floor was him painfully clawing his way up the side of the tree.

Looking down into the clearing, he sees a large bonfire explode into flames around a giant smelting pot. Lawrence looks down the length of the tree next to him. He starts to cry when he realizes Brett is no longer there. If he ever was.

While fixated on the molten gold and silver swirling in the pot below, he is hypnotized by its beauty. The bait he has covered himself in is magnetically pulling him toward the boiling pot. Some force is trying to bring the two of them together.

The last two weeks have been leading up to this moment. He no longer has a choice. Lawrence mutters a quick prayer for his sister and niece before offering up a sincere – and most likely futile – apology for all the wrongs he has ever done. Especially of late. "Amen."

Lawrence leans forward and lets himself fall to what he hopes will be nothingness. If not heaven. The rope snaps and breaks his neck instantly.

He is free of the agony and suffering that comes with being human. For a moment, he is free of everything.

While his earthly suffering has ceased, the suffering of his eternal soul has yet to begin. His spirit floats down to its destiny. Below him, the fiery liquid glowing in the smelting pot boils furiously. With every bubble that pops, Lawrence hears the agonizing, desperate screams of some lost soul.

His disembodied spirit continues floating toward the boiling metal. When he is within a few feet of the rim, Lawrence realizes the molten liquid is not silver or gold.

The bubbling fluid is a radiant collection of souls he has helped reap along the way. The street vendor with the leather duster... the tourist and his wife... the migrant worker... the drug dealer and his girlfriend... the pawn shop owner... the three Cash4Gold clerks... John... Richard... and a multitude of other people he has never seen.

All of them are swirling around in a molten pit of torture. Their souls have been sowed and reaped as if by some evil farmer. They are now condemned to burn forever like so much smelted gold.

And soon Lawrence will be joining them.

As he continues his slow drift downward, Lawrence closes his eyes and accepts his fate. The heat from the bubbling liquid starts to burn and he can feel flaming hands reaching out for him. Finally, one of them grabs him by the ankle and hastens his inevitable journey into a liquid hell of his own creation.

THE END

Epilogue

"Listen Pete, I just got out of jail and I need some cash. If you want in on this, fine. If not, I'm fucking doing it alone." Brett's cousin Joe is trying to motivate an acquaintance from prison to either shit or get off the pot.

"I just wish your cousin'd called you back. It'd be nice to know if it's worth the trouble before we go stealing shit from the freakiest section of the forest. I heard they found two bodies here a few months back. Some married couple came out and offed themselves together. Come to think of it, they didn't mention finding shit on either one of them."

That's enough arguing, Joe's ready to get on with it. "Let me tell you what then. You stay up here and I'll go down there. I'll do all the work, get all the rewards, and then I'll come back here and pick you up. I don't know how late it'll be, but I can promise you it'll be after dark if I have to do it alone."

Check out my other book:
My Dad Versus Mr. Hearst
(Bertrand James Hampton)

Coming Soon:
The KingMaker: Be The Fire
(Bertrand James Hampton)

Follow me on Twitter:
@Clearing_Novel

23510832R00158

Printed in Great Britain
by Amazon